The Edge of Yesterday

By the Author

New Horizons Series

Unknown Horizons

Savage Horizons

False Horizons

An Intimate Deception

Just One Taste

The Edge of Yesterday

The Edge of Yesterday

by

CJ Birch

2021

THE EDGE OF YESTERDAY

ISBN 13: 978-1-63679-025-1

This Trade Paperback Original Is Published By
Bold Strokes Books, Inc.
P.O. Box 249
Valley Falls, NY 12185

First Edition: November 2021

Credits
Editor: Shelley Thrasher
Production Design: Susan Ramundo
Cover Design By W. E. Percival

Acknowledgments

It's taken me a while to write this book. It started as a vague idea in 2016 about an operative from the future who studies historical anomalies and corrects them if needed. But that one was missing a sense of urgency. And then at some point it was going to be about all the feet that wash up on British Columbia's coast without bodies. But that idea was missing heart. Then, in October of 2018, I hit on this idea about a pandemic that decimates the population and leaves them unable to live above ground and an operative is sent back through time to stop that from happening. And this was the idea that really got me excited. I began outlining it while writing *Just One Taste*. And then March of 2020 hit. And I stalled. It actually took me about two months to figure out why I didn't want to write a book about a pandemic. And I thought the idea was dead until my partner said, very casually one day, "Why not make the reason something other than a pandemic?" And that was the go switch. A year later, it's done.

I would like to thank Maire for giving me that push in the right direction and for taking lead with the chaos that is our house in order for me to eke out some time to write each day.

I'd like to thank my editor, Shelley, who's always honest when my writing is lazy. She's great at telling me to do better.

I would also like to thank everyone at Bold Strokes for being so supportive and for finding creative solutions for how writers can promote their work during a pandemic with lockdowns. They've gone above and beyond this year. And, of course, I'd like to thank my readers. Without you, my stories wouldn't have any place to land.

Dedication

For Maire.

Chapter One

As Easton's eyes adjusted to the dying light of dusk, she saw, for the first time in her life, the sky and grass, and began to cry—something she hadn't done since her father died. The grass was cool beneath her naked body, the dampness from the dirt seeping into her skin. The trees surrounding the field were full of reds and oranges, and a soft wind brushed through the leaves. It was such a contrast from what she'd left behind, so surreal it looked like a simulation.

She squinted into the light of the day. Even fading, it stung her eyes, not used to the sheer brightness of the sun.

In the distance, backed into the trees, stood an old farmhouse, the roof patched in parts and the porch with wood so new it was unpainted. The slap of a door brought her attention to the back, where a small boy with floppy hair bounded down the stairs, cheering as he rushed toward a rusted pickup truck. His fist struck the air as he yelled, "Pizza" and hopped into the back.

She ducked out of sight as an older man came through the front door. "Down, Mikey. I don't want you riding in the truck bed. It's too dangerous."

"Aww, man. But Tiger gets to ride in the back."

"That's because he smells." A young girl burst out of the front door and skipped down the stairs, her hair as dark and floppy as the young boy's.

"You smell."

"I do not. Dad, I don't want to go if Mikey's going to be mean all night."

"Enough." A woman with a slim build and the most golden hair Easton had ever seen stepped out of the house and locked the front door. "You two have been at it all day."

It felt wrong to be watching this glimpse into their lives. It wasn't that it was secretive, but in its own way, viewing the mundane interactions, with their guards down, was intimate. This was a gift, a look into who this family was without any outsiders around to intrude. Except there she was, crouched in the bushes, naked, like some depraved grunt who got their jollies from hacking computer cams to watch women undress.

A sadness that she'd never known such freedom with her own family washed over Easton. Restaurants, if you could call them that, were a luxury they couldn't afford. She'd eaten in one only once—the night of her mother's memorial. Restaurants were for politicians and Ministry heads.

Easton and her sister would never have argued in front of their parents. They were under too much stress to begin with. Why add to it with more? Of course they had their disagreements. But they kept those private and quiet. One time Calla took a puzzle game their dad had made her, wanting to solve it before she'd had a chance, to prove she was smarter. In many ways she was. Calla was one of the most talented thinkers she knew. But back then she was a brat. They'd waited until they were in the tunnels on their way to class before scrapping about it. Arguments back home were seldom resolved with words. Words create sound, and sound, most times, is the enemy.

From her vantage point, hidden out of sight, the family of four loaded into their pickup truck, arguing and chatting as they left. Easton longed for this, wished she'd had it with her family—the simplicity of jumping in the family truck and going out for pizza.

The dust kicked up from their wheels as they lumbered out of the yard. She waited several more minutes in case they doubled back. Her first task was to gain access to their house and find clothes that fit. The thing about time travel is that you can't take anything with you that's not attached to your body. She was lucky she'd arrived on a mild day. Soon the weather would turn much colder, judging by the colour of the leaves.

As she stood, a soft breeze filtered through the trees. Easton closed her eyes, a small smile lifting the edges of her lips, which eventually grew to a large grin. The wind swept through her hair, caressing her with delicious tendrils skipping over her skin. The wind felt alive and its action the most incredible experience Easton had ever had. It was one thing to see a breeze on video, but to actually feel it move around her was another thing altogether.

Trees isolated the house. No neighbours were in sight, but she still took no chances walking in the open. Staying to the brush Easton inched along until she reached the back of the house. If necessary, she would break a window, but she found no need. The boy hadn't locked the back door when he emerged, and she gained easy access through the side entrance. Hooks with coats in various hues and sizes lined one wall, and below that was a shelf with muddy boots and shoes.

They didn't have mud where Easton was from because it never rained. It must do so up on the surface, but they hadn't lived on the surface for over two hundred years.

Only the constant hum of running appliances greeted her. Persistent white noise. She recalled the boy mentioning a tiger, hopefully not a real one, but more likely a dog she would have to deal with at some point. The side room had two doors, both shut.

She chose the door on her left, since the one on the right most likely led to the main living area. A fresh, clean smell bombarded her senses. A washer and dryer sat against the wall under a long, skinny window looking into the side and back yard. Beyond was a sprawling expanse of land, where laundry dried on a line, blowing in the breeze. Underneath it, a bright-yellow dog lounged in the grass.

For a moment she stopped. Later she'd realize this was the moment that almost broke her, and while it didn't at the time, a crack occurred, and it was only a matter of time until that crack grew and shattered. That moment of peace, of wishing her life had been different, that life had been different for everybody she knew was bittersweet. She wanted it to last forever, for that house to be hers, that dog out in the yard, hers, the laundry blowing, hers.

Easton hadn't expected this scenario. She'd trained for years to resist going rogue. The plan, her slipback, the goals of her people were more important than one person's happiness. They had drilled that belief into her from the start. If she did go rogue, the repos would hunt her down, and the repercussions were deadly.

She wasn't there yet. This was only a moment of wishful thinking, only a tiny second when she let her guard down to the possibilities of life in the past.

Yet it seemed unfair that she and Calla should be born into their world, which was like contrasting the warmth of a hot, blazing sun—the past—to the cold, dead surface of the moon—their present. The first time Easton heard about air travel, of humans taking planes to fly to other parts of the world, she couldn't comprehend such freedom. In her reality, they could barely travel between cities.

But once that split second ended, the moment passed, and she focused again on her slipback. She opened the dryer and searched for clothes that might fit. The mom didn't look much bigger than her, so she should be able to find something to wear. The only clothes in the dryer were small and pink and purple, which probably meant they belonged to the young girl.

With Tiger safely outside in the yard, she risked trying the other door. As she suspected, it opened into the house proper, a kitchen with dark counters and pale-blue cupboards. Children's drawings and family photos were plastered on the fridge, one of them on a beach, something Easton had seen only in videos or old digital photos. The colours in the photo were so vibrant she could almost feel the sand under her feet. She imagined it would feel like the sand pits at the quarry, granular and unstable. In the background, a giant wave was about to break onto the shore.

She stood listening for a few minutes to make sure no one else was home or no other animals lurked about. Everything appeared safe so she ventured out in search of the bedrooms. The house was a maze of rooms, each with its own purpose, it seemed. She found a room for watching TV, a room for preparing food, a room for eating, and several rooms she couldn't figure out the use for. As she climbed the stairs, the air became still. The wall leading upstairs was full of more family photos, these much older, going back decades. She looked at black-and-white photos from earlier times. Easier times. At the top of the stairs hung two baby pictures. One child lay in the grass sucking on its fists, the other strapped into a chair, a death grip on a fluffy stuffed lamb.

Again she felt a twinge of something close to jealousy, which was pointless. Her trainers had taught her that negative thoughts and self-pity were the fastest way to fail at your slipback. You could do nothing to change your own past. Instead, you had to work to change your future, and the only way to do that was to change humanity's past.

The house opened up to several rooms at the top of the stairs, brightened by a skylight in the ceiling. The sun had almost sunk below the tree line, turning the sky several shades of orange and purple. It would be dark soon. The timing of her arrival was off by several hours. It would be harder to navigate in the dark. Slipbacks were never perfect because too many variables were involved. It was best to make do.

She chose a room at random. The mess of clothes on the floor and the bed, and the general purple nature of the room told her it wasn't the room she was looking for.

The sun had fully set by the time Easton had found clothes. In the kitchen she stopped and opened the fridge and paused. For some strange reason, wearing someone else's clothes didn't bother her, but taking food did. Both were stealing, and both were necessary for survival. The crammed fridge told her they wouldn't miss anything. The light from the single bulb cast strange shadows, and for a moment she thought she saw something move in her peripheral vision. Despite the rumble in her stomach, she closed the fridge. She couldn't bring herself to take food that wasn't hers.

At the snick of a door closing, a low growl started beside her. The yellow dog stood a few feet away, teeth bared, less than friendly. The dog must have an entrance. Her heart began to pound the second she saw its teeth. Those were not something you wanted to encounter. The second she moved a step back, the dog launched itself at her, barking and snarling. She stumbled, her head bouncing off the hard tile floor. Dazed, she flung her arms up to protect her body. The foul stench of fish smacked her in the face. The dog was snarling and drooling

She threw her arms up in time, and the pinch and agony of teeth ripping into her forearm propelled her farther back. She kicked and screamed, lashing at it until she'd kicked it off. She scrambled up, cradling her arm, and ran for the front door. Any hope of getting in and out undetected was now trashed. She'd fucked up the first part of her assignment because she hadn't secured all the entrances.

She ripped open the door, slamming it behind her, and dashed down the front steps toward the road, hauling air into her lungs, dripping sweat, blood, and saliva. Definitely not a pretty entrance into this world.

The air was crisp with the sun long gone. Easton stumbled down the country road holding her arm. It was too dark to see what kind of damage she'd done, but guessing by the low, dull throb, it wasn't as bad as she'd imagined. The bleeding had subsided by that time as well, so it wouldn't need stitches. She'd already ripped up the long shirt she'd taken and wrapped it around her forearm a couple of times. The evening was warm enough, even wearing just a tank under the jacket.

They might not have set her down at the right time, but she was almost sure they'd gotten the place right. She'd seen a sign a few minutes back with a notice saying Smokey River was only five kilometres ahead. She could make that by mid-evening if she kept up a steady pace.

Tiny bugs that lit up every few seconds darted along beside her, almost as a guide. Deep forest blanketed either side of the road, and the bugs would swoop in among the trees and back out on the road as if they were drunk or lost.

Very few cars drove by on the road, nor were any houses down the lanes she occasionally passed. A small sliver of a moon was the only light.

The stars though. She'd never seen anything so beautiful. Logically the galaxy must contain billions of stars, but pictures couldn't do this scene justice. Standing on the centre line craning her neck, she saw tiny dots of white that filled the sky almost entirely. Some of the constellations were easy to make out—the Big Dipper, the Little Dipper, and Orion's Belt. After that she got lost. She was tempted to lie down in the middle of the road and just stare up at the sky for as long as possible. Why not? After this slipback, who knew what would happen. A big part of her wondered if everything would just stay the same.

Twenty years ago, one of the ministry's scientists had made a breakthrough and changed their idea of the past forever. What if they could do something about their world in a profound way? What if they didn't have to live like they did? Underground, constantly hiding? What they did was secret. Even Calla didn't know what Easton did. But with all the slipbacks, with everything they'd been working for, nothing changed. Nothing ever had. Operatives come back, and still they lived in that nightmare of darkness.

Easton kneeled, running her hand in the tall grass along the side of the road. The breeze was sharp and carried a sweet smell of water, far off and cold. This was real, yet she kept having to tell herself this because it didn't feel like it should be real. She rubbed the grass between her fingers, the texture so subtle it had to be genuine.

Calla told her about one of the VR cafés she'd been in, with tiny booths you could pay money to submerge yourself in the past. One of the contracting companies had paid for it as a thank-you to her team. She'd chosen to go to the beach, a place called Cancun. The experience had been both amazing but disappointing, she'd said. Bittersweet because the tiny imperfections in the simulation kept reminding her it wasn't real. Easton wasn't surprised she'd chosen the beach. As a kid she must have made her watch the same movie, called Jaws, over and over. She didn't love the action, but the way they sank into the sand. Back home, everything was so hard and unrelenting, made of metal or cement, but sand was soft and springy.

When she stepped into that booth in that café, she was still standing on the metal floor, even though her mind saw the soft waves sucking at the sand by her feet. She said she never wanted to go back. It was too sad to be so close and know she'd never get to experience it. She said the café was better for patrons who purchased stripper shows so they could get off in privacy anyway.

But Cancun would exist for real in this world, and the only thing stopping Easton from seeing it was a plane ride. Something so simple, everyone took it for granted.

But her trip wouldn't include planes or beaches. She wasn't here to enjoy herself. She had one simple mission: to locate Dr. Zachary Nolan and kill him. And apparently sometime in late fall of that year, he would be in Smokey River, B.C. She just had to find him.

In the distance she heard a loud rumble from beyond the bend, and a minute later, two headlights careened around the corner, barrelling down the road. Even from that distance she could hear the loud music blaring through the open driver's side window. It had a fast beat and screeching guitars. A small, grey lump scurried out from the bushes, and the truck swerved in its direction, missing and overcompensated before landing in its lane again.

Easton stepped back off the road, skirting the edge of the ditch running along the side of the road, and knelt in the brush waiting for him to pass. Instead of streaking by, the giant grill of the truck swerved toward her side of the road. She pushed herself out of the way before it slammed into her but couldn't catch her footing. She slid back and stumbled down into the ditch and rolled a few times, ending up smacking into a dead tree lying in the stagnant water at the bottom.

She flipped onto her back and groaned. Her whole body hurt. The tree branches had done a number on her face and ribs. She lifted her shirt to feel for damage and returned with wet, bloody fingers.

"Shit." So far, this wasn't going well. She'd managed to be attacked by a dog, almost run over by a truck, and ended up lying at the bottom of a ditch in awful-smelling water.

However, she'd gotten her view of the stars.

Chapter Two

Tess Nolan groaned as she pulled into the clinic parking lot. She rarely worked this many hours in a day. The early morning false alarm that Benny's mare had started foaling had occurred before she'd spent a full eight hours in the clinic. And then came that emergency call out to the Geary place. Their husky had gotten into their cannabis edibles and eaten most of a chocolate bar, so on top of a long-ass day, she was also covered in dog vomit. It certainly wasn't the worst thing she'd been covered in. That prize belonged to Misty, a standard poodle with an anal-gland abscess. That had been a two-shower day.

She turned to the ball of fur lounging next to her. "One more stop, Lou. Then I promise some warm snuggles and a dental treat." Maybe a glass of wine and some indulgent TV were in the mix. A shower definitely.

At the mention of his name, Lou jumped up, tongue lolling, ready for the next adventure. Tess scrubbed his head and peeled herself out of the truck, while Lou waited patiently as she came around to let him out. He bounded onto the tarmac and hopped a little to get his balance, his three legs compensating for the lack of his left hind one. Tess hefted her toolbox from the bed of the truck, Lou circling her legs as she extended the handle and rolled it behind her, appropriately a Husky brand.

When she'd first started, she'd used a small duffel bag for house calls, but it was impossible to keep it organized and didn't provide enough room. After a colleague suggested she use a toolbox on wheels, she couldn't believe she'd ever used anything else. It was stackable, so had lots of room, easy to clean and disinfect, and contained tons of compartments to store everything she needed.

She definitely didn't want to be back in the clinic, but if she didn't refill her house-call bag, she'd find herself here again at an ungodly hour tomorrow. She believed in getting things out of the way sooner rather than later.

Since she'd taken over the clinic four years ago, she'd expanded her home visits. The majority of Smokey River residents were older and couldn't always easily wrangle their pets into a car to come into the vet.

Joe, the vet she'd bought the clinic from, hated making house calls, saying that's why he'd built the clinic in the first place—to make people come to him. But Joe wasn't much of a people person to begin with. He preferred animals, but sadly they always came with humans attached. In that way, the two of them were very similar.

Tess loved not being stuck in some office and could meet new, interesting animals in their own environment, though sometimes the people weren't always worth the trip. The man who'd owned Bruce, a mastiff whose only problem was that he had nipples, had demanded she remove them, not believing that male dogs should have, in his words, "titties." Needless to say, she hadn't removed them. But she enjoyed gems like Mrs. Boucher, who owned the most beautiful Bernese Mountain dog, a descendent of Hilton Boucher, one of the original prospectors who had founded Smokey River almost two centuries ago.

Once a booming town of over twenty thousand, with settlers racing to the area with hopes of cashing in on the Cariboo Gold Rush, the place was now home to only a few more than twelve thousand, most over the age of forty. Tess didn't mind. In fact, it was a welcome distraction from Vancouver. No one commented on her lack of spouse, even if some of the residents were a little too much in her business. She could handle them, but not the horrible dates and one-night stands back in Vancouver.

Tess had grown up in Smokey River and only recently returned. Vancouver had been great at first, but after a while, she'd grown tired of everyone's constant need for newer and better. She missed the old days. Smokey River was small and slow, just how she liked it.

When Zach and she were kids, they would pack lunches and head out into the woods all day for what her brother called a hunting party. He'd heard the term once and thought it sounded like fun. Mostly they hiked, ate their sandwiches when they got hungry, swam in the river when they got hot, and watched the animals sprint away from their stomping boots.

During their treks in the woods, Tess fell in love with animals and decided she eventually wanted to pursue helping them. She'd thought Vancouver would be a better choice, but the lifestyle didn't live up to her expectations.

The second date she'd gone on in Vancouver had been the worst of her life. With only one grainy picture and a couple of messages back and forth, she'd made the colossal mistake of going on a date with lovergirl85. She should've saved everyone the trouble and named herself needylovergirl85. Dating was a definite downside of living in the city. So much pressure to be paired made it seem as if only certain parts of the city were available to couples.

In Smokey River, she felt no such pressure. When she first moved in, a few people offered to introduce her to a son or nephew, but they quit when she explained she was gay. Only six lesbians lived in Smokey River as far as she knew, and they were all paired, which suited her just fine. She preferred the company of animals. They were easier to talk to, and most didn't talk back.

As soon as she unlocked the door, Lou froze at the door. Usually he rushed to his bed in Tess's office and settled in, planting his snout on his front paws. This time a low growl escaped, almost like an engine starting up.

"What is it? You smell something?" Lou was probably part coonhound, so Tess took these warning signs seriously. It was probably a damn animal that had climbed in the back window. She debated going in herself, but what if it was a bobcat or, worse, a bear looking for food? Lou began sniffing the ground. "It's probably just a stupid marmot." One had gotten in last spring and made a giant mess of the staff kitchen area. If that's all it was, it'd be one hell of a mess to clean up, but nothing dangerous. Marmots could have ticks and carry Lyme disease or Rocky Mountain spotted fever, so she held Lou back.

"Let's call someone to take a look." She headed back for the front door, and Lou bounded through sniffing, searching for whatever had him spooked. He stopped at the door leading into the surgery room and pawed at it.

"Shit." Though more frequent when she'd worked in the city, they'd sometimes get break-ins—people looking for drugs. "Hello?" Tess grabbed a roll of printer paper—the only thing handy—and stepped closer to the surgery. "We don't keep narcotics on site." She pulled out her phone and dialled the local RCMP station. Then she stepped back toward the front of the clinic, patting her leg and urging Lou to follow. He did, reluctantly. A new smell for Lou was like a mug of hot chocolate and a good book on a cold night for her.

Finally someone picked up. "Hey, Colin. It's Tess. I'm pretty sure something's broken into the clinic. I'm not sure if it's an animal or a person. Can you please send someone to check it out?" Satisfied she wouldn't have to wait too long, she turned to leave, and as she did, Lou yipped and rushed through the door to the surgery.

Tess stopped at the door. Blood was spattered all over one of the tables, along with a pile of bloody gauze and empty bandage wrappers.

Was it smart to be armed while looking for trouble with only a printer paper roll and a dog with one eye and three legs? She found Lou squatting in front of something shoved under a desk. When Tess got closer, Lou was desperately trying to connect his tongue to the face of a terrified woman curled up tight. He yipped again, wagging his big bushy tail as he turned back to Tess as if to gauge her excitement level at finding a new friend.

"Lou, down." Tess pointed to the place beside her, and Lou's whole body sagged. Tess was not as excited as he was about this new friend. He hopped over and collapsed in a pile at her feet, resting his head on her foot. "Good boy." Tess bent down and scratched his head. To the intruder she said, "He's harmless." When she didn't move, Tess added, "I'm harmless too. You can come out." Tess set the printer paper down beside her to prove the point that neither she nor Lou would hurt her.

A few seconds passed, and then the woman peeled herself out of her spot and stood. She towered over Tess, and even though she looked terrified, she wasn't necessarily harmless. Tess stood too, evening out the height distance somewhat. At five foot nine, Tess wasn't exactly short, but this woman still had a few inches on her. The woman's pale skin was offset by her black hair that hung loose around her face. Her deep-green eyes pierced Tess as if she could read her intentions by looking at her. A readiness to her pose resembled a wild animal's—she could flee or strike, depending on how Tess chose to handle this situation.

Tess, of course, chose to state the obvious. "You're hurt." She pointed to the woman's face, which had lacerations, like someone had scratched her, and a dark bruise on her cheekbone. From where Tess was standing, it looked like she'd taken a pretty bad beating. "What happened?"

The woman eyed Lou in an uneasy way, until finally she said, "I fell."

How many times had Tess heard that? Her Aunt Pam used to "fall" a lot when she was younger. At the time Pam was married to the town's only honest contractor. What Fred earned in karma during business hours, he squandered at the bottom of a Crown Royal bottle with Pam's face. Tess's mom eventually persuaded Pam to leave, and Fred was never the same after. He began drinking more, started messing up on the job, and eventually closed down and moved out of town. No one ever forgave Pam for that. Just the memory had Tess grinding her teeth.

Tess stepped forward to take a closer look, and, obviously spooked, the intruder stepped back, stopping when she reached the desk. "I won't hurt you. I want to take a look. That's all."

"It'll be fine." She waved Tess off, and that's when Tess noticed where all the blood had come from. It coated her arm, and a distinct set of teeth marks showed on either side of her forearm. It was no longer bleeding but was also covered in dirt—a solid invitation to an infection.

Tess didn't wait to be invited. She grabbed the woman's hand to examine the bite mark. "What attacked you?"

"Nothing. I just made a mistake."

Pam had made mistakes too, though, luckily, they didn't own a dog. "When was your last tetanus shot?"

"All my vaccinations are up to date."

Tess didn't comment. Instead, she pulled the woman over to an operating table and switched on the light. The woman groaned, then closed and averted her eyes. "What's your name?" When she didn't answer, Tess looked up. She still hadn't opened her eyes. "It's okay. No one's going to hurt you. I want to make sure the wound is clean and doesn't need stitches." The gashes weren't as deep as she'd suspected. They also didn't explain the excessive amount of blood. Tess worried she'd been injured somewhere else. It would be best to take her to the hospital and have her looked over. Now she wished she hadn't called the RCMP.

The woman motioned to Lou, still curled up like a pretzel on the floor. "What happened to your dog?"

"I found him two years ago on the side of the road, bleeding and broken. Some careless asshole hit-and-run. I wasn't able to save his left hind leg or his right eye. Couldn't find his owner, so I kept him. But he's recovered fine. He's a badass squirrel hunter." Tess motioned for the stranger to sit on the operating table. "I mean, he'll never catch one, but I love that he thinks he can. Plus, he's a champion snuggler, and that's all you can really ask for in a dog."

The woman hopped onto the exam table, still eyeing Lou, although she didn't look frightened anymore, only curious. "He hunts squirrels? Are they big?"

Tess laughed. "Hunt is the wrong word. He stalks. Sometimes he'll sit at the back window and watch them in the trees. If we see one while we're on a walk, forget moving until it disappears. But his real superpower is being my bed warmer. Especially in winter. He'll snuggle right up to you on the pillow and keep you warm." As she talked, Tess prepared the syringe, all her movements quick and efficient. She swabbed the stranger's arm and then quickly jabbed the needle in.

"Ow." She peered down at her arm, frowning. "What was that for?"

"A tetanus shot. Just in case. Animal bites tend to get infected easily. A lot of bacteria lives in their teeth, so I always like to be cautious."

The woman slid off the table. "Is it okay if I pet your dog?"

Tess nodded, watching her kneel next to Lou and run her hands through his fur. He was fluffier than other coonhounds, so he was probably mixed with a poodle. What were they called? Coonoodles? Tess was tired of all these designer dogs, especially when a lot of them ended up abandoned after they didn't turn out the way the owners were hoping.

"His name is Lou." He was now on his back, legs in the air, tongue drooping out the side of his mouth, getting his belly rubbed.

"Lou?"

Tess shrugged. "It's short for Louis Xavier the third, but that's a lot to say in one breath...so, Lou." She began cleaning up the various wrappers left on the exam table, worried the woman had nowhere to go.

"Not a bear then, I see." Both of them turned to see a middle-aged man with a Tim Hortons cup in each hand. He held one out to Tess. "Thought you might need one, seeing as it's been a long day." He shrugged. "Ran into Nancy Geary earlier. She filled me in."

Tess took the offered coffee. "Thanks." She knew it would be just the way she liked it. No milk and two sugars. Colin had a Persian cat named Mimi, who was a bit of an escape artist and tended to get into scuffles with burr plants. He always brought a coffee when he came.

"Who's your friend?"

Tess turned toward the woman, who had suddenly calmed and looked cool and collected.

"Easton," she said.

"Easton...?"

"Gray."

Colin nodded and sipped his coffee.

"Colin, it's fine. She had an accident. I'm going to take her to the emergency room, see if she needs stitches. I'm sorry to have bothered you." Tess wasn't sure that would be enough for Colin. He hadn't started his career here, but he was more small-town than by the book. And if she wasn't willing to press charges for breaking and entering, she wasn't sure Colin could do anything. She hoped.

He nodded again. "As long as you're fine. You want me to check the place out? Make sure nothing else might have spooked you?"

"Really, we're fine. Thanks for coming down."

Colin nodded, gave a little wave, and turned to leave. She noticed him scoping out the place as he did. He would have questions later, she was sure.

When the door had slipped shut, Tess turned to Easton. "I'll take you to the emergency room. I was serious when I said I wanted them to check you out."

Easton stood, her right hand resting on her hip for extra support. Her face remained expressionless.

"I'm not going to the emergency room. Thank you for your concern, but it's not necessary."

"Whoa." Tess put a hand on Easton's arm but pulled back after the icy stare she got. "You can't just leave."

"Why not?"

"You broke into my clinic, and you're lucky you're not in jail."

Easton smiled. "Technically I walked into your clinic. The front door was unlocked. If I'm guilty of anything, it's taking a few bandages. You were the one who administered the syringe. It was pleasant meeting you, but I have to go." Easton walked past her and Lou toward the front door.

"Where are you going?"

Easton stopped, her hand on the door frame, and turned back. "Why?" Easton seemed genuinely curious.

Tess raised both her arms and let them drop at her side. This was one of the strangest encounters she'd ever had. She could insist the woman go to the emergency room, but she also knew Easton Gray was not the type of woman who would do something if she didn't want to.

"At least let me give you some clean bandages. For your arm."

Easton stopped at the door to Tess's office and waited as Tess rushed to grab a pack of gauze bandages and surgical tape. Easton's eyes wandered to the nameplate that read Dr. Tess Nolan. "Is this your office?" she asked.

"Yes." Tess slipped the bandages into a canvas bag with the logo of the clinic on it. Smokey River Veterinary Clinic was written in gold letters around the face of a golden retriever. The logo came with the clinic, but Tess would've preferred something a little less cutesy.

Easton took the bag without looking at it. Instead, she stared deep into Tess's eyes and nodded.

Chapter Three

Three months earlier

It was the last place Easton should've been.

Last week was the anniversary of her mother's death, and until that morning, she hadn't remembered. Twenty years had passed, and she was ashamed she let that milestone go by as if the intervening time could make up for what she'd missed. It felt strange to have grown up with almost no memories of her mom. Calla and she had honoured her death, according to what little they remembered. They had some childhood pictures and videos their dad took of them, but she didn't "remember" much of it.

A whole forgotten world was wrapped up in who her mother was, and the only people alive who remembered even a shred of that were her sister and her. And in a few months, no one might remain to bear witness to her mother.

On the morning they were to announce who would be on the next team of slipbacks, Easton had stood in the great hall, in front of her mom's memory plaque. It was a tiny square, ten centimetres by ten, containing only her name, year of birth, and the date she died. Hundreds of thousands of them were in the hall, most of them with names long forgotten.

She hadn't gone to the great hall only for the anniversary. She already knew she was slotted for the next slipback team. Her supervisor had told her that morning, and so it might be the last time she got to visit her mom.

She'd spent the majority of her life dreaming of a world that could be different. When she watched a film or read a book, it wasn't about her life or about how they lived. They were always about before. Before. A word she'd spoken more than any other in her life. They all had, because not a single living person remembered before. They knew only the present. And that wasn't something worth remembering most of the time. Of course it wasn't all drudge and dreary; humans were, after all, still human. They still loved, ate, fucked. They were still able to experience joy, but those moments were brief, disjointed, and sometimes hollow. Easton couldn't even remember the last time she'd laughed. Perhaps when she was a kid? Her sister was always the less serious of the two. But something truly joyful, something that could make you forget where you were? That was harder.

Sometimes they'd hear kids in the tunnels playing tag like she and Calla used to. But any laughter was usually hushed before it could echo any farther down the space. Too many things that could hear were listening above, and it took only one mistake for disaster.

That evening Calla was home before Easton, which wasn't unusual. Easton's job required long hours. But what was different was the smells coming from the small contraption on the counter. Calla had gone all out and purchased a premium pack for dinner. More often than not, they were fine with the basic pack, which meant less work for the printer, but also bland and unexciting food.

While it wasn't impossible to grow food underground, the space and resources made it inconvenient. Over the decades, scientists had found ways to provide nutrients without having to grow them, well, in the traditional sense. Instead, they printed their food. And like all economies before, a correlating scale existed between price and quality. The basic was the cheapest, and most lived on that day to day. The basic pack consisted of blocks of food that Easton's dad had once said were similar to army rations. They had the nutrients their bodies needed but tasted more like eating dirt with just the hint of salt. A step up from the basic was the deluxe pack. Think mashed potatoes or lentil soup. The premium packs were the closest thing to real food they could get.

Rumours floated around the complexes of people who had makeshift gardens in their apartments, hidden under beds with special lamps. They weren't illegal per se, but frowned upon because they could cause friction. The concept that others had more was not encouraged. Everyone should feel equal, the operative word being "should."

That night Calla had made a feast. The smell of roast chicken wafted up and over Easton as she entered their apartment. Calla's grin reached all the way to her eyes. Easton took a moment to appreciate her sister's smile, which was always easy to come and ready to engage and infect those around her.

She bent low to the food printer on the counter and watched as the last strands of the roast were layered upon each other. "It's almost ready."

"What's the occasion?" Like most apartments, their place wasn't very big, but it was space enough for one less person than lived there. They made it work by converting the common space into their everything room and using the den as a second bedroom. Most of the apartments were modular in some way to account for this handicap.

Calla shooed Easton toward her room. "Get out of your work clothes. I'll tell you over dinner."

"So we are celebrating something?" Easton pulled the curtain closed across her door—enough for privacy but not much else. She could still hear Calla when she spoke from the other room. She stopped before opening her drawer, a dreadful thought having occurred to her. What if Calla had met someone? Was this her way of telling her she was moving out? Would some stranger show up later, wanting an introduction? She shook the thought off as soon as it came. Calla was an open book. Easton would know the second Calla met someone.

"Of course, I'm not going to blow a week's worth of food packs for a random Tuesday night."

Easton pulled her heavy-duty cargo pants off, folded them, and placed them back in their drawer. "I thought it might have something to do with Mom's anniversary." The other room went silent. Calla had stopped setting the table. A second later, she pulled Easton's curtain aside.

"You don't still go to the Great Hall every year, do you?" Calla took a seat on the bed, crossing her legs and looking up at Easton with the same brown eyes their mom had. In many ways Calla looked more like their mom, Ada Gray, than Easton did—feminine and delicate. Easton had more of her father in her—his dark hair and green eyes and a brooding nature that he wore as a cloak. Or maybe that had surfaced only after their mom had died. She'd left him alone with two daughters to raise in a time when raising even yourself was difficult. Maybe her father had been lively before that, but Easton couldn't remember. Her father's cautions invaded too much of her life.

"Of course I still go." Easton pulled a lighter pair of pants from her drawers. "It's important to remember."

"Why?"

"What do you mean, why? Because she was our mom, and she gave her life so we could have a better one." The death of their mom—an accident at work—had come with an insurance payout from the government. The work she'd been doing was dangerous, and the more dangerous your job, the more the government paid out if something went wrong. That money had given them a much better life than if she'd stayed alive. Calla was able to go to school and become a surveyor, and Easton had succeeded in joining the Ministry of Discourse. They had a good education, and with that came better jobs.

"Please, Easton. You can barely call what you have a life. Mom didn't sacrifice hers so you could work and sleep through yours."

Easton fastened her pants. This was an old argument. "I'm not interested in dating, so whatever flimsy setup you've worked together, you can forget it."

"How do you know they're flimsy? You've never actually gone on any of the dates I've set you up with."

Easton shoved the curtain aside and stepped into the common room at the same time the buzzer for the food printer chimed. How could she explain to Calla what a frivolous thing it was for her to date? She couldn't even tell her what she actually did at MOD. The Ministry of Discourse wasn't just the research arm of the government. It had several levels that dealt with areas of testing that weren't shared with the general public. And Easton worked in the most highly classified level of government.

Many of Easton's coworkers felt the same. They saw no point in getting attached to this life, not when they might be able to change it for the better. But few talked about the fact that if they succeeded, the people who existed in their time would never know anything had been altered. They would simply cease to exist. Easton and her whole department were, essentially striving to wipe everyone they loved from existence. Easton wasn't delusional. She knew what that would cost her emotionally if she succeeded. Only the greater good kept her going. If they could change the past for the better, humans wouldn't have spent the last two centuries underground afraid of any and all sounds that could penetrate the surface and reveal them to their unwitting captors. That was the prize they were all striving for. And they were close. So close.

Calla emerged from Easton's room. "We're supposed to be celebrating." She opened the front case of the printer, revealing a medium sized-chicken, crisp and golden brown. Surrounding it in the roasting pan were potatoes, green beans, and carrots.

Easton's mouth watered. She'd never actually eaten a premium pack before. Who could justify the credits? The best she'd ever had was a bowl of chicken noodle soup. "Are you ever going to tell me what we're celebrating?"

Calla pulled the meal out and placed it on the table she'd unfolded from the wall earlier. "Oh, God. That smells so fucking good. Do you think some people splurge on this every night?"

While it was possible to spend all your credits on premium packs, it was unlikely anyone did. Everyone was allotted the same number of credits a month, and what you did with them was up to you. But everyone needed somewhere to live, clothes, food—the basics of living. Some people lived in basic cubicles and never bought new clothes so they could afford better food packs, but the idea of eating like this every night? Too decadent for words.

"Let's eat before it gets cold. You don't want to waste this."

Calla took her first bite and closed her eyes. "Doesn't matter what temperature this food is. It would taste good frozen."

Easton doubted that, but she couldn't disagree that it was the best thing she'd ever tasted. The textures and flavours swirled in her mouth, and a little part of her was sad. If she'd never tasted it, she wouldn't know what she was missing.

They were halfway through the meal, both engrossed in eating, before Easton asked, "Are you ever going to tell me the good news? I'm assuming it's good, or we wouldn't be eating so well."

Calla set down her fork and held up her glass. "Guess who got promoted to the red team?"

Easton had also raised her glass, but now she lowered hers. "Red team? That's the front line."

"I know." Calla's excitement had eclipsed everything. "That means I'll be travelling to other cities. It's been years since they've upgraded the tunnels. And they want me to go with the first wave to scout whether we can use the existing structures or dig new ones."

Easton looked down at her plate of half-eaten chicken. She wanted to be happy for Calla, but this was dangerous. People died on the red team, which was why they promoted only people who'd worked for several years as surveyors.

Calla placed her glass on the table, her excitement gone. "You know I deserve this."

"You can ask to be reassigned."

"Why? So I can do what you do? Sit at a desk all day and read about the past? It's done. They fucked up, and now we have to live with that. Why can't you move on?"

"Dad—"

"Dad worked the construction side. I'm not anywhere near the tunnels when they're digging." Calla slapped her hand on the table and stood. "Why can't you be happy for me? I know it's too much to ask in your own life. You'll never be satisfied until everyone around you is miserable." Calla stood. "I'm going for a walk."

Before Easton could stop her, she'd rushed out of the apartment. Easton knew better than to follow her. In this state Calla was unreasonable. She needed to walk off her anger. Easton, on the other hand, was a cleaner. She busied herself with erasing any traces of dinner, one thing playing over in her mind: why couldn't she be happy for Calla? Sure, she was worried about the dangers, but her own job was much more dangerous, and not just potentially anymore. In three months, she would slip back, and even if it were successful—which wasn't guaranteed—anything could happen in the past. The return rate was dismal, the success rate even more so.

After cleaning up, she made herself a tea and sat, still contemplating Calla's news. What worried her so much about Calla's promotion? Why should Easton be allowed to take all the risks? Very few safe jobs existed in this life. It was just the nature of their situation. They'd lost both their parents to work accidents. Their dad had been caught in a tunnel that collapsed, his entire team crushed in an instant. Why should Easton assume her sister would be spared from the dangers? And what right did she have to be angry that she should have the opportunity to do something that she loved? It was good work, and Easton should feel proud.

Logically she knew all this, yet the worry was still there, deep inside like a bad stomachache. Maybe it was the dread of being informed that someone she loved had been killed in an accident. First her mom, when she didn't fully understand what it meant to never see her mom again. And then with her dad, when she knew exactly what it meant. Never again would she get to hear his baritone voice, booming from his barrel chest, or the crinkle of his eye when he teased her. It wasn't like humans had never known loss like this before. Part of her job at MOD was to study history, which revealed plenty of times throughout human history when life seemed bleak.

In general, life expectancy throughout the ages was not great. In prehistoric times, if you could reach your teens, you might be lucky to reach the age of forty. And that really didn't change much until the early twenty-first century, when life expectancy soared, not to mention the probability of reaching your teens or early twenties. One of the worst times to be alive, in Easton's opinion, was late medieval Europe and during the early industrial revolution. Human life was cheap, and too much of what mattered was wound up in nobility and wealth. Sadder still was the fact that most of their data pertained only to males, because before the twentieth century, females were chattel. And even after that, it took a couple more hundred years for women to reach true equality.

That was one thing she dreaded about seeking the past. Would she be able to see beyond her own prejudices? It would be a challenge to crawl back behind the curtains, so to speak, and pretend the injustices in the world were normal. But Easton loved history, and one of the things she loved about it was the freedom that had once existed. In the past, people were free to travel from one place to another. And, if anything, her studies had taught her that it was human nature to want to explore and discover. So, of course Calla would want to do everything she could to explore. Very few in their society could transport from city to city. The government limited movement because it took energy. Even though they'd done their best to make transport as silent as possible, noise always could travel up to the surface.

Easton had never been outside their city, but she'd never desired to go anywhere else. She knew every city would consist of the same modular structures, the same tunnels, same dark-grey walls and daylight lamps dotting the cavern ceilings. That was why VR suites were so popular. They gave you a chance to see what the world had been like, never mind that it would never look like that again.

Both Calla and Easton had promised each other they would never fall into that trap. It was better to be happy with what they had instead of dreams and make-believe. Some people spent all their credits on the VR suites escaping reality, as if they could pretend the bleak tunnels were make-believe and the sunny cities they visited reality. Easton wasn't willing to engage in that delusion. Her dad had always told them the inability to face reality made life more difficult. Hiding from it was denying your existence. The spell would always break, and you would wake up more depressed than if you'd faced reality in the first place.

She couldn't fault Calla for following her dreams. She was living the best reality she could in these circumstances, and it wasn't Easton's place to tell her she couldn't. None of them lived safe lives, least of all Easton.

CHAPTER FOUR

Lou's tongue slipped across Tess's cheek, waking her from a dream that had something to do with wild hogs shopping for apple pie. She opened an eye to see Lou bending over her panting, the reek of dog breath wafting up her nose. Tess had never been a morning person, but the nature of her job and the vast amount of fur balls in her life had trained her to be up at the ass-crack of dawn.

First light had not yet reached the meadow behind her house. From her cozy place under the covers, it was going to be overcast and stormy. She ran through what she had to do that day and groaned. She had several house calls to make, including one to Barbara Fowler's alpaca farm. Tess loved the floofs. However, not all of them liked her. One in particular always managed to get spit in her eye. If she could help it, Tess preferred working in the clinic on days like this.

Lou made a low whimper, signalling that he had to pee. Tess peeled the warm cocoon from her body and slipped on a sweater. Whether she liked it or not, her day had begun.

Tess didn't love getting up in the mornings, but she did like being out in the back fields at dawn. It was a strange paradox about herself she couldn't explain. How could you love the result of something you hated? That morning the air was fresh from the moisture—thick enough to feel as she tramped through the knee-high grass. It left its mark on her pants and dark-green Kamiks.

It was more than the quiet she loved. This time, few things were stirring except some birds, but the breeze was hiding somewhere beyond the trees, away from the meadows that backed onto her property.

She'd bought the place two years ago, tired of living in town with all the traffic, although it had nothing on Vancouver. She'd lived most of her time there above a record shop that played late-seventies punk during the day and closed before nine, which suited her fine. She couldn't remember a time when she couldn't hear police sirens or firetrucks. Cars were always honking and trucks jangling by, not to mention the crowds once the bars closed. She lived in East Van, close to a lot of pubs, which meant the noise never really died down until two in the morning, especially on weekends.

Here it was calm. Not until she'd bought this place and spent her first morning roaming the fields with Lou had she realized how much she'd needed calm in her life. Even though she'd been close to her brother Zach, she'd always felt disconnected, like she didn't belong. However, if she was being truthful, she'd never felt that overwhelming sense of belonging. Out here, where life was slower, it was easier to forget that lack. That was also why she liked animals so much: she never felt out of place around them. For some reason it was easier to understand animal social cues. With people, she was never sure where she stood. Zach said she was hiding, and maybe she was, but it was her life. So if she wanted to hide out here in their hometown where she could find some modicum of peace, that was her business.

Except she hadn't found the peace she was looking for. She was the only full-time vet around, which kept her busy. Not to mention break-ins at her clinic. To be fair, last night's had been a first, but it was no less unnerving. Tess still didn't know what to think about that. Should she have let Colin take the intruder in? Tess didn't think she'd been there to steal drugs. And she felt a certain empathy toward the woman. She'd looked so beat up and out of place. She didn't, however, believe the front door was open. Donna was always so good about locking up at night. Tess had to believe she'd made the right decision. She wouldn't have to see this woman again, so she could put her mind to rest with the belief that she'd helped out someone in need, and that was the end of it.

Tess could hear the cry of the fawn from half a kilometre away. The scream seemed to pierce the air, cutting through the morning fog. She hurried toward the sound and found the small animal caught in a broken chain-link fence. Tess roped Lou off on a nearby post and knelt next to the fawn. It panicked and thrashed about, its eyes wide. When she was close enough to hear its panting breath, she spoke low. "It's okay. I'm not going to hurt you." She rested her hand on its head, waiting until it settled to assess the damage. The jagged edge of the fence had snared its hind legs. In a blind panic to free itself, the fawn had gotten twisted in the wire. She eased the fence down closer to the ground and pulled the part ensnaring the young animal away from its back legs, careful not to jab it with any sharp points.

The second it was free, it sprang forward to bolt but collapsed in the wet grass. Figuring it must have broken something, Tess reached down and scooped it up in her arms. It mewled and fought against her for a few seconds before settling down to its fate. She unhooked Lou from his spot and headed back to the house. While walking she lifted one of the deer's legs to see that, as she'd suspected, it was a female.

"Hi there," she said in a soft voice. "I wonder where your mama is?" Tess retraced her steps, making good time now that she had somewhere to be.

Tess took the tiny animal to her garage out back, where she had a tiny clinic set up for such an occasion. She placed the small fawn on a cushion that Lou usually used and set about grabbing supplies to disinfect the cuts on the deer's back legs. Lou circled the room, watching like a nervous dad.

While washing some of the matted blood off the legs, Tess guessed she'd been stuck there a while, possibly overnight. She looked cold, tired, and hungry.

Originally, Tess had planned to do house calls today, but her first stop would have to be the clinic. She could ask Prisha, her technician, to get X-rays of the fawn's hind legs to see how bad the fracture was. If Prisha had the time to take care of this, Tess would be able to finish her house calls before heading back.

Later, she'd give Gary a call. He owned a wildlife-rehabilitation centre outside of town and was great at this sort of thing. With the town so isolated, they had their share of run-ins with the local wildlife. Tess found the biggest problem was education. The residents weren't so bad, but the tourists were. Last year she'd listened to Gary gripe about how many fawns tourists brought in, saying they'd found them abandoned. More likely the mother had gone looking for food and would be back in a few hours. But people would assume she'd left her baby there and scoop it up, some thinking they'd found a new pet. The poor mother would come back later, only to find her baby gone. He worked to reunite them as best he could, but it wasn't always possible.

In this case, Tess felt certain she'd done the right thing. Even if the mother did come back, it was unlikely she'd be able to help her baby escape the wire on that fence.

As she prepared the fawn for a ride into town, one question kept circling her mind: where had Easton Gray spent the night? Honestly, the thought of Easton hadn't really left her mind since she met her. She should've been furious that this woman broke into her clinic to patch herself up, made a mess—which Tess had to clean up—and had the gall to just walk out without any kind of thank you. However, the look and certainty in Easton's eyes as she'd turned and left had Tess intrigued. Okay, more than intrigued. Something about those deep-green eyes and the way Easton had stared at her, like she'd been discovered, something rare and captivating to be explored, had an almost physical effect on Tess.

Without a doubt, Tess wanted to see Easton again.

Easton's attention was glued to the window or, more specifically, the kaleidoscope of colours turning in the breeze outside. The yellows were so pure they were almost luminescent, as if they were providing colour to the gloomy day. Easton had never seen such colours in nature. To her, nature was the bamboo plant her sister had given her for her birthday a few years ago.

Plants weren't forbidden. People grew many of them in their apartments, especially several species that helped purify the air. Her mom always kept an aloe plant handy in case of scrapes. But this was something else. During her second year of training, she experienced various scenarios in the simulators so being here wouldn't seem such a foreign experience. But the simulations always seemed somehow unreal. Obviously they were fake, but the colours were always a little off too. Sometimes glitches or render errors took her out of them. Also, the simulations never got the smells right. They could pump in scents, but they were artificial.

Easton spent the night in the back of a car. It had taken her half an hour before she'd found one left open. She'd used the blanket the owner had laid out across the backseat for their dog as warmth, which was enough once she was out of the wind. Her arm ached, but she felt content that she'd achieved two of her first goals: locate her target and find shelter. Tess Nolan wasn't her main target. Her brother was. The AI gave a 75 percent chance that Tess Nolan would share his work if she were to live. With her death added into the algorithm, a 92 percent chance existed that his technology would die with them.

However, being displaced in time meant that as soon as you tried to interact with that world on a logistical level, it was obvious you didn't belong. In the mid-twenty-first century, where Easton found herself, most people didn't leave the house without some form of ID and money. Easton had neither, which was why advance teams existed. If Easton had been arrested at the clinic last night, they would've run her name and found an up-to-date driver's license, because an advance tech team had come in earlier to set up her profile. Several teams were in motion working on this part of the timeline puzzle, not just Easton, which was why it was so important that each operative complete their assigned slipback.

But being present in the database didn't solve all issues of being displaced in time. Easton didn't have any ID to prove who she was, nor did she have any money, and the last one was the most crucial for survival. Level five had spent years working on this issue. It didn't matter how much you trained your operatives, being displaced in time, with all the short-term and sometimes long-term memory loss it incurred, sending your operatives back without a solid plan was doomed to fail.

The first night was always the hardest. Disoriented, alone, disconnected, operatives invariably struggled to find that thread of hope. Easton was more than confident she could succeed. She woke the next morning at first light, a grey fog muting the background of the town somewhat. She made sure to leave the car as she'd found it. Debating whether she should lock it for the owner. Seeing as she had already broken into it, and nothing bad had happened, she left it as is.

She crossed the street, heading toward town. In order to succeed, Easton had undergone several augmentation surgeries to account for the fact that she wouldn't be able to bring anything with her. One of these was an NFC chip placed below the skin in her hand. The technology was a bit antiquated for her time, but most devices in the mid to late twentieth century used them to talk to other devices. A small computer imbedded in her forearm allowed the chip to override whatever it was near.

With this thought in mind, Easton spied a café at the end of the street. Her chip would allow her to pay for things as if she had a wearable device connected to credit, wherever tap was available.

In her research of Smokey River before her slipback, she hadn't spent much time on restaurants or cafés. Food was a low priority for her. Of course she'd have to eat, but she hadn't given much thought to it more than as a survival aspect.

At this hour, the streets were empty, with only a few cars parked here and there. The café beckoned her with its warm lights and promise of warmth and caffeine. She hadn't thought to grab a hat or a scarf when she'd been at the farmhouse choosing clothes, which had been a mistake. A light frost covered everything, and the vapour from her breath formed a cloud as she breathed. Easton was too cold at the moment to find the vapour mesmerizing. She'd grown up in a strictly controlled atmosphere, where the temperature barely dropped below twenty-one.

When she entered, a young woman looked up from the book she was reading, as Easton was the only customer at the moment, and jumped off her stool.

"What can I get for you?" She had a pleasant voice. Easton guessed she was in her early twenties, maybe late teens, and her name tag said her name was Sara.

She looked up at the board behind the counter. Tea was one thing they had in abundance, thanks to the hardiness of camellia sinensis, the tea plant. From this one plant, growers could make green tea, black tea, and oolong tea, which was Easton's favourite. But she didn't see oolong listed on the menu in the shop, so she ordered green tea instead, second best. But it was caffeine she was after. While Sara busied herself with steeping the tea, Easton took the time to look at the pastries on display. They were unlike anything she could even imagine, full of colourful fillings and dusted in white powder. She hadn't eaten anything in two days, thanks to the slipback protocols. She would've thrown up any food in her system the second she arrived. Her stomach growled at the images. The only thing she recognized was a Danish, something she'd seen in a movie once. A pretty woman in a black hat was shown standing outside a jewellery store eating the pastry while wearing fancy gloves. So when Sara asked Easton if she'd like anything else, she pointed to the Danish on the top shelf.

While she was at the cash register, a few more customers came in talking of the weather, a topic that dominated, no doubt.

"Bunch of wimps, if you ask me. Rented a place down in Arizona for the whole winter." An older woman with short grey hair unwrapped the scarf from around her head. She was talking with a gentleman with equally grey hair, although there looked to be less of it than there had once been. "As if they haven't spent their lives up here and suddenly it's too cold."

"What do they call themselves again?"

"Snowbirds."

"That's right." The man held out a chair for the woman at one of the tables in the back near the windows.

"And now their place is just going to sit empty for the entire winter. Such a waste."

"The Pattersons know what they're doing. I'm sure they have someone looking in on it."

The woman shook her head. "That's not what she told me."

"Well, if it isn't Ms. B and E herself." A jolt of recognition. Easton turned to see Tess Nolan standing at the counter watching her. She had bundled for the cold with a green scarf wrapped elegantly around her neck and shoulders. Her strawberry-blond hair poked out of a matching knit hat with a white bob at the end. Her cheeks were red from the cold, and in all her life, Easton had never seen anything so beautiful. Her reaction surprised and disturbed her.

"B and E?"

"Breaking and entering."

"Is it breaking and entering when the door's left open?" Even though she knew it was a mistake, Easton couldn't help the flirty side grin as it spread across her face.

"I'd imagine it is, yes." Tess's face was serious, her mouth formed in a long line. She did, however, have a twinkle in her eyes, enough of an invitation for Easton to press her luck.

"I'll pay for whatever she's having," Easton said to Sara, who'd finished ringing up her order and was about to pass the card reader to her.

Sara turned to Tess. "The usual?"

Tess hesitated for a moment, then relented. "I'll have my usual coffee." She hooked a finger in the top of the paper bag Easton was carrying and peeked inside. "And I'll have a Danish as well."

Sara smiled as she moved to complete her order.

"I don't think I've ever had a thief buy me breakfast before." She rested her arm against the counter, watching Easton.

"Thief. I don't recall stealing anything. You were the one who gave me the bandages. I may have entered—without breaking—but I didn't take anything I wasn't given."

Tess nodded and smiled. "Hmm. Okay. I'll accept that explanation for the time being, but I still think you should've gone to the hospital."

Easton waved her arm around. "Feels fine. I'm sure I got the best treatment around."

"If you're a dog or a cat maybe."

Sara returned with Tess's coffee and Danish and rung them up. Easton held her breath that her chip would work. She hadn't tested it yet. She held her hand over the card reader as if she were wearing a smart device. The first time the card reader came back with an error, and the second, it declined it entirely.

"I knew this was too good to be true." Tess rolled her eyes. "It'll be my treat, B and E."

Chapter Five

There's talk of a blizzard this week, which is ridiculous. I haven't even put my snow tires on yet." Donna stood in Tess's office doorway conversing with one of their clients. It was a habit Tess was not fond of. She'd come to ask Tess something while still in conversation with someone else and then forget what she'd come to say. As a result, Tess knew way too much about every one of her clients, as well as most of the trivial things happening around town.

Tess wasn't a gossip. Her parents had lived by very simple rules and raised her to mind her own business. If the topic of conversation did not involve anything within the boundary of your property, that topic was best left for other people. Donna had clearly not been raised with these rules. Of course, she'd also grown up in a completely different town during a very different decade than Tess.

Donna, in her early sixties, had dark bottle-red hair and a darker artificial complexion. She looked almost as if she were wearing foundation too dark for her skin type. Coupled with the beige lipstick she wore, she had a strange, makeup-free appearance. And while she might have looked bland, her personality more than made up for it. You could usually hear her from the parking lot around the side of the building. As soon as you entered, she would greet you loudly and enthusiastically. She owned two cats, Rosaline and Russell, and Russell had diabetes.

Donna was standing in her doorway with a paper compost container, which was probably her lunch order from Rob's. "That can't be true." Donna turned in the doorway to address Tess. "Dr. Nolan, that can't be true, can it? Did we have a break-in here last night?"

Tess shut her eyes for a second. Where had the leak come from? She'd trust Colin with most things in her life, but his sister was about as trustworthy as a paper boat. If she'd managed to get ahold of this fact, the whole town knew. Of course, Sara, from Bean There, Doughnut That, might have overheard her conversation with Easton that morning. However, Sara wasn't much of a gossip.

Now Tess had a choice. She could substantiate that claim, and open the clinic up to even more gossip, or stop it right here.

At first she'd thought Easton was running away from an abusive relationship. Her last encounter, however, had led her to believe that she was running away from something else. Maybe even the law. Last night she hadn't pressed charges because she wanted to help Easton. She'd felt sorry for her. In the end she decided to keep the clinic business private. She saw no reason to involve anyone else because she could figure this out on her own.

"I don't know where that story came from. It's not true."

Donna tutted the person in the reception area. "I didn't think so." As if she'd now remembered what was in her hand, she gave a perfunctory knock on Tess's door jamb and set the container on the desk. "Samantha and Fuzzy are here."

Tess shoved her food container to the side and plastered a smile on her face. "Can you please have them wait in exam-room two, please." She opened the container and nicked a slice of cucumber from her salad while she listened to Donna usher the young girl, Sam, into the exam room.

Tess gave them a few minutes to get settled before she entered and stopped at the door. Fuzzy's fur was matted with a sticky blue substance, and knowing Sam the way she did, it was probably gum. Barely ten, Sam had been a handful since Tess had moved there. She had a menagerie of small animals that always happened to "find" their way into sticky situations. It was possible Sam meant well. The first time she came in with Chub, her white cat, covered in red lipstick and silver eyeshadow, it was easy to believe she'd been trying to give him a makeover and didn't know animals didn't wear makeup. This was probably the fifth time she'd seen Sam this year.

She placed her smile firmly on her face again. "Hi, Fuzzy. What have you got all over your fur?"

Sam pulled the light-brown English Lop out of his travel cage. Almost the size of her, he spilled over her arms as she placed him on the exam table. "Well, I was trying to see if I could give him a mohawk."

Tess gently lifted paws off the table to see how much of him was covered. "And what did she use to give you a mohawk?" Thankfully his belly was free of blue gunk.

"Hubba Bubba sour gum." To illustrate, Sam blew a giant bubble and let it pop against her face. "Want some?"

Tess shook her head. "Well, Fuzzy. I hate to tell you this, but instead of an awesome mohawk, you're going to have to have a shave."

Sam began to cry, and Tess rolled her eyes to the ceiling. What did you expect when you stuck gum in your rabbit's fur? She tried to pull Fuzzy off the table, but Tess quickly scooped him up.

"Now don't worry, Fuzzy. This will not hurt, and I promise all your fur will grow back. It probably won't take that long at all. But you have to promise you're not going to stick gum in your hair anymore. Okay?"

Sam wiped her nose with the back of her arm. "You'll be okay, Fuzzy." She wiped her own eyes, restored suddenly. "Can I watch?"

"Sorry, Fuzzy. It'll just be me and you, but I'll take good care of you." Tess walked out as fast as she could.

Tess escaped to the back surgery, where Prisha was folding blankets. She held Fuzzy aloft to showcase his new look. "I'm about to perform a shave and a haircut. Care to join?"

Prisha dropped the blanket she was holding. "Oh my God," she mouthed. Prisha always talked in a low whisper at work, afraid someone might overhear her. When not at work she was the loudest person in the room. "What happened?" She walked over and touched the sticky blue stuff clinging to the poor rabbit's fur. Fuzzy wiggled his nose at them.

"Apparently bubble gum is the new hair gel. I swear, that child should not be allowed to own pets." Tess set Fuzzy down on the table, arranging him so he'd be comfortable.

Prisha had come with the clinic, which was a windfall for Tess. As a vet technician she knew her stuff and wasn't afraid to get her hands dirty. She had two cocker spaniels named Dipsy and Doodle. Tess didn't think those names suited two very prima donna dogs. However, she wasn't one to talk.

"Oh, come on. She's a kid. It's not like she meant to hurt him. She was having a little fun." Prisha fished out their electric shaver, usually used for preparing animals for surgery, and plugged it in.

Tess gave her a look that told her what she thought of Sam's idea of fun.

"You are such a hard-ass. What are you going to be like when you have kids of your own?" When Tess didn't say anything, she asked, "Don't you want kids?"

"God, no. Why would I want those?" She started to laugh, but Prisha's stony expression stopped her. Why did everyone take this conversation so seriously? She felt like she'd been having it her whole life. It had been a bit of a relief when she'd figured out she was a lesbian. She assumed that fact would keep people from asking her, "So, when are you planning to have children?" But no. They still asked. And she knew lesbians who had some. At no point in her life did she have the urge to have something shoved up her lady bits in order to plant a seed so she could carry around another human being for nine months, only to have to clean up after them for the next eighteen years. Why did people think that prospect sounded inviting?

"I have more than enough animals to keep my life fulfilled."

"Would you say your life is fulfilled?"

Tess bit the inside of her cheek. Her life was far from what she'd expected as a child. But then she wasn't living in Hawaii rescuing dolphins by day and enjoying her spacious condo overlooking Waikiki beach by night. Goals changed. Reality set in. If she had to sum up her life now, content was the best word she could come up with.

Tess waved the shaver in the air. "Doesn't this scream 'fulfilled'?"

❖

After her run-in with Tess, Easton retreated from the town. She felt too exposed on the streets. Not that they were busy. The streets back home were more crowded than this. Easton soon realized the open sky was giving her anxiety, making her feel small and obsolete, putting into perspective the enormity of being on the surface. A few weeks ago she was worried she'd be too elated to be out in the open, breathing air and watching day fall to night. Elation was the last thing she felt right now. Her NFC chip hadn't worked, and now she had to figure out why, or else she'd be adrift.

Easton had found a quaint old farmhouse on the outskirts of town, close enough to walk, yet far out enough to be isolated. The name on the mailbox read PATTERSONS in bright-red paint. She'd spent an hour walking the neighbourhood, keeping an eye on the place to make sure no one was home or watching it. With only five houses on this street, all much newer than the farmhouse, this part of town had few neighbours. At one point this had been a farm, possibly during or after the gold rush. Some prospector had decided to put down roots and find a better use of their time than sifting through rivers for gold flecks.

Easton didn't understand the desire to attain wealth very well. Of course, some people would always be better off than others. In her time period, it was the politicians and the enforcers, the people who held the power. But you didn't get there with wealth; you had to be elected. If you didn't hold any of those positions, you were in the same position as everyone else.

It seemed, at least to Easton, that most of human history had been focused on amassing as much wealth as possible, because in this time, wealth equalled power, and having power meant you got to hold on to your wealth. Only who could try to collect wealth had changed from one century to the next. That didn't mean they would succeed. In fact, few did. This preoccupation with money was a waste of time and one of the reasons humans had practically destroyed themselves.

The development of nanotechnology had been big business, with ramifications across a whole herd of fields. Zach Nolan had spent so much time creating something that would make him wealthy, he'd never considered the downside of that greed.

She'd gained access to the farmhouse through a basement window that hadn't latched properly. The woman had said they were gone for the entire winter, and while Easton believed that was the case, she still wanted to be cautious. What if the Pattersons had hired someone to take care of the house and hadn't told anyone? So far that didn't seem to be the case. She'd been watching the house for a while, and no one had slept over, or if they had, they'd been gone early in the morning.

Though the basement was freezing when she entered, the upstairs was better, yet the house was chilly. Still, Easton wasn't going to complain. She had a roof over her head and was out of the wind and elements.

She found a closet upstairs with extra blankets that smelled of laundry soap and wrapped herself in one. Then she chose a quiet corner to sit down and figure out what had gone wrong with her NFC chip. The chip wasn't the only augmentation surgery she'd had. They'd also implanted a small computer in her forearm that communicated with the chip. It had an encryption algorithm that should let her unlock doors and pay for items with any device that used near-field communication. However, if the algorithm wasn't correct, it would render the chip a useless piece of silicon in her hand.

Nestled in a cocoon of warmth, Easton slipped her arm out of her jacket and pressed four fingers to the area right below her wrist on the inner part of her left forearm. When in sleep mode, the display appeared skin-like, but it came to life by fingerprint recognition. After ten seconds a screen four centimetres by ten appeared on her arm, followed by a soft purple glow. The logo for her ministry appeared, followed by a simple GUI interface.

First, she checked to make sure she was in the right time and place, and as suspected, she was. Next, she opened her list of algorithms and scrolled the list until she came to the one she needed. If this was wrong, she worried others would be too. The chip wasn't only for payments. She could also use it to access areas locked by access control systems, as well as retrieve information on devices that used NFC chips, such as smartphones and some laptops. She was limited to the uses in this century, but as time went on, this type of technology was used for almost everything. It was almost like a skeleton key, allowing her entry into some of the most used systems of everyday life.

It was growing dark by the time Easton finally figured out that the algorithm wasn't updating dynamically but was stuck on the date she'd arrived. It wasn't a huge issue since she could change that setting manually. It just meant she'd have to remember to do that each day, or her chip wouldn't work.

Hungry, Easton wandered down to the kitchen. She was careful not to turn on any lights in case one of the few neighbours noticed. She hadn't eaten anything since that pastry this morning. But, truth be told, she wasn't sure what she'd do if she did find something. The contents of the fridge were sparse—only a few condiments. She left the fridge open as light to check the cupboards, most of it things she didn't recognize. The cans of soup seemed obvious, but a jar of something called peanut butter mystified her. While she could read the labels fine, she had no idea what most of it did. She pulled out a canister of baking powder, opened the lid, and sniffed. It didn't smell like anything. Was she supposed to do something to it, like add water?

After she poured a small amount into a bowl, she held it under the tap to add a bit of water. A little at first, then a bit more. She set it on the counter and watched it closely. It did nothing. She stirred it with her finger. Still nothing. "Magic baking powder, my ass. You're about as magic as a bowl of oatmeal."

She found better luck in the freezer, which held a few boxes of frozen meals. She pulled out a box of chicken korma and read the directions on the back, which described three different methods of reheating. "Why does it have to be so complicated?" She had no idea how to even turn on an oven, so that option was out. She wasn't sure what a toaster oven was or if the Pattersons even had one, so that left a microwave, which she'd also never used but had seen in a video once.

After several attempts to start the microwave and select the right time, she had a hot meal in front of her. She didn't feel comfortable sitting at the table. Standing felt less intrusive. After the first few bites she realized she needed to stir the contents to make the heat consistent instead of containing pockets of hot and cold. On one hand, she wasn't entirely sure what she'd eaten, but on the other, it was probably the most flavourful thing she'd ever tasted. She couldn't decide if it was a flavour she liked or not. Perhaps over the years her tastebuds had gotten used to the bland porridge she ate the majority of the time.

Easton still hadn't turned on any lights. The night was clear, and the moon had risen to shed a beam of white light through the window over the sink.

The Pattersons struck her as practical people. The house wasn't ostentatious, with minimal furniture and decorations. Mostly oil paintings and family pictures from over the years hung on the walls. They had three kids, now grown with their own kids. Two sons and a daughter. She guessed something had happened to the daughter because she didn't appear in any pictures past her teenage years. Maybe they had grown apart.

On the fridge, fastened by a couple of magnets, were pictures of famous landmarks and sentences like Welcome to Cancun. A magnet held a postcard of the Eiffel Tower, and another one showed a picture of a white sand beach and leaning palm trees. It said Longboat Key, Florida on the front, but when she turned it over, nothing was written on the back.

It dropped from her hand when the doorbell chimed.

Tess stared at the half-eaten blue doughnut on her desk. She hadn't had anymore run-ins with Easton, which wasn't surprising. She was surprised that she'd noticed. She kept coming back to whether she'd made the right decision to press charges or not. This person was a stranger, and still Tess hadn't stopped thinking about her since she'd met her.

She waved her hand in front of her face to bring herself back to reality. It was a puzzle, and she didn't entirely trust this woman. No, correction. She didn't trust this woman. Tess knew she would worry until she got to the bottom of what this woman was doing in town.

She looked down at Lou, curled up in his bed in her office. "It's none of my business, is it?" Lou harrumphed and doubled down on his snuggled position. "No. You're right. I should let it go."

Tess's cell buzzed on her desk. It was Benny. She answered on the second ring. "Dr. Nolan." She pulled back at the loud, frantic voice on the other end. "It's okay. She'll be okay. How long has it been since she went into labour?" Tess was throwing her coat on as she listened. Benny was the calmest person she knew, besides Colin. If he was this worked up, she didn't want to waste any time.

"I'll be right over." She pulled her jacket and hat off the coat rack. "I have an emergency. Benny's mare gave birth, and there's been a complication," she called to Donna as she sailed past and out the door, only waiting for Lou to squeeze by before letting it go.

As soon as she pulled up to the old ranch, she knew something was very wrong. Benny was standing on the edge of the drive waiting for her, shifting from side to side as if the sheer act of standing still was too much for him. Tess slammed the truck into park and leaped down into the muck in the drive. Lou followed her out, taking a moment to sniff around before joining Tess.

"What happened? How's the foal?"

"The foal's okay. He arrived about three hours ago. But Diz, she hasn't shed the placenta yet, and I don't know what to do. I've never had this problem before."

First, Tess had to calm Benny down. It didn't help to get riled up near horses, or any animal for that matter. She walked a few paces behind as he led her into the barn. In a stall halfway down, she could hear shuffling and soft neighing. Benny's mare, Discriminate Save, Diz for short, was pacing the stall, keeping her flank against the far wall. Tess placed a hand on Benny's arm. "Do you have any hot water, water that's been boiled and cooled, and a clean cloth?"

Benny stood a moment, blinking, then nodded. "I can get some."

"Great." Tess smiled in what she hoped was a reassuring way, thankful he had something to occupy his time. Next, she stepped into the stall slow and easy, so as not to spook Diz. In the corner she could see the foal all curled up in a ball, resting while he could. They didn't stay still for long at that age. After a brief external examination, Tess walked back to her truck to grab her kit.

She wanted to try the least invasive way first, which was a dose of Oxytocin. They'd wait it out, and hopefully that would do the trick. If not, things could get tricky. She hoped like hell it did work. Horses died from this. While it was serious, it wasn't time to panic yet.

Chapter Six

Two weeks earlier

Easton sat in a stark room with five other operatives, her hands clasped in her lap and her attention on the front screen with their slipback breakdown. In two weeks she'd be slipping back a little over two hundred years to change history. If they could prevent the invention of nanotechnology, they might be able to reverse their current fate. It wasn't the first time they thought they'd had it. But like most significant inventions, they happen more than once and sometimes simultaneously.

In the third century BC, eighteen hundred years before Nicolaus Copernicus, Aristarchus of Samos came up with what would be known as the heliocentric system. Even Edgar Allan Poe had speculated accurately about an infinitely expanding universe that began from a denser unified state, almost fifty years before a multitude of scientists theorized it.

But more commonly, starting in the seventeenth century, discoveries and inventions were happening at the same time. This increasingly became the norm, so much so that scientists began to speculate as to why. The theory of mimetics, of self-replicating culture, was applied. Ideas and experiences can be passed through culture, the building blocks for inventions.

And such was the case with nanotechnology. This science that began in the late twentieth century saw numerous pushes by many different scientists from all over the world, each building on one another's ideas. But actual individual nanobots were invented a total of five times by twenty-five different individuals over a period of sixty-six years.

Level five of the MOD had become most interested in this technology because it would eventually cause the human species to be relegated to a few underground colonies in the twenty-third century.

In 1959, Richard Feynman's talk, "There's always room at the bottom," presented the general concepts of nanotechnology, as it began to be called in 1981. At first, humans considered it a boon, a benign device to get things done faster, cleaner, and more efficiently. But in 2102 a mutation in a nanobot created an army that began to target humans as a threat to the planet, and therefore themselves.

Now, even though teams of people had invented nanotechnology over several decades, removing just one instance from the timeline wasn't enough. They all had to be removed. But not only that, because of the way inventing depended so fully on mimetics, all references to the technology had to be removed, including fictional references, which included thousands of works spanning centuries.

Also, given that stimulus affected everything in the universe presented an even larger problem. If they removed or changed something, an alternative evolved to replace it in some way. It was like a bucket of water that refilled itself every time it rained. You could knock it over, but the next time those storm clouds rolled in, it would be full of water again.

Eventually they realized they had to eliminate the references to fiction all at the same time, including the physicist Richard Feynman, who put the idea in people's heads in the first place. But dealing with time was tricky. It was the most malleable yet the most static thing in the universe, and the only real way to change it was to warp it from multiple angles.

Operatives were never sent back again. You had one shot. Once you returned, if you returned, you were transferred to the research and training department. Firsthand knowledge of the past was vital to instruct new operatives.

Easton sat on the edge of her seat, ready to take her place in history, literally. She'd been training for this mission for the last five years, when she'd been recruited to level five. Never would she have thought she'd get a chance to see the world she'd dreamed about as a child. But here it was, laid out in front of her. In two weeks she'd be sent back to a time when humans lived above ground, a time when they didn't have to be afraid of the noises they made or the slipbacks coming from their industry. They were the dominant species of the planet and had been for hundreds of thousands of years. It only took technology to fuck it all up. She had always wondered how dinosaurs could dominate the earth for two hundred and twenty-eight million years, and the only thing that stopped them was a giant asteroid hitting the planet. Humans? They'd managed to screw it all up in the span of three hundred thousand years, and all because they had opposable thumbs.

"Now, this is not going to be a Sunday morning sleep-in." Harper, her supervisor, strolled in front of a screen that encompassed the entire front wall of the briefing room. It had several graphs showing the different teams and which year and slipback they were assigned to. "Because of the nature of slipbacks, each of you will be sent back alone. We can't pinpoint the exact time and place, especially if there are two operatives. Therefore, once you arrive, you will be on your own." She flicked to the next screen, still pacing in front. "These are some of the side effects you may experience once you arrive. Nausea, short-term memory loss, muscle fatigue, and, most seriously, time-dysplasia. This happens rarely, and less so now. But certain times operatives have become confused and disoriented. It happens when their body doesn't take well to being displaced in time. If you experience fainting, double vision, or extreme headaches, use your recall immediately."

Someone in the group mumbled. A few months ago, an operative who'd been sent back for reconnaissance had used their recall to come back after experiencing time-dysplasia, and the results had not been pretty. He died on the slipback floor before the medics could even get to him. All the operatives now had that extra worry to take with them.

Harper pressed a button on the side of her screen, and a timeline with dates and places popped up on it. "If you're being sent before the twenty-first century, you're on what's known as a deep-time slipback, meaning you are to destroy ideas and information."

Easton looked down at her slipback tablet. She hadn't been selected for a deep-time slipback, which was good. Such individuals were generally sent back during one slipback and then pulled forward several times. Mainly, they destroyed documents related to nanotechnology.

The other type of operative went back to destroy people. Easton hadn't been given her assignment yet—sometimes you didn't find out who your target was until the day before your slipback—but she knew she would eventually be forced to kill someone.

This was a far cry from where Easton had started. She'd always been fascinated with history, more so than most. Calla had never understood her desire to know the past. She felt it would only make Easton feel worse about their situation since you could do nothing to change it. Their father had been the same way. Why worry about the past? Focus on what was good in the here and now. Their mother had been more like Easton, and in fact, Easton was sure her mother had instilled a love of the past in her in the first place. She used to tell stories so real Easton felt like she was there herself experiencing these wonderful things.

When Easton started school, it had seemed natural for her to take history. And when she graduated, the Ministry of Discourse, which researched the past, trying to preserve it for future generations, hired her. And deep down, Easton hoped they were also trying to find a way out of their current situation. She'd had no idea how right she was.

When she was first promoted to level five and informed of what their real purpose was, she didn't actually think she would ever be selected. Not everyone was. So she hadn't given it much thought. She was more excited at the prospect that actual people were working to change the past so they wouldn't have to live like this anymore. Never mind that, if they did change the past, she and her sister would no longer exist. The whole thing had been a fantasy, a story from her childhood her mother told. None of it seemed more than that.

Everyone at level five went through the same training. They learned about the past as much as they could, knowing some of history had been lost forever. They were skilled in combat and participated in the same boot camp as if they would be chosen. None of it had sunk in until the day Harper had called her into her office three months ago to tell her she'd been promoted to team three. That meant she would be given a target to assassinate sometime in the late-twentieth or early to mid-twenty-first century.

Even now, with more than three months to think about it, she found it unreal. She knew she would do it, however, because millions of people were counting on her ability to do her job.

Easton sat at one of the empty desks on the probability floor, referred to by most people as the math room. The room was dotted with desks, places for people to work with minimal distractions. Very little talking happened in the math room. It was a place to read or work out the probability of a certain event with the AI, which was fairly accurate when predicting the outcome of a certain slipback.

For instance, if someone predicted what the outcome of removing a certain work of literature or a research paper from the timeline would do, the AI could forecast the outcome within 60 to 90 percent certainty. The problem arose only regarding something significant within history, like removing a person from the timeline. An obscure research paper or little-known work of fiction might have touched perhaps hundreds of people in its lifetime. A person had trillions of connections a year.

But this wasn't as impossible to calculate as one would imagine. Far from it. During a single lifespan, a human being formed only a certain number of significant connections. And even fewer of those impact the timeline in any meaningful way. A marriage, a divorce, having kids were significant, but the chance elements of the day-to-day have very little impact on the world. Time seems to speed up as people age because they have fewer new experiences in a given day, so the brain dismisses the average to save space for the unexpected.

When the AI is asked to look at only these significant milestones in a person's life, it becomes easier to foresee the result of their absence. According to the MOD scientists it is easier to remove someone and affect the timeline only slightly than people would like to think.

When Easton first heard this fact, it struck her as sad beyond measure. If her mom had been an erasure, the powerful sorrow her family felt didn't register in the timeline, and ultimately the only thing her mom contributed was having two daughters. And even having children isn't as significant as people think.

Take, for instance, Eliza Grace Symonds. Say someone was to travel back to the year 1840 and remove her. She would never have met and married Alexander Melville Bell and, in turn, would never have given birth to Alexander Graham Bell in 1847. Now, you could argue that removing the inventor of the telephone, one of the most important inventions of the nineteenth century, would bring chaos to the timeline. But without Bell, Elisha Gray would have been awarded the patent for a device that relayed speech through a water transmitter. Both patents were filed on the same day. Time would've moved on perhaps a little differently, but the foundation would've remained the same.

The scientists at MOD were finding that time was very fluid and very forgiving, except when you did want to change something. In the end, they found they had to work backward and forward at the same time.

This next slipback, which had been in the planning stages for over two years, would send out twenty-five operatives. Fifteen deep-time operatives would work their way up from the beginning of nanotechnology's introduction into the timeline, each jumping several times in what were known as sideslips, and ten operatives were sent back to remove specific people from the timeline. The result, according to the AI, was a 99.5 percent probability of the erasure of nanotechnology in the timeline. They hoped this would set society back on track and that they would no longer find themselves living underground, targeted by armies of nanobots.

The day after she'd been assigned to the slipback, Easton had asked Dr. Filby what would happen if they succeeded. He gave her his lopsided grin. "Well, if it works, we'll never know it."

"What do you mean?"

"If the timeline changes as we're hoping, my timeline will never exist, meaning I'll never have been born."

"What about us? Doesn't that create a paradox? If we're not around to go back in time to change it, how does that all work?"

"If time were linear, it would create a paradox. But as far as we can tell, once you pass into a particular time, you belong to it. So everyone who is not in this time when the changes take effect will still exist, because in your past, you were born, you lived, and you travelled to the past. That can't change. But your future is uncertain, as is the world's, because it hasn't happened in that timeline yet."

Easton shook her head. She thought she should understand, but some elements didn't make sense to her. Their conversation had taken place after one of the briefings in the math room, which had emptied out almost as soon as the meeting ended, so they had the place to themselves. Filby was the only person she felt comfortable talking to about this concern. Most of the other doctors gave such a disconnect she once wondered if they were even human. Filby was one of the few who talked to her like she wasn't an idiot.

"So what happens when we return to our old timeline?"

Filby perched on the desk behind him. "That's the great mystery." He shrugged. "I have several theories, but we won't know until it happens."

Easton waved for him to continue. He folded his arms and said, "One of the most likely scenarios is that when you press your recall to return, nothing happens, and you just stay in your current time. Or you could return to the here and now, but it's the continuation of your current timeline, meaning nothing would be the same."

"Meaning we would see all the effect our actions caused, good or bad, but…"

"No one you knew in this life would still exist."

Easton had been thinking about that ever since, because Calla wouldn't exist.

She bent her head to the desk to study the files displayed on the monitor imbedded in the surface. The next file that popped up was Dr. Zachary Nolan. He held a bachelor's degree in advanced sciences from Waterloo, one of the first to graduate from the university's nanotechnology engineering program. He had a master's in physics from the University of British Columbia and a doctorate in cellular and molecular biology from the University of Toronto.

He'd spent the first half of his career working for a company called BioNxt, but little was known about them beyond their name and the names of several CEOs over a ten-year span. After BioNxt, he didn't surface again for two years, until he began working for a company with no name. They only knew it was a contractor for the Canadian and US military.

Nolan had helped develop a weapon that, when shot or damaged, could repair itself, and his development of the team unit helped usher in a new era of warfare. But this particular application hadn't led to the destruction of the human species, though a side project he had developed to patrol borders and identify threats created the devastating combination.

Easton stopped and rubbed her eyes. She hadn't eaten all day, and her stomach was telling her it was time to rectify that oversight. She closed her station and exited the math room.

The MOD building was built far below the crust, and the general public was aware of only its top six floors. Easton stepped onto a lift and rose from the depths of the MOD to crust level, where the remainder of the species lived, huddled together in carved-out tunnels in the earth's crust roughly a hundred kilometres below the surface.

Four cities in all were connected to each other by tunnels and high-speed trains. Originally there had been five, but an earthquake fifty years previously had collapsed many of the structures of one city, and they'd abandoned it.

The lift doors opened into the empty lobby. It was past working hours for most, but Easton liked working late. It was nice to enter the lobby when she and the night clerk were the only ones there. She nodded to the man whose name she didn't know but she'd nodded to almost every night for the past five years. She passed through the scanners, pausing for an instant until she heard the tiny wisp that signalled she was free to exit the building.

Few crowds were on the street. The lights had dimmed to simulate evening, so above was nothing but darkness, the lights too low to see the ceiling of the cavern. Easton tucked her hands into her pockets and turned left toward her apartment. What would happen to her memories of Calla if she were to succeed and Calla no longer existed?

Chapter Seven

Easton stared up at the ceiling above her bed, although it wasn't her bed. Hers didn't have a view of the morning sky. She'd chosen one of the upstairs bedrooms with the nicest view. She was sure it wasn't the Pattersons' because it didn't have any of the personal touches, nor was it the biggest. Instead, it had huge windows that almost reached the floor and looked out into the backyard.

She felt more secure in the house after her encounter with one of the other neighbours, who'd seen the light of the fridge from across the way and come to investigate. Easton was more than happy that they'd rung the doorbell instead of called the police, which she mentioned to Thomas, the neighbour.

She'd explained she was house-sitting for the Pattersons, expecting him to be suspicious and ask a million questions. An older gentleman who'd lived in the area for decades, he was more concerned that no lights were on in the house, and she'd explained they weren't working. He'd offered to help, but she said she had it under control.

For the next several hours she'd worried that he might come back with the police, but he never did. That incident gave her confidence to be a little more brazen.

Now as she lay between the soft, warm sheets of the bed she'd commandeered, she primarily worried that none of this was turning out as she'd expected. Periodically, throughout the day, she kept returning to the conversation she'd had with Tess at the coffee shop. Tess had seemed flirty but cautious. She'd also shown kindness. At the clinic she could've easily had her arrested, but she hadn't. Not that she'd expected her targets to be mouth-drooling assholes. But she wasn't prepared for charming and beautiful.

That was one of the main issues they'd covered. What happens if you sympathize with the person you're preparing to remove from the timeline.

The majority of the people they would encounter would be decent, moral people, whose only crime was being intelligent. Easton and the other operatives were being asked to weigh these lives against the suffering of billions, not just in the past but over centuries. It was a classic case of the few for the many.

Easton had often heard questions about removing a parent and not wanting to leave the child behind. The man sitting next to her had asked if they could take out the child as well, and Easton had gone cold. It was if he were playing chess in his head, and the pawns at the front of the board were disposable. He had little care for people who had lived centuries before him. Before that lecture, she hadn't thought much about the short-term consequences of removing someone from the timeline. If that person had taken Calla, she could imagine the hole it would leave in her life.

Before that day in class, she hadn't worried what it would be like to remove someone from the timeline. Reading this argument in a textbook, she found it more than logical. If you had the chance to save hundreds of billions of lives and make life better for an entire species and all you had to do was murder—because that's what it was, even if no one called it that—a few hundred people, would you join the cause? The theory was far simpler than the practice. After that class, the thought consumed her.

It promised to be another overcast day, which made Easton happy. Her eyes were slowly adjusting to the light, but it was hard not to squint when she was outside. Indoors was better. Slipbacks are hard on a person's body, not only because of the light sensitivity, but mild short-term memory loss, as well as dehydration and muscle aches, all of which Easton was feeling tenfold because of her injuries. Yesterday she felt like that truck had hit her. Sleeping jammed into the backseat of a car didn't help. Today she felt like she'd fallen down a steep hill and landed on a pile of rocks at the bottom, which was an improvement.

She checked the time: a few minutes past eight. Today she would stake out Tess's house. Thomas, her lovely neighbour across the way, had been very talky and mentioned that the town vet lived across the fields, where the street dead-ended past the Pattersons'. She'd also managed to snare Tess's schedule from the clinic with a simple fishing phone call and knew that she had house calls that morning so she would be out, which made it a perfect time for Easton to take a look.

She couldn't have planned it better if she'd tried. There were no houses past the Pattersons' on this side of the street, which made getting to the fields without being seen easy, even in the day.

She saw no point wasting time in bed, even if it was particularly cozy. Easton pulled the covers off and grabbed the jeans she'd been wearing for the last few days. When she went into town to grab supplies, she'd have to remember to pick up a few more things to wear. While she was sure she could fit into Trish Patterson's clothes, the woman didn't exactly share Easton's taste. Where Easton tended toward shades and darker colours, Trish was more of a pastels-and-busy-patterns type of person. She really liked her florals.

Sam Patterson, on the other hand, had a few good wool sweaters Easton could borrow and an old pea coat that, while bulky, at least was warm, with a good layer underneath.

She left the house through the backyard and went out the gate. Staying along the side of the road, she made her way into the first field, surrounded by trees and tall grass on three sides. It didn't look like it had been farmed anytime in the last century and a half. But at one point all had been plowed, judging by its geometric shape.

Easton pushed on toward a copse of trees at the far end. They had to lead to another field, which could meet up with Tess's property.

It was a grey morning, with mist hanging in the field's dips and furrows blurring the edges of reality. Once out of sight of any buildings, she almost felt like she was in another world. When she made it to the adjoining field, where the land dipped and most of the surrounding houses disappeared from view, Lou pounced with a happy bark.

"Where did you come from?" Tess called. Lou pawed at Easton, licking and demanding scratches behind the ear.

Easton hitched a thumb behind her. "Across the street. I'm house-sitting for the Pattersons." Easton bent down to give Lou the attention he demanded and, by the look on his face, felt he deserved. As soon as she stood, Lou pawed at her leg, asking for more. This was not what she'd hoped for when she'd ventured toward here. She'd expected Tess to be out by now doing house calls. Unfortunately, she'd timed it wrong.

Tess caught up to them, a little out of breath. "Don't let him guilt you like that. He gets plenty of scritches from pretty much anyone who comes near him."

Loud sirens were clanging inside Easton's head. This was a bad idea. The last thing she should be doing was spending time with Tess. She didn't want to get to know her, even though she could tell that Tess was very much someone she'd want to get to know if things were different.

Lou bounded off across the field, and Tess turned to follow. Easton wasn't sure if she should follow as well or back off and return another time.

"So you're house-sitting for the Pattersons'?" Tess asked. Well, that answered that. Easton followed them through a small patch of forest into another larger field. "For the winter, while they're in Arizona." She'd done a little snooping while she'd been in the house so she'd have some talking points. "Is all this yours?"

Tess pulled a ball out of her pocket and tossed it out into the field for Lou to fetch. "Nope. We're trespassing right now."

Easton froze, peering out over the empty field to see if she could spot anyone. "What happens if we get caught?"

Tess shrugged. "Get asked in to tea and have our ears talked off." Lou came looping around and dropped a slobber-covered ball at Tess's feet. "This property belongs to Rita Modine. She's seventy-eight and could talk the petals off a flower." Tess picked up the ball and flung it as far as she could. "Her property backs onto mine." Tess pointed back the way they'd come.

"She doesn't mind?"

"That we're here? Why would she? We're not doing anything bad. You don't have neighbours that you chat with?"

Easton had several neighbours she chatted with. It was hard not to when you lived on top of each other like they did in the west end of the city. But in order to be on someone else's property without their permission, you'd have to be in their apartment. The idea of owning land along with your living space was foreign to Easton. Calla and she were considered well off because they resided in a building with less than ten floors. The taller building apartments were like tiny coffins that housed people. At least she and her sister had their own rooms. "I know my neighbours. I just wouldn't go on their property without their permission."

Tess turned to look Easton square on. "Where are you from, Easton?"

"Nowhere important."

"And where's that?"

Some of their best researchers had prepared Easton's backstory. Operatives who had been back and studied the time had helped create a reason for Easton to be in a small town. However, the fact that Tess had found Easton in her clinic after hours beaten and broken rather badly made that explanation a little harder. She was originally supposed to be from Ontario and had given up a job in finance to pursue her dream of travel. She'd gotten a little lost along the way and fallen in love with this town and planned to stay for a while. The story about house-sitting for the Pattersons had fallen into her lap and could be adapted. But she could already tell Tess didn't entirely trust her.

"I'm more interested in where I'm going than where I'm from." That was true. In a week or two, the place she'd come from very possibly wouldn't exist anymore.

Tess pointed to a copse of trees up ahead. From this vantage point, Easton could see a small path weaving through the thick of them. "And do you know where you're going?"

Easton shook her head. “Not yet.” She turned to look at Tess and smiled. The moisture in the air had settled on Tess’s strawberry-blond hair, painting it in tiny prisms. “But I’ll let you know when I get there.” She knew she was playing with fire but didn’t care in the moment. There was something to be said about giving in to your whims.

As Tess led them through the path in the trees, Easton steered the conversation toward family and home. “Where is it you’re heading?” she asked.

“I grew up around here, but only my dad’s left.” Tess stopped abruptly. “That sounded horrible. My family’s still alive. They just moved away. That’s all. Not many people feel at home in Smokey River.”

“But you do?”

“Feel at home here?” Tess was still stopped on the path. She gazed up at the trees and then back from where they’d come, almost as if she were judging her surroundings. “I’m not actually sure. I moved back here to be close to my dad mostly. But I guess I thought it would be comforting to be here. And while I wouldn’t say I miss Vancouver—because I don’t, I really don’t—I’m not as at home here as I thought I’d be.” She started walking again, stuffing her hands into her coat pockets. “Don’t get me wrong. I have a great life. I love my job, my home, and Lou has been the best part of that. Wow. I can’t believe I’m telling you all this. I wouldn’t even tell Zach this much, although only because he’d shove it back in my face and say, ‘I told you so.’” She covered her mouth with her hand. “I’m truly sorry for the overshare.”

“Don’t be. Just because we want something to be true doesn’t mean it is. Maybe you don’t belong in Smokey River either. There are more than two places in the world.”

“I wouldn’t leave my dad. He’s had a rough go since my mom left.”

“Oh? I’m sorry. When was that?”

“Over two decades ago. He has a hard time letting go.” Tess smiled. “I know it seems strange to think I’d hang around to make sure someone else doesn’t feel lonely.”

"All the while feeling lonely yourself."

"I didn't say that."

"Sure you did. Lou, your dog, is the best thing in your life."

"Lots of people think their dogs are the best thing in their lives."

"You're right. I'm sorry." They walked a little more in silence. Easton hoped it wasn't an uncomfortable silence. She hadn't meant to offend Tess but merely to point out something that seemed so obvious to her. She would never claim to know Tess well, but she'd seen her and felt she understood her a little because she'd experienced the same thing. An outsider looking in. Tess had her work and her dog, which were small comforts in a larger life. Easton used to watch Calla, a person who was so much more comfortable in her life than Easton ever was. She had lots of friends and an actual social circle. She went out on dates and did things other than work and sleep.

Easton could be off base with Tess, but she didn't think so.

"Is Zach your brother?"

"Yeah."

"Where's he now?"

"He lives in Vancouver. He was pretty bummed when I moved back here."

"Do you see him much?"

Tess shook her head. "Not really."

Tess bent down to unlace her boots. She hadn't been able to get what Easton had said out of her head all day. She thought Tess was lonely. Was she? Was that what she'd been feeling all this time? Sure, she filled her days with work. On the weekends she went for long walks with Lou and over to her dad's for dinner every Sunday. But beyond that, what did she do? Had she even carved out a life here?

When she'd first arrived she'd felt happy to not have to worry about the pressures she'd faced in the city. Very few people were pushing her to date or be part of a couple. At work, they tended to mind their own business. As small towns went, Smokey River was a pretty low-key place to live.

But what more could she want? She'd left Vancouver because it was too much of everything. Too loud, too stressful, too much drama. She'd definitely left all that behind, but was she also running from life? She'd balked at striving to be part of a couple, but was that what she was missing in her life? Someone to share the mundane with? It seemed so stupid to run from something only to find it was the one thing she needed.

She didn't think Easton had meant her comment to be cruel. It had only been an observation. But should she take it at face value? Could she trust that this stranger had seen something she hadn't?

Tess placed her boots on the tray near her back door. Her knees cracked as she stood. The light had left the day behind a while ago, leaving the driveway dark. She peered out the mudroom window. A couple of fields to the north, Easton was settling in. She couldn't quite get her feelings about Easton in order. On the one hand she really didn't trust her, but another part of her had felt comfortable telling this stranger all this personal stuff. A part of her that had felt seen.

The next morning, she woke early and felt something she hadn't in a long time, anticipation. Lou stirred, lifted his head and cocked it to the side. "Don't be so surprised. I get up on my own all the time." Lou whined and put his head back down on the bed. Tess grabbed her phone off the side table to see if she'd missed anything important from the clinic. It was unlikely because they had only a few clients scheduled on any given day, and Donna was always really good at taking care of mundane stuff on her own.

She did find a text from Zach though. He said he was coming up for a visit this weekend and didn't know how long he'd be staying. She snuggled back down under the covers to reply. The air had gotten colder overnight. She'd have to remember to turn the heat on finally. She hated doing it because it was kind of expensive to heat the old place. Too many drafts she hadn't had a chance to fix yet. There was a woodstove in the kitchen she could use. However, that felt like too much work so early on in the season, especially when conditions could easily shift. Unlike Vancouver, Smokey River did get a fair amount of snow throughout the winter. Usually by late December, early January, there was about ten to twenty centimetres of base snow at any given time.

As she replied to her brother, she tried to rack her brain for when he'd been up last. She didn't think he'd been to the farmhouse, which meant he hadn't showed up in at least two years. She decided to include her address as well. The only time he ever visited was when their dad called to guilt-trip him. She hadn't talked to her dad in a couple of days. Maybe she should stop by and see him today.

Tess prepared coffee in the kitchen, looking out the window at the fields. She'd called the clinic and left a message on the machine to say she would be doing rounds, but was available for emergencies. She wanted to go check on Benny and see how he was holding up. Dr. Arnold, the vet she'd taken the clinic over from, was in today. He still worked two days a week, which allowed her to make more house calls, which she liked. Less chaos, most of the time, when you were at someone's house. She loved the clinic, but at times it was a lot to handle.

"Parrot's pussy," a strangled voice called from the other room.

"Shit."

The phrase was repeated a few more times before Tess entered the living room to find her African grey clinging to the door of his cage. "Alexa, all lights on," he chirped. The lights in the living room illuminated.

"Good morning, Geoff."

"Fuck off."

Tess sighed. She'd rescued Geoff from a family with young kids. Their dad had a colourful vocabulary, and their mom was tired of getting calls from her kids' teachers about their vocabularies. Tess had taken pity and adopted Geoff a year ago. Besides being versatile in every known swear word, and a few Tess had never heard before, her parrot had an attitude and liked to bite.

"Alexa, all lights off." Also he'd come with his own virtual assistant.

Tess groaned as she filled a bowl with seeds and placed it in the bottom of the cage. "I'll be back at lunch to give you some pears."

"Fuck off. Alexa, all lights on." Generally Tess was able to ignore Geoff's more colourful language. Perhaps he was why she didn't have much company.

Next she turned her attention to a giant table on the far wall, which housed a long structure with five-inch plexiglass walls. "Morning, girls." Two noses poked out of little homes, followed by three more. At the sight of her, the guinea pigs all began squealing. Glinda and Belina, her two youngest, began popcorning around the cage, hopping and racing, excited because they knew it was feeding time. "I'm in a hurry, but I'll be back at lunch." She replenished their timothy hay at the far end.

Somehow Tess had become the unofficial guinea-pig rescue in the area. She'd gotten her first two, Ozma and Dorothy, from a family moving out of province who were unable to take them. The next one, her only boy—whom she'd neutered immediately, the Nome King—had come from a family that had lost one of theirs and didn't want to get another so gave him up.

Guinea pigs were social creatures, so much so that it was cruel to keep them alone. Her next two, Belina and Glinda, each came because they'd been surprises. Their owners had thought they had two boys. It turned out they had a boy and a girl, and ten weeks later were gifted with a little one. This had happened to two different families, and Tess for some reason was always the obvious choice to take them in.

These weren't their original names. She'd renamed them. After all, it wasn't the name they responded to, but the tone of her voice.

After feeding her animals, she poured a thermos of coffee and clicked for Lou before heading back out the door.

Tess groaned the second she saw the red and blues flash behind her. "Shit." She checked her speed. She hadn't been going over the speed limit. Much. She watched Colin shuffle out of the car and stroll toward her. She rolled her window down before he had a chance to rap a knuckle on it.

"Don't you have better things to do, Colin?"

"I was on my way into the station and saw you run that stop sign back there. Thought I might make sure you weren't high or drunk."

He leaned in and sniffed the truck bed. Lou sat up and yawned, then turned three times and flopped back down. He'd had a good, long run in the fields, and now he was ready for one of several naps he'd take that day.

"A stop sign?" Tess turned in her seat to look out the back window. She hadn't even seen it, even though she knew it was there. "Sorry, Colin. My mind's been elsewhere this morning."

"Yeah. I heard." He leaned against the car. "You just come from Benny's?"

"I'm on my way there. Check to make sure he's doing okay."

"I'm really sorry about what happened."

Tess nodded again. She was sorry too. They let the silence lengthen, mourning the loss. The diffused light of the day cast a dull gloom over the hood of her truck. The wind was silent, the birds—it made for an eerie moment.

"You need me to escort you? Make sure you get there okay?"

Tess didn't need coddling. She'd been a vet long enough to experience these kinds of days many times. Sometimes you lost animals. It didn't make it any less sad. "Did you get my text from earlier?

Colin huffed. "I did, and I'm not going to do it."

"Oh, come on. It's a small favour."

Colin pushed himself back from the truck, checking for traffic. "It's also illegal. I can't just look up anyone in the system." No cars were coming from either direction.

"Okay. Fair enough. But just say, for a minute, that the other night you had looked her up—"

"I didn't."

"But say you did. Would it be illegal for me to peruse that informa—"

"Yes."

Tess groaned. She and Colin had been in school together, though not in the same grade. He was a few years older than her. "Can you at least tell me if there are any warrants out for her arrest."

He frowned and sucked in his bottom lip. After a few seconds he shook his head. "No warrants in the database."

"Ha. You did look her up."

"I merely checked the database for outstanding warrants. As a business owner you have the right to know that it doesn't appear she's ever been caught before."

"You sound so uptight, Colin. I didn't get the impression she'd done anything like that before."

"People also thought Ted Bundy was a really nice guy, even after he was charged."

Tess rolled her eyes. "Did you just compare this woman to a serial killer? You need a hobby." She was about to throw the truck into drive when she had another thought. "Does that database cover only Canada? Or did you check other countries too?"

Colin chuckled. "So you don't think she's done anything like this before, but you still suspect her of something?"

"I can't explain it. I'm sure she broke into the clinic for some DIY medical attention, which she definitely needed, yet she refused to go to the hospital with me. That tells me she's hiding something, and that doesn't sit right with me." Tess shrugged. "I guess I don't trust her."

"Nor should you. You should've let me haul her in and charge her."

Tess sighed. That didn't seem like the right call either. She couldn't figure out what was bothering her about the whole encounter. She waved to Colin as she pulled away and headed out, careful not to run any more stop signs.

Chapter Eight

Easton doubled back after saying good-bye, waiting until Tess had pulled out of the driveway before venturing closer. She approached from the back field. Tess had no neighbours, but Easton was still cautious.

The house was massive and looked like a family of ten could live there. What if their intel was wrong, and she did have a whole family living here? One woman in this giant house somehow didn't seem right, and she stood by her earlier assessment that Tess must be lonely. She chose this town and this house. She had chosen to remove herself from life. Had something caused these decisions, or did she simply not feel like engaging in life? Easton could relate. At times she couldn't get up the energy to engage in life either.

She entered through the basement, which wasn't much more than a crawl space and storage for an ancient furnace. She dropped to the stone floor with confidence that Lou was with Tess, and she wouldn't be encountering any animals. For someone who had gone their whole life obeying the law, since she'd gotten here, she'd been doing a lot of breaking into places.

That happened when you were somewhere you didn't belong. She found it such a strange concept. Belonging. How often had Calla lectured her about not trying harder to fit in? Calla would often invite her to come out with friends. Easton had accepted only once, and that had been enough. She loved Calla, but her friends she did not. They were loud and vulgar and talked about things that didn't matter. Gossip. Who was dating whom. What so-and-so had said to whom. They would play a game where they would pair up two people and predict the outcome. When it was Easton's turn, she'd told them it wasn't polite to talk about people behind their backs. They stared at her as if she didn't get the point of the game.

By then she was aware of the MOD's true purpose and couldn't focus on anything but reversing humanity's fate. From the moment she'd heard about it, she wanted to be one of the operatives sent back, which meant she had to work her ass off to get noticed.

Well, here she was in a world she'd always dreamed of, and she was spending most of her time breaking into other people's houses.

Easton found the stairs leading up into the main house, which opened into a modernized kitchen. The only antiquated thing in the whole place was the woodstove tucked into the corner. It was a nice touch—made the place look homey and welcoming. Easton decided to search the whole house before deciding what her plan would be.

As far as their intel went, Zach Nolan would be coming to Smokey River in late fall of this year. They had narrowed it down to within a couple of days, but it was hard to be accurate this many centuries out. He would most likely be showing up within the week, which, as planned, had given Easton time to adjust to her surroundings and plan how she would remove him and Tess from the timeline.

As she made her way upstairs, she noticed black along one of the wood beams, which looked like old smoke damage. An old furnace, a woodstove—these were dangerous liabilities. On the landing stood a side table with drawers and picture frames lined up under the windowsill. She picked one up at random. It was Tess and her family when they were kids. She had pigtails, and a little boy, most likely Zach, was sticking his tongue out at the camera. They looked like a normal, happy family. It was hard to believe that they would end up, both dead, removed from time because of a fire Easton started.

She replaced the picture and continued through the house. Tess's room was on the top floor. She hesitated before entering. For some reason this invasion felt more intimate than reconnaissance.

She could see why Tess had taken the quaint, cozy attic bedroom, with its slopped ceilings and tiny fireplace at the end. Through the window fields, and beyond the road, the tip of the Pattersons' roof.

On the bed—hastily made—lay a long-sleeve chemise and boxer shorts with roosters in rainbow colours.

Easton didn't stay long. It felt wrong to snoop through Tess's personal space. Besides, she'd made her plan. As she headed back down through the house, she noted all the entrances. It would be best to enter through the basement because it had been easy to pry open the old window. She would block the clasp so she wouldn't have to force her way back in.

A spark from the woodstove in the kitchen igniting some nearby newsprint would start the fire. Easton would help it along by making sure it had adequate natural fuel. She didn't plan to use accelerant or anything that might look suspicious. She wanted it to look like they had lit a fire in the woodstove and not latched the door properly. The house was old and obviously had a history of fire, so no one would question it.

Easton climbed down the basement stairs, ducking as she reached the bottom. The first part of her plan was set. Now she had to figure out how to keep them in their beds long enough to die from smoke inhalation. Most people who die in a fire actually die from inhaling the toxic gases. She had to make sure they wouldn't wake up before that happened, which was tricky. According to the hundreds of cases she had pored over, the fire most likely wouldn't completely destroy the bodies, so she had to make sure that what she gave them to knock them out wouldn't appear in an autopsy. This part of the plan would take more thought.

Out in the open fields, Easton retraced her steps, breathing in the crisp air. The farther away she got from the house, the more her mind moved to the future. If she did succeed, what would it look like? Her computer had a tracer as well as a recall function. As soon as her slipback was complete, she would activate the recall and travel back to her own time. However, what would be there when she arrived? It wouldn't be her present but the one created by the result of their slipback. Would all operatives arrive at various times, clueless about how to navigate that world? Would they remember? One of her coworkers had worried that they would cease to exist the second they returned, because if time had changed it was unlikely any of them had ever been born. Level five didn't believe this to be the case since they did exist and would already be in the timeline when it was changed. However, no one else from their timeline would.

As they were coming back at different times, it would also be unlikely that they would run into each other, because as each slipback was completed, it would create a different timeline that would be woven into the future. Two things were certain: if they did all succeed, then level five probably would not exist when they did return to their timeline. A few operatives wondered if it would be better not to hit the recall button. Why not remain in the past if their family and friends weren't there to greet them? And, depending on the agent's slipback, some weren't guaranteed to return to a particularly good time. It was such a gamble.

Lou whined and plopped his head down on the passenger seat next to Tess. He could sense her mood, which was low. The last time she'd travelled up this particular driveway had been for an emergency, but emergencies can have good outcomes. This time, Tess knew the outcome, and it wasn't good.

She parked in front of Benny's barn and stepped down, and Lou whined again but didn't budge. "Suit yourself." Tess closed the door and went looking for Benny. She found him ten minutes later in the barn office, his head in the books, a thermos of coffee on the edge of his desk. Tess knocked and leaned on the doorjamb. "How're you doing?"

Benny looked up, pulled off his glasses, and stretched. "Jesus. What time is it?"

Tess checked her watch. "Quarter past nine."

"In the morning?" Benny threw his glasses on a stack of papers and reached for his thermos.

Tess entered and grabbed a seat, moving a stack of books to the floor to make space for herself. "Please tell me you weren't in here all night."

The room was jammed full of stuff—shelves rammed with books and ledgers, a desk with an old PC pushed to the side. The furniture was office chic circa 1956. Tess angled her chair toward the heater in the corner of the room.

"Would you like a cup?" Benny offered her the lid, which she took and smiled, leaving the thermos for himself.

"How is she?"

Benny shrugged, sipping from the thermos. "She's not eating much. I just don't know what to do for her. Hell. I wouldn't know what to do if it was a human mother who'd lost her baby."

"I'm so sorry. If there was—"

Benny waved her off. "Nah. Don't talk like that. It wasn't your fault. I called you up to help with Diz, and neither of us was thinking about the colt. I mean, she's healthy, right? She can have more?"

"That's one reason I came today. I wanted to check up on her, see if she's healing well. I also wanted to see how you were doing. It's not easy, especially because it was so unexpected."

"If she's healthy, how long?" Benny placed the thermos down, hard. "Damn. That sounded so crass. I just... I hate seeing her so sad. She hasn't moved from the spot where he...died. I guess I'm hoping it will make her feel better."

Tess stood and placed a hand on Benny's shoulder. "It'll take time. While I don't think we could ever deny that horses grieve, the emotions they feel are less complex than ours. She will get over this. It's a part of life. And if she's healthy, she'll most likely be ready in about a month."

Benny nodded, cupping his hands and squeezing them between his knees. "It all feels so pointless, you know? And I keep playing it over in my mind, how happy I was to finally see the placenta, only to realize that he wasn't moving. I just can't keep the two thoughts in my head at the same time. I don't know if that makes sense."

Tess crouched next to him. "You're going to grieve too, which is normal, and maybe even worse than Diz. I think you should seriously think about talking to someone. A doctor. Not just me. I'm not good at this shit."

Benny waved her off. "I don't need therapy. I've been raising animals long enough to know it doesn't always go as planned. And like you said, it's part of life. It's fresh, that's all."

Tess patted his knee and stood. "If you're not feeling better by the time you start trying to breed Diz again, I want you to promise me you'll see someone."

A look of extreme distaste flitted over Benny's face, but after a second or two, he nodded.

"Let's go take a look at Diz."

An hour later, when she climbed back in the truck with Lou, she was emotionally spent. He gave her sympathetic eyes. "Why do I have to deal with people, Lou? Why can't it just be animals?" He didn't have an answer for her, not that she was expecting one. She sighed as she pulled out of the drive. She wanted to help. Her heart broke for what Benny was going through, but she felt as powerless as he did trying to help Diz. She never had the right words for situations like this. And if she did occasionally seem to say something helpful, it always felt false, even when she meant it. Responding to grief was trite. She could never experience what the other person was feeling, so everything she said sounded clichéd.

On her way to her next appointment, she decided to stop at the hardware store. The latch for her woodstove had broken last winter, and she needed to fix it before she could use it again.

Lou jumped out of the cab after her. He was always welcome in the hardware store. Bill and Cindy, the owners, had a husky named Burk, who had a soft spot for porcupines. Unfortunately he kept trying to make friends, and the porcupines weren't interested.

The doors slid open, and Lou beelined for the back. Tess, on her own mission, headed in the opposite direction in search of a woodstove-door replacement.

She was discovering she might have to order a new one online when she heard a familiar voice.

"Well, hi there, Lou. Are you off on your own today?"

Tess followed the voice to find Lou splayed on the ground, belly up, tongue out, enjoying belly rubs from the familiar dark-haired woman.

"You're such an attention whore, Lou," Tess said. Coming upon the scene she couldn't help but smile. "I wish you'd show more restraint." Lou cocked his head like he had no idea what she was talking about.

Easton smiled up at Tess but addressed Lou when she spoke, which actually softened Tess's heart more than she'd care to admit. "You told me you were out and about on your own today. Have you wandered off?"

"He mentioned he had a few things to get." She suspected Lou had grabbed her scent the second they entered the store and went in search. He seemed to have a soft spot for her.

"So. We seem to be bumping into each other a lot."

"Almost like it was planned."

"How's house-sitting going?" Tess looked down at Easton's basket, which was filled with a box of strike-anywhere matches, gardening gloves, and duct tape.

"Great."

Tess didn't know the Pattersons very well. They were much older and generally kept to themselves. Some of her neighbours would have BBQs in the summer and invite lots of people in the area, but the Pattersons hadn't been ones for parties. From what Tess could remember, they had retired here from Calgary about five years before Tess moved back. They'd run a business there that had something to do with horses.

Now, according to Benny, they didn't want anything to do with them. He found that strange and had remarked on it several times. "You're either horse people or you're not," he'd said. "You don't just stop." He'd said a lot about it being in your blood and whatnot, but she'd tuned him out at that point. Benny was definitely a horse person. He lived, breathed, and slept horses. As far as she was concerned, if the Pattersons wanted nothing more to do with horses, that was their business. She couldn't understand why Benny had gotten so bent out of shape about it.

Lou had settled on the ground between them, his tongue still lolling out the side of his mouth.

"How long are you going to be house-sitting?"

"A few weeks?" She seemed uncertain.

"Aren't they usually gone the whole winter? Is someone else coming in when you leave?"

Easton shrugged. "They only hired me for a few weeks. I'm not sure what they have planned."

"Fair enough."

"How was your…appointment?" Easton asked.

Tess shrugged. "Not great. A friend of mine's mare gave birth a couple days ago. The mare's placenta hadn't dropped, and I went to check her out. While I was there the colt died. I'm still waiting on lab results, but I'm pretty sure he had an infection of some sort. He wasn't nursing properly, which we didn't notice at first." She shrugged. "I wish I could do more, but right now I can just give him some answers."

"If you had known, what would you have done differently?"

Tess looked up to the ceiling, thinking. It was easy after the fact to say what you'd do because now you knew something was wrong. It was silly to speculate. She shook her head. "I can't do anything now."

"See. You can't blame yourself for not knowing the future."

"If I had a magic ball to see the future with, my job would be a hell of a lot easier. For one thing, I'd know when to triple-glove." Even though she'd meant it as a joke, Tess didn't laugh. It had felt good to shed some of her worries. But she still felt guilt for not noticing the colt sooner.

Chapter Nine

Tess pulled into her driveway at dusk to find a strange car in front of the garage. She eased behind the dark-grey Beemer and put the parking brake on but left the truck running.

The lights were on in her house, but no one was moving around inside. Lou was still lumped on the seat next to her. She didn't doubt for a second that if a burglar were inside, as a team, she and Lou wouldn't stand a chance.

Instead of putting herself in that situation, she struck the horn, hitting it several times to get the attention of whoever was there. If they were friendly, they'd come out and see what was going on, and if they weren't, she still had the relative safety of her truck and could back up and be out of the driveway in seconds.

It took less than a minute for the side door to slap open. Light spilled onto the darkened driveway. Zach, her brother, stood in bare feet, a sandwich in one hand. "What the hell?"

Tess jumped out of the cab, both relieved and furious with him, which was pretty much how their entire relationship had gone. "I thought you weren't coming until tomorrow." She waited for Lou to jump out behind her before shutting the door. "How did you even get in? I don't keep a spare key around."

Zach took a huge bite of his sandwich. "The basement window has a broken latch," he mumbled around the food in his mouth.

She smacked him on the arm. "You scared the shit out of me. I thought someone was breaking into my house."

"Who the hell would want to break in? You don't even own a TV, and your laptop looks like it's from the 90s."

"And how would they know that unless they broke in?"

"Are you kidding? This place doesn't look like it's holding any special treasures." Zach grinned. He had the same dark-blue eyes as Tess, but his hair was a darker blond, and he was a foot taller. His laugh came easily, and she could almost forget the anxiety and fear in his voice the last time they spoke.

"You should've seen the place when I bought it. It was a real shit hole." Tess followed Lou into the house, Zach trailing behind her.

"So naturally you had to have it."

"Did you eat all my food?"

"Not yet."

The kitchen looked like someone who didn't live there had made a sandwich and left everything out in case they wanted another. "By all means, make yourself at home."

"You should really fix the furnace in this place. It sounds like a dead cow's come back from the dead to be murdered again."

"That's an image I never want in my head. Besides, the furnace is fine. It just takes a few days to get into its groove."

"If I bought cars the same way you describe furnaces, I'd be dead."

Tess screwed the lid on the mayonnaise and placed it in the fridge. "Why are you here again?"

"When was the last time you talked to Dad?" Zach took a seat on one of the stools to watch the cleanup happen from a more comfortable place. He licked a spot of mayonnaise off his thumb and stuffed the last of the sandwich into his mouth.

Tess shrugged, grabbing a cloth from the sink to wipe down the counter. "Last week sometime? Have you called to tell him you're in town?"

Zach rescued a cucumber slice from the counter and popped it into his mouth. "I'm putting it off until I'm mentally ready to deal with his shit."

"His shit? He misses you."

"The first thing he always asks is, 'how's your mother?' The fact that it's been decades since she left him and he's still sitting there in his BarcaLounger with a Molson in one hand and the remote in the other waiting for her to walk through the door irritates me so much…" He shrugged. "I just don't know what to say to him."

"You talk to her more than any of us." Tess hated that their dad chose to hold on to memories of their mother, especially since he felt Zach was the one to connect with her. She'd left when they were ten and, as far as Tess knew, hadn't been back in B.C. since. Tess was more than happy to cut her out of their lives like she had, but Zach took it a little harder. He wasn't as close to their dad, and Tess always suspected he was upset she hadn't taken them with her. But Tess knew why. She'd been ten years younger than their dad and hadn't been ready for kids or life in a small town. What had once seemed cozy and safe quickly turned cloying. She'd fled to Ontario and met a man and started a whole new family that didn't include any of them, although Tess wasn't exactly sure of the order of things. It was possible she met the man before moving to Ontario, but none of that mattered now.

"When was the last time you talked to her?"

Tess rinsed the cloth in the sink. "Christmas? We had our annual awkward conversation where she pretends to care what's going on in my life, and I pretend to care that she cares." Tess folded the washcloth and placed it over the tap in the sink. "I agree that Dad needs to move on. She doesn't give a shit about any of us, and she's definitely not going to leave her cushy life in Oakville to come back here and join Dad's couch-potato lifestyle."

"Because who doesn't want to live in the same town they grew up in?"

"It's not the town. It's how he lives his life."

"Is this how you want to live your life? Hiding away from the world?"

Ever since she'd brought up leaving Vancouver, he'd been sore about it. In a way he probably felt like she was abandoning him as well. That wasn't how she thought of it. Sometimes Zach couldn't see past his own feelings.

"I like it here. I have Lou and the clinic and this house. I don't need anything else." Why was everyone on her case lately about how she lived her life?

"M'kay."

Tess poured herself a glass of wine, presenting the bottle to Zach to ask if he'd like one as well. She shouldn't have bothered. Zach only drank beer.

"Alexa, all lights on," came the scratchy voice from the living room.

"Let me guess," Zach dead-panned. "A cockatoo."

"No. An African grey."

"A bird is a bird."

"Tell that to a penguin."

When they were settled on the couch, Tess with her glass of red wine and Zach with his craft beer, he turned a discerning eye on her. "When was the last time you got laid?"

Tess laughed deep in her throat. "Oh, we are so not having this conversation. Keep your little psych-minor hands in your own lap, please and thank-you."

Darkness descended outside while they talked, catching up on life. Before Tess knew it, Zach slapped his knees, which reminded Tess of their dad, and stood for bed. She watched him leave, choosing to stay a few more minutes and finish her glass of wine. She'd almost made it through a whole bottle as they chatted. She couldn't remember the last time she'd had someone over for drinks, or dinner, if ever.

Was she hiding? When she'd moved here it didn't feel like it, but at times she certainly felt a bit like a recluse. She'd only stopped dating and didn't miss it one bit. Inexplicably her thoughts shifted to Easton. Since she'd met her, Tess had recalled more often all the things she'd left behind in Vancouver, namely women. She couldn't think why Easton had her thinking about this subject. Sure, she was beautiful, and if things were different, Tess would be lying if she said she wouldn't jump at a chance to see what she was like in bed. However, things were different. Easton was certainly not the person she pretended to be.

❖

Tess followed Lou down the rickety back stairs into the kitchen, where Zach was already sitting at the island with a cup of coffee. He'd probably been up for an hour puttering around her place, waiting for her to get up. She was surprised he hadn't knocked on her door to wake her up sooner. Zach was very much an extrovert. He needed the attention. Tess was the opposite. It's why she liked waking up with Lou.

"Pour me a cup of that, please." She slid onto a stool and waited for the much more awake and alert person in the room to feed her caffeine addiction.

"You know this thing has a timer. I could set it so it automatically starts before you get up and always have hot coffee immediately."

Tess accepted the coffee, staring into his face trying to decipher what he'd said. Several sips of coffee and a couple of minutes later, his words finally assembled into order. "I don't always grab coffee here. I like leaving my options open."

"Just trying to be helpful."

They sat in silence for a few blissful seconds before Zach laid his hands on the counter, his blue eyes staring unblinking into hers. "I have to talk to you about something."

Tess practically turned in the opposite direction, cradling her coffee. "Here we go. Can I at least have coffee first?"

"This is important."

"If it's so important, why didn't you tell me last night?"

"We were hanging out last night. It was nice, and I didn't want to ruin that."

Lou came over and placed a paw on Tess's knee, his one good eye giving her the most pitiful look she'd ever seen. "Can I have five minutes, Lou?" Lou doubled down by patting her knee again. "Ugh. Okay. We'll go out." On the word go, Lou twirled around and headed for the back door. "Why don't you come? You can tell me what the issue is on the walk."

"Why do you assume I have an issue?"

"Because you came all the way up to Smokey River to tell me in person. If it were good news or something easy to say, you'd have left me a text."

"Oh, come on. You make me sound heartless." He slipped his arm into his jacket, an exaggerated pout on his face.

"Am I wrong?"

In the back fields of her house, Zach waited until he'd tossed the ball to Lou before scanning the horizon for anyone else. "I think someone's following me."

Tess crossed the street, narrowly avoiding a deep puddle. Zach was waiting by the front door of Rick's Bar and Grill. It was his favourite place to eat, which she couldn't understand. The place smelled like beer and grease.

"You done for the day?"

Tess shook her head. "I still have a few appointments this afternoon." She'd spent her morning doing house calls, even though she'd prefer to be in the clinic. House calls reminded her too much of Benny.

She stopped next to Zach and followed his line of sight. Someone across the street. Easton. She was standing motionless, watching them. She waved and stepped out onto the street. A figure behind her yanked her back, and a car sped by.

"Who's that?" asked Zach.

Tess couldn't take her eyes off her. Such a bizarre feeling washed over her, almost like she knew she'd never see her again. "Easton Gray. She's house-sitting while the Pattersons are away."

"Who're they?"

She turned away to answer Zach. "They moved in a couple of years ago. You wouldn't know them." When she turned back, Easton was gone.

They went in and took a seat in a booth. Zach sat facing the door, Tess noticed. Usually he liked sitting at the bar, but he'd said it made him feel too exposed. She wondered if someone really was following him and couldn't imagine why they would want to. He'd said it had something to do with his work.

Zach picked up a menu. "So what's the deal between you and Miss Jaywalk?"

"There's no deal." Tess didn't even bother picking up the menu. She always ordered the least offensive thing on it, which was a Caesar salad and a cup of tomato soup.

Rick's had opened in the '80s. Walking through the door felt like entering a time warp, as if you'd stepped back to 1983. The floor tiles were the same shitty brown, the walls covered in the same record albums that had been hits in the late '70s and early '80s, and even the music was the same '80s rock they'd been playing for decades. Every time Tess entered, she was reminded of almost every Friday she'd spent as a kid. Their parents, and later her dad, would bring them here for dinner. Back then she was into cheeseburgers and crinkle fries.

He waved a finger at her. "All your blinky bits are turning on."

Tess raised her eyebrows. "I'm not even sure what that means."

Hannah, Rick's wife, stepped over to the booth. "Welcome home, Zach." Her smile was warm and infectious. "What's the occasion?"

"Someone's trying to kill him."

Hannah laughed. "You two always were good for a laugh."

"I had a huge craving for your gold-rush burger and hopped in my car and came right up."

"Mmmhmm? That what you're having?"

Zach looked down at the menu one last time, then back up at Hannah. "That and a pint of Naked Fox IPA."

She took his menu back and looked over at Tess. "The usual?"

Tess nodded and handed over her menu. "Just a ginger ale for me, please."

"Alrighty then." Hannah flounced away, her energy no match for her sixty-plus years.

Zach leaned back, a relaxed smile on his face. "Where were we? Oh yeah. Blinky bits."

Tess's phone rang. Saved by the bell, she thought. She checked the caller ID. It was Colin, her police buddy. "I've been trying to reach you since yesterday."

"I got ahold of the Pattersons. Tess, they never hired a house sitter."

Tess physically turned so she wasn't facing Zach and his look of concern. "So Easton—"

"Broke into their house and—"

"For what?"

"I'm not sure, but she's gone now. I stopped by earlier, the place was empty. It also didn't look like anything was missing. Appears she was using it as a place to stay. She found an opportunity and was exploiting it."

Tess stood to pace. She'd suspected something was off. However, she hadn't actually thought she'd be this on point. "Have you found out why she might have been here?"

"She's most likely on the run from something or someone and was only passing through on her way to somewhere else. It's possible she gave us a fake name. Truth is, we'll probably never know." Tess was looking out the restaurant window at the last place she'd seen her. "If you see her though, don't engage. Call me instead."

Should she tell him about seeing her across the street? She was long gone now, doubtless already out of town. Colin must be right. She wasn't planning on staying. "Okay." Tess turned back to Zach. Their drinks had arrived, but he hadn't touched his yet. She motioned for him to start, that everything was fine. But that's the thing about being twins. You knew how to read the other, and Zach could probably see that everything was not fine.

Easton watched the cop car roll out of the Pattersons' driveway. Her time was up. It didn't matter. Things had finally fallen into place. With the arrival of Zach Nolan last night, she was ready to complete her slipback. If everything went according to plan, this time tomorrow, Zach and Tess Nolan would be removed from the timeline.

Her first move was to locate Zach's paperwork. The AI said there was an 86 percent chance he had it with him. But just in case, operatives were sent to destroy the servers his company used and wipe all data from it at the same time as her slipback. That way, when Easton completed her mission there existed an almost 100 percent certainty that all of Dr. Zach Nolan's work on nanotechnology would be destroyed with him. As other operatives completed their work, the idea of nanotechnology would fade from existence.

That wasn't to say it would never exist. The AI had placed the probability of it popping up in future sciences at 55 percent. And it wasn't higher, which Easton thought it should be, because ideas were not a certainty. Of course the idea of tiny machines seemed such a natural concept in this timeline, but that's because the idea had been around for centuries. It was built into the collective brain, part of a culture and an important science. But concepts took time to build and evolve.

Paper money, for instance, took hundreds of years to catch on. First conceived in the Tang Dynasty in China, it wasn't until the eleventh century that it became more integrated into everyday use—almost three hundred years later. It took even longer still to travel to Europe and become an accepted form of currency. Why? Because the concept of making a piece of paper worth the same as precious metals was more than the average person could wrap their head around. As the centuries wore on and paper money turned into a more common use of currency, no one questioned the idea of paper representing value. Yet once the idea that something could be given in place of another took root, it became easier to transfer that value onto other things. It required an even shorter time for the idea that codes on a server could represent money.

In the early twenty-first century, where Easton found herself, people rarely used paper money. Instead, they transferred ideas from one machine to another.

One day the idea of nanotechnology would resurface. Easton was sure of that. She could only hope it would come in a more docile and less deadly form.

She had only one stop left to make, and that was at the clinic. While talking to Tess at the hardware store, she'd thought of what to use to keep her and her brother knocked out. Horse tranquilizers, which she knew she could find at the clinic. It was possible they might test their blood and find it afterward. But if she did a good enough job of making the fire look like an accident, they wouldn't bother with an autopsy.

For only a moment, she thought about the lives she would be destroying. But in her heart she knew it was the right thing to do. It was the only thing she could do. Even if she changed her mind, another operative would arrive to finish her slipback. Instead of these lives, she thought about the future lives she was saving. Billions. Hundreds of billions saved from a future no one wanted to live in.

Easton waited several minutes to make sure the police wouldn't return, then made her way into town. By the time she made it back to Tess's house, it was dark. It didn't look like anyone was home when she arrived, and she debated whether she should set up in the furnace room now or wait until after they were asleep.

In the end, she opted to wait.

Chapter Ten

Two days before slipback

A few drops of Easton's blood fell to the armrest of her chair. She stared at the three dots and the triangle they formed. One dot for the past, one for the present, and the other for the future, each neatly aligned as if they informed the other. In a way they did, just not in the order you would think. If she drew a line from the top dot, representing the present, to the left dot (the past), would it transform the future? Were they ever going to get this right?

"Sorry about that." A sterile glove and hand wiped them up, in an instant reverting the space to its disinfected state.

And what if, worse than changing nothing, it made it worse? What if humans weren't meant to influence the past for their own gain, were prone to the ultimate form of greed—of avarice? Who were they to assume the Earth should be theirs to shape and morph how they pleased? Time beyond comprehension had passed without them on Earth, and humans represented only a tiny drop of blood in an ocean of time. Why were they special? Because they could be? Was that the defining factor?

As Easton neared her slipback date, she had more concerns that what they were doing was wrong.

Level five operated in secret because not everyone thought their situation was horrible. True, the average citizen did wish for more—more space, more food, more variety. More of something. But a select few were thankful their species had survived. Humans, yet again, had adapted to their surroundings. Yes, they lacked daylight and the freedom that most humans had enjoyed throughout history. However, maybe there was something to be said for too much freedom. Look what they'd done with it. They'd nearly destroyed a planet and numerous ecosystems.

Humans had caused the mass extinctions of the mid and late twenty-first century. By the end of the twenty-first century, more than 75 percent of the species on Earth had become extinct, and humans were no longer dominant. If there wasn't a correlation there, a direct result of humanity's actions, what more proof did people need to realize humans were destructive. It was their one universal trait, it would seem.

When a population size grew too big, it took on a life of its own. It became its own monster, an enemy from within. If they changed the events that brought them to this place in history, what was to say their destruction wouldn't come later, from some other event? Easton had spent years studying the histories of civilizations and found only one truth, they fell. All of them. Not a single civilization hadn't fallen at some point.

When Easton had joined, she'd been full of optimism, convinced they were doing what was best. As years went by, she wondered if arrogance alone had gotten them here. Most of life throughout history consisted of misery or, at the very least, hardship.

Early humans probably lived a happy life, so few of them, travelling around the land looking for food. They traded certainty for freedom. Most would starve or die of unknown diseases. Some were eaten by larger, stronger animals. As the nomads began to settle and the first civilizations started, very few were at the top. Most worked as slaves or serfs or lowly workers providing the comfort to others. Slavery was rampant, wars, vicious genocide, poverty, disease. In fact, from what Easton could see, only one century stood out above all others—the twentieth century. Technology had caught up to provide a majority of people comfort. The middle class expanded. People bought homes, had babies, went to cushy jobs. And then by the end of the twentieth it began to unravel, as it always does. The powerful got greedier and took more until no middle class remained, and poverty, disease, and hardship prevailed.

"All right. We're almost done here. Can you please step up onto the scale, and we'll get your measurements." One of level five's doctors indicated where Easton should stand.

Easton slid off the chair. This was her final medical before the slipback. They had to make sure everyone was healthy before sending them back. She had gone through several inoculations for diseases that hadn't existed for centuries just in case she encountered them. They also had to make sure she wouldn't take anything back to the past. What could be worse than succeeding at their slipback, only to cause a pandemic that decimated the timeline?

A few months earlier Easton could think of nothing else because her mission was no longer a construct, a fantasy that things would be better for humanity. Now she had to face the real possibility that her sister would no longer exist. You could argue they would be better off. What about Calla? She enjoyed her life here. She was one of the few who didn't question it. She liked her job, she had good friends, a life. She was settled and not pining for the past. Who were they to take that away from her? And how many others were happy? They talked about sacrificing a few for the many. In truth they were trading billions of lives for billions of others, almost like swapping one in and another out.

Easton hadn't discussed this subject with anyone. She didn't consider any of her colleagues close enough to confide in. And even if some of them were of the same mind, having similar doubts, she couldn't be sure they would keep her reluctance quiet. She knew what they did to people who went rogue.

Easton was in the final stages before her assignment, which meant endless days of tests and briefs. It felt like a whirlwind after years of waiting. Operatives joked that level five was more like a waiting room for an appointment that was never made.

For the last five years Easton had trained in a wide array of areas. She had sweated her way through every training course they had, studied weapons throughout the centuries, immersed herself in various cultures, all in the hopes that she would blend in once she reached the past. However, you could prepare only so much.

❖

Easton was shown to a seat in the minister's office. He hadn't yet arrived. This was her first time in the Ministry of Transportation office. Was it strange that she'd never seen where her sister worked? It had something no other office she'd ever seen had—unused space. His desk was the size of her bed and yet had nothing on it. The room could've held ten of his desks but had only two chairs angled in front of his glass monstrosity. Adding to the sense of space was a floor-to-ceiling window overlooking the city square. The neon lights dappled the glass desk, sending light in every direction.

"Neat, huh?"

An equally sparse man arrived, walking in that hurried fashion she'd seen all politicians and people who want you to think they're busy do.

He stood behind his desk and jammed his hands into his suit pockets. Without bothering to find out if Easton thought it was neat too, he asked. "What can I do for you? You're Calla Gray's sister, right?"

"I'm here to ask you to take her off the red team."

"No small talk for you, huh?" He took a seat and arranged his suit jacket so that it fell in tidy waves down his body. "And why would I do that? She earned her promotion. She's one of my best surveyors."

"It's dangerous work."

He clasped his hands on his desk and leaned forward. "And so is what you guys do on level five. Does she know the nature of your work?"

Easton sat back. Until this moment she hadn't been sure how much the ministries shared with one another. The up-tops obviously knew what went on below the surface. Was he worried, Easton wondered, about their success? "No. She doesn't."

"And do you think it's fair? Asking her to give up something she wants so you can sleep better at night?"

"Life isn't fair."

A woman arrived with two tiny glasses with what looked like steamed green matcha and set them on the desk with a clink.

The minister, whose name she'd already forgotten, lifted the glass and downed the contents in a single gulp. "Excellent."

"Extravagant."

"Do you know what the difference between our two ministries is?"

"Besides the fact that they do entirely different things?"

"Not true. All ministries do the same thing. They make lives better. Except yours. Your ministry is working hard every day so that perhaps, at one point, maybe, down the line, none of this will have existed." He waved his hand toward the window as he talked. "It's not what they say at the ministers' meetings, of course. It's all greater good, for the people. But what they're really doing is preparing to take our lives from us."

"Many people don't want these lives."

"That's a fairy tale."

Easton reached over and lifted the glass of matcha, examining it in the neon lights. "This is worth three meals to me and my sister." She drank the liquid, letting it slide down her throat. "And while you can preach of equality, we all know that some of you are more equal than others. Perhaps it's time to descend from your glass castle and see how your ministry is really helping people. You spend money on tunnels that go nowhere, and you lecture me on making lives better." Easton stood. This had been a mistake. Not only shouldn't she have meddled in her sister's life, but pissing off her boss was not going to win Calla any favours. "Thank you, and I withdraw my request."

"It's already done."

"What?"

"Your boss asked me to do her a favour. I may not agree with what the MOD does, but it is higher up on the pecking order, and I have an obligation to follow that if I like my job."

Easton turned and left. She didn't think him worth the energy it took to respond. She should've been happy she'd gotten what she wanted, but now she felt like it had cost her more than she had.

Chapter Eleven

Easton awoke in a field, the sun almost set, the air on her body alerting her to the fact that she was naked. This time the experience was just as jolting, just as unnerving. A moment ago, she'd been standing in a different field at night watching a house burn.

She checked the display in her arm, and sure enough, it was the exact day and time she'd originally arrived. At the sound of voices, she moved behind the tall grass at the edge to watch as the young family, arguing as they went, climbed into the family pickup and took off down the drive.

She'd forgotten how sweet the air had smelled, floral with the hint of dirt, which was raw and made her feel present in a way that being underground couldn't. There the smells were homogenous and sterile. Here, walking a few feet could earn you a different aroma.

Easton didn't move. She stayed hunched in the grass contemplating what had happened. As far as she knew, once her slipback was complete, it was up to her to activate the recall system through her computer. Once that happened, she would be transported forward to the exact time she had left for her slipback. She recalled speculation and whisperings that some operatives planned to stay in the past because, if everything went as planned, then the future they knew wouldn't exist, nor would any more repos to come get them. Easton had seriously thought about it. After all, what did she have to go back to? It could very possibly be worse. Also, the repos might still exist, and it wasn't worth the punishment. When she'd met Tess, it seemed a real possibility that she might want to stay. But with her gone and the memory of what she had taken from this timeline, it didn't feel right to stay.

She examined her ribs and around her face. No hint of the cuts or bruises from the previous timeline. It was as if time had reset.

This scenario hadn't even occurred to her, and she hadn't heard any talk of a reset if she failed. Had she? The fire had been set. She'd seen it engulf the house and consume most of the upper floor before she woke up in the field at dusk. That was the only explanation though. Perhaps they hadn't included this scenario in their brief in case people decided to fail on purpose and live in an endless loop of failure. Of course, if they failed the first time around, they would discover this loophole. Easton suspected something else was going on. It seemed more obvious to bring the operative home and try again with someone else in place. After all, if the operative couldn't succeed the first time, what led anyone to believe they would succeed a second time? Perhaps something was wrong with her computer or recall system that had led her to reset. The best course of action was to continue her slipback as if this were her first time. Now, however, she was more prepared.

After twenty minutes, Easton stood, sure no one was watching. When she entered the house this time, she knew to watch for the dog and closed both doors leading to the laundry room and the kitchen. She was quick about selecting her clothes, as she knew where to find them, and was out of the house in less than five minutes.

The last time around she had created a story that she was house-sitting for the Pattersons. It had worked for several days before the police became suspicious. She could use that ruse again, and this time she would be out before they knew she wasn't supposed to be there.

As night fell in Smokey River, Easton made her way to the Pattersons' and let herself in through the basement. She had learned the secret of the thermostat last time, and when she was in, she immediately turned up the heat.

Staring out into the silent backyard, eating the heated chicken korma from the freezer, she wondered why she was back here. Had it not worked?

True, this time around things were going much better. She hadn't been attacked by that dog, nor had she ended up in the clinic trying to patch herself up, which was where she first met Tess. She was apparently still alive, which gave Easton the chance to see her again. It was strange to think that Tess had no longer existed for a moment so fleeting it didn't seem real to Easton.

A loud clang came from outside in the backyard. Easton stopped chewing, placed her food dish on the island, and unlocked the side door leading to a raised porch in the backyard. Once outside, she paused to listen for the noise again. Below, she could hear a disturbance that sounded like someone scuffling under the porch. With a silent stealth she walked, barefoot, to the steps leading down into the backyard. The stairs were cold, but Easton ignored the sharpness seeping into her skin. When she reached the bottom, she paused again to listen. A scuffling sound came from behind her under the stairs.

A lone black-and-grey animal sat on top of one of the garbage bins prying at a cord wrapped around the lid. The second it saw Easton, it hissed. She picked up a broom leaning against the railing and began swatting at the animal. At first this had no effect, but the second Easton began advancing, it took off into the woods behind the house.

She replaced the broom where she'd found it and went back inside to finish her dinner. This time around she planned to be more focused on the details. She'd been so engrossed in the larger picture she hadn't had time to take in what it meant to be here.

She'd also fixed her computer so her NFC chip would work on the first try, which would certainly lead to less embarrassment.

Whatever the reason she was here now, she planned to take every advantage of it.

❖

Tess scrubbed behind Lou's ear. "Give me a few minutes, buddy." She'd parked across the street from her favourite coffee shop, Bean There, Doughnut That. It was cheesy as hell, and she loved it. Back in Vancouver she used to visit a shop called Brewed Awakening. The coffee wasn't always the best, but she loved the name so much it made up for the burned brew. Usually she'd make a mid-morning stop when she was ready for a latte. They had a vanilla rooibos latte that killed. Bean There at least had decent coffee, not that bitter taste that too many passed off as decent.

She sent a quick text to Gary from the wildlife rehabilitation centre to get in touch with her. At some point that day she'd find time to drop the fawn she'd found earlier. Hopefully they'd be able to reunite her with her mom, but at the very least she'd be released into the wild when she was ready.

She opened the door and turned back to Lou snuggled in his blanket bed in the passenger seat. He tilted his head and gave her that begging look she knew so well. "Sorry. No way am I bringing you a doughnut. You know they're bad for you. Me as well, if we're being honest." Tess pulled a small bag out of her middle console. "Here. Have a pig's ear as a treat. This at least was made for you." With Lou settled, she jumped from the cab, anticipating a pumpkin-s'mores doughnut, one of her fall favourites.

As she entered, a mixture of sweet, sugary doughnut goodness and coffee beans washed over her, instantly warming the chill from her skin. She loved this about fall. She could be cold to the bone from doing house calls all day and then step into Bean There and all that would be gone, replaced by anticipation.

The shop wasn't as busy as usual. She waved to Pete and Janice sitting at the far table and then stopped. She literally halted mid-walk, startled at the vision at the counter. A woman with raven hair and pale, porcelain skin—it sounded like a Jane Austin novel, but it was true—was busy studying the pastries. Her skin reminded Tess of a fancy teacup. She was examining the pastries in the display case as if it were the only decision she had to make that day. Her concentration was so complete she didn't even turn when Tess lined up behind her.

She exuded the faint scent of lavender, similar to a soap her grandmother used to use. Her hair looked soft and had fallen over her shoulder. Tess had this sudden desire to pull her hair back so it wasn't obscuring those beautiful dark-green eyes. Confused and disoriented for a second as to why she could see this woman's eyes, Tess realized the woman had turned around and was staring at her.

"Sorry. Why don't you go first? I'm having a hard time choosing this morning." She couldn't tell if the woman had an accent or not, but a few words sounded different. It hardly mattered. Her voice had a husky quality that Tess could listen to for hours. "Do you have any recommendations?"

It took Tess's brain a second to kickstart into action. "Um, I definitely recommend the pumpkin-s'mores doughnut. They're not too sweet, so they're great if you can't stand that cloying sweetness that most doughnuts have." She was fully talking with her hands, a sign that said she was nervous. She knew why, although she shouldn't be. She talked to strangers every day. It was part of her job, for crying out loud. Tess forced her hands down at her side, where they stayed for about two seconds until she opened her mouth again. "But if you don't like pumpkin spice, which I totally understand, then I would recommend the blueberry-bourbon-basil doughnut."

The woman's eyes widened. "Which ones are they?"

Tess pointed to the blue glazed doughnuts in the top tray. She preferred those in the summer, but they were still delicious any time of year.

"And which one were you going to get this morning?" The woman's mouth formed into a saucy grin that sent a zing straight through Tess. She peeled off her hat and scarf. It had suddenly become too hot to wear them any longer.

"The pumpkin-s'mores. It's definitely the most indulgent."

An eyebrow quirked up. "I like indulgent." She turned to Sara and ordered two pumpkin-s'mores doughnuts and a green tea. "And put whatever else she's having on my bill."

Tess waved her away. "I can't let you do that."

"Why not? If it weren't for you, I'd still be standing here trying to decide what to get. You saved me a lot of time today. The least I can do is pay for your food."

This was flirting, right? This is what it looked like? It had been so long since Tess had experienced this kind of interaction with her preferred sex, she was forgetting how it was done. "Um…"

"Say thank you." Even the twinkle in her eyes when she'd given the order felt indulgent.

"Thank you."

Sara rang up their order, and the woman extended her wrist to lightly tap the debit machine. A small beep showed the transaction had been approved. She grinned as if buying Tess a coffee was the highlight of her day.

"Impressive."

"If that impresses you, I have a feeling we're going to get on very well."

"Are we now? And what makes you think we're going to get on at all?"

"Because you haven't been able to take your eyes off me since you came in."

Tess smirked. Okay, this woman was definitely hitting on her. She amped up her smile and extended her hand. "Tess Nolan."

The woman took her hand in a firm grasp and shook it. "Easton Gray."

"Are you new to Smokey River?"

"I'm house-sitting for the Pattersons while they're in Arizona for the winter."

"Did you just say you're house-sitting for Sam and Trish?" Janice at the back table had fully turned in her seat. Easton nodded. "They told me they hadn't gotten anyone." She turned back to Pete. "Which I said was ridiculous."

"They changed their minds at the last minute."

"Finally someone talked sense into that woman." Janice turned back around as if that was all she needed to know, as if it had been troubling her and now the matter was settled and she was at peace.

"So you're here for the winter?" Tess guided them to a table in the front so she could keep an eye on Lou. He'd be fine for a few more minutes.

Easton pulled out her pumpkin-s'mores doughnut, which was piled high with gooey marshmallows and slathered in a deep caramel-coloured icing. She looked confused about how to eat it, which Tess could understand. It was a lot.

"You just have to go for it," Tess said. "It's going to get messy, but that's how it's supposed to be eaten. Here." She handed Easton several napkins. "This should help."

Tess watched Easton take her first bite. It was a small, tentative bite, her eyes closed, a smile forming on her face as she chewed. If she wasn't already wildly attracted to this woman, this would be the moment it happened. She had this mixture of childlike delight and vulnerability that had somehow been wrapped in sophistication. The combination was proving to Tess that she did still have a libido and perhaps she hadn't been meeting the right women in Vancouver.

"Well?"

Easton shook her head. "It's almost too much. It's so sweet."

Tess took a bite, not as dainty as Easton's but not too much that she'd have the pumpkin-spice icing dripping down her face. The taste instantly reminded her of everything she loved about fall. The smell of fallen leaves, the rainbow of autumn colours, sitting by the fire with hot chocolate reading a book while the wind whipped at the trees. The anticipation of Christmas just around the corner.

"Wow," said Easton. "You're really enjoying that."

"I think part of the thing I love about food is its ability to transport you places in your mind. These flavours always remind me of my favourite time of year."

Easton looked down at her doughnut, something like confusion and awe on her face, as if the thought that food could transport you somewhere had never occurred to her. "These flavours will now always remind me of this moment. I've never had anything like it."

"You've never had pumpkin spice before? How is that possible? I see it everywhere. Even dog biscuits come in pumpkin-spice flavour."

Easton shrugged, which didn't give much away about her. Tess wanted to know more but wasn't sure how to instigate that move. The best way to get to know someone was to take them on a date, and that thought actually terrified Tess. The last date she'd been on was one of the worst nights of her life and the main reason she'd decided to give up Vancouver and move back home. She hadn't been on a date since. Right now, watching Easton enjoy her doughnut was the highlight of her week. Hell. It was the highlight of her year.

"How do you know the Pattersons?"

Easton wiped her face with a napkin. "I don't. My parents do. I think it was my mom who convinced Trish to have someone look after the house while they were gone."

"And you were able to pick up and just come out here to look after someone's house all winter?"

"It was a bit of a lucky coincidence. I had decided to take a year off work and travel a bit, de-stress as it were, and this came along."

"That is lucky." Tess checked her watch. She hadn't planned to stay so long. "Listen, since you don't know the area, why don't I show you around sometime. It's small, not much to see, but what we have is very pretty."

Easton wiped the sticky icing from her fingers with a napkin, which brought Tess's attention to Easton's long, elegant fingers, and suddenly all thoughts of her morning clients vanished. "I would love that. I'm sure there's enough to keep us occupied."

They stood together, collecting their garbage. Tess still had half a coffee, which she was grateful for. She was going to need all her wits about her today. Easton followed her out of the café, and they stopped in front of Tess's truck. Lou jumped up, panting excitedly, which Tess found odd. Lou wasn't the bouncy-ball-of-excitement type dog. He was much more laid back. Usually when she came back from a coffee run, he only turned onto his back to get belly rubs.

Tess opened the cab door, and Lou bounded out and jumped up onto Easton, trying to lick her face. "Well, hello."

"This is Lou. He's apparently very excited to meet you." Tess stood in amazement as she watched Easton scratch behind his ears, a place he particularly liked. This evidently was Lou's seal of approval, although she still couldn't understand why he was suddenly acting like an excited puppy. "Down, Lou. Give her some space."

Lou hopped down, circling a couple times, his tongue hanging out. Tess tapped Lou's seat a couple times and waited for him to jump up.

"Sorry about that. He's usually better behaved."

"He's adorable…and soft."

Tess's smile spread across her whole face. Anyone who found Lou adorable grew leaps and bounds in her estimation of them. Most people were wary of Lou because of his eye and leg. Tess didn't think it made him look scary like some people seemed to think. It made him more unique. Tess shut the door and waved good-bye to Easton. Her day had taken on a whole new glow. And as she drove away, watching Easton in her rearview mirror, she realized she hadn't felt like this before, ever.

Chapter Twelve

Tess hopped down from her truck and held her hand up for Lou to stay. “Sorry, buddy. You can’t come in. They sort of frown upon dogs in restaurants.” Lou plopped back down on the seat with a whine and a huff. “I know. I don’t get it either, but it’s the rules.”

She’d pulled into the parking lot of Rob’s Bistro, which sounded fancier than it was. The bistro part was Rob’s way of pulling in some tourists, but it was your average bar and grill sandwiched between Service B.C. and a Skidoo dealership. Tess could order a Reuben here and not feel like she’d swallowed a litre of grease when she’d finished. Plus, it wasn’t overpriced like some of the places on the other side of town with a nice view of the mountains. Too many trees were in the way here, but they made it cozier. As someone who’d grown up in the shadow of the mountains, she’d gotten used to them a long time ago. They were simply there, always present, watching over everything, never judging. Maybe they judged. Who knew? Humans could do some pretty dumb things sometimes.

Last week she’d overheard a client, the one with Bruno the black Lab, complaining about the students down at the high school organizing a walk-out in support of the Fridays for Future protests happening all over the world. Bruno’s owner couldn’t understand how walking out on your education was a good idea. Tess disagreed but had kept her opinions to herself. Protests weren’t going far enough. All governments needed to make some serious changes in the next couple of years, or they were going to be in serious trouble.

She'd called ahead with her order, so she wasn't too worried about letting Lou stay in the truck. She had her hand on the handle when she spotted Easton Gray across the street entering the IGA. Her stomach did a somersault that would make Rosie Maclennan proud. They'd spoken only that morning, but Tess couldn't stop thinking about Easton. They'd hit it off rather well. God. Now she was starting to sound like her dad. She'd promised to show her around but realized she hadn't gotten her number and didn't know the Pattersons' house line. Or even if they had one.

On a whim she decided to "bump" into her. She could do subtle. She let the door shut and banged on her truck as she passed. "One minute, buddy. I'll be a little while longer." Lou whined, but that was nothing new. He always wanted to go where she went. And dogs were definitely not allowed in the IGA. Hank, the owner, disliked dogs. He wasn't an animal person in general, but Tess suspected that was because his wife had three of the bitchiest cats she'd ever met. Whenever they came in for anything, Tess always made sure Joe was working that day.

The IGA was dead at lunch hour on a weekday. She saw only two other customers besides herself and Easton, whom she hadn't spotted yet. Tess grabbed a basket and headed for the back. As she passed the "family planning" section she started to second-guess herself. What if she walked up to Easton, and she was grabbing a prescription for something embarrassing? One of her assistants at the clinic in Vancouver had told her the story of bumping into one of their clients when she was buying Preparation H. Jen had recently given birth, but it was still mortifying. Even Tess was embarrassed, and it wasn't even her story.

When she did finally spot Easton, she almost knocked over a display showcasing leftover Halloween candy.

Tess was transfixed. As in she couldn't have moved if a stampede of bulls had barged into the store. Easton was in the vitamin section comparing two different brands of vitamin D. Her raven-dark hair was loose around her shoulders, creating a stark contrast to her pale skin. Tess's eyes were drawn to her dark, full lips, which were moving as if she were debating with herself which ones to get.

Easton had an aura of absolute confidence and insouciance that Tess found magnetic. It's why she hadn't stopped thinking about her from the moment they met. Look at her, for Christ's sake. She was practically stalking the woman, which was so unlike Tess. Usually she would play coy until the other woman made the move, and if she didn't, Tess chalked it up to fate. But something about Easton Gray had Tess sitting up and paying attention. She refused to leave it up to chance and wait for Easton to make the first move. She wouldn't be able to live with the consequences if she didn't.

"Oh, hi, Tess. Did you call in a refill for your prescription?" Tess whipped around to find Hank standing a foot behind her, wearing his ever-present white lab coat. She knew all pharmacists did it, but on Hank she found it pretentious. Possibly because she'd known him since he was a teenager and he'd always thought he was better than everyone else. "If you did, they're not ready yet."

Tess turned back around, and sure enough, Easton was watching her and Hank. "No, Hank. I came in to grab..." She looked over at the shelf she was standing next to and picked up the first box she saw. "Some...Nair." She'd picked up a box of Nair, bikini zone. She could die right then and there.

"Because, you know, we've just gotten the generic brand of—"

"It's okay, Hank. I have plenty." She hoisted her box of Nair and shook it as if it were the only thing in the world she needed. "I'm good." She stalked off before she could embarrass herself further.

Easton had a tiny smirk as Tess approached. She wasn't sure how much she'd heard, but if there was a God, then Easton was partly deaf.

"Hi." Tess waved—with the hand holding the box of Nair. She dropped her hand. "What are the odds?" Smooth, Nolan, smooth. Maybe abstaining from dating for four years hadn't been such a great idea. "Of bumping into you...more than once." She had just met the woman of her dreams, and here she was, blathering inanities. "In one day." Stop. Talking. Now. Tess set the box of Nair on the shelf in case she started using it as a prop, because suddenly she had no idea what to do with her hands.

Still smirking. "Hi," said Easton.

And that was all she said, leaving Tess to come up with a conversation in the midst of her sudden awkwardness. She talked to people all day. Okay, she pretended to talk to people all day, when she was actually talking to their pets. Maybe she felt awkward because Easton didn't have a pet she could pretend to have a conversation with.

Tess sighed, her shoulders dropped. This was not going well. Usually when things were this bad, she found it best to be honest. "I was grabbing lunch across the street." She pointed to Rob's Bistro. "And saw you come in. I realized I hadn't gotten your number or anything and…" And this is where her train of thought stopped because Easton's smirk had turned into a full-blown smile. And that smile had made Tess's insides turn to mush. Easton had the most kissable lips. And they were moving. "Hmm?" Tess hadn't heard a word Easton had said.

"I said, why don't you give me your number? I dropped my phone in a puddle earlier, and it no longer works."

Tess grabbed that lifeline as if it were pulling her out of a tempest. "Oh, no. That sucks."

Easton shrugged like losing a thousand dollars to clumsiness was no big deal.

Tess looked around for something to write with. She didn't have her purse; it was still in the truck with Lou, so she didn't have her business card with her. "Do you have a pen on you?"

"Tell me. I'll remember."

Tess wasn't sure if this was a brush-off or the sexiest thing she'd ever seen.

"Okay. It's 778, 536, 1603. How are you going to remember that?"

"You'll see when I call you."

Tess left the IGA with her heart in her throat. She wasn't sure she was going to survive Easton Gray. If she could stand waiting for a phone call that she hoped to God would come, she might not survive the first date. Easton was dead sexy, and Tess wasn't sure if her heart could handle that.

❖

Easton banged her head against the door. The echo of the deadbolt sliding home was loud and definitive. "What the fuck am I doing?" she asked the empty house. She took her bag of items into the kitchen and set it on the counter. Last night she'd had every intention of steering clear of Tess Nolan. Every intention. As much as she knew she wanted to see her, it was a horrible decision. And in less than five hours she'd managed to bump into her twice.

This morning had been her fault completely. She'd forgotten that Tess had been in the coffee shop that first morning. Running into her had been an accident, but one that she could've avoided if she'd paid better attention. That was the problem with repeating time. It wasn't always easy to remember what had taken place when.

The second time in the pharmacy hadn't been her fault at all. And from the sounds of it, Tess had sought her out.

But the flirting? The blatant flirting? Both times? That was on Easton. It was easy to say she couldn't help herself. Seeing Tess like that—non-confrontational, with all her walls dropped—was stunning. No. That wasn't the right word. Of course she was stunning. She'd been stunning before. This time, however, she hadn't been guarded, and that had made her softer somehow. More approachable. More irresistible.

Easton began to pull the items out of her bag and place them on the counter. She hadn't meant to agree to a date. It was one of those off-hand remarks you make but don't mean to follow through on. Easton, of course, had put the ball safely in her own court. As long as she didn't call Tess, everything would be fine. It helped that she wasn't sure how to contact Tess. She didn't have a cell phone, which was what most people used for communication, and she wasn't sure if the Pattersons had a phone in the house. She hadn't seen one yet. Of course, it didn't mean there wasn't one. She'd thought about getting a cell phone. This way she would have access to the internet, GPS, and maps, but that required a credit card, which she didn't have. It was better if she stayed off grid as much as possible.

Today, her best bet was to stay in and wait. Tomorrow she would go to the hardware store to pick up all the tools and items she needed, which would save her from bumping into Tess later in the week. She should also get more frozen dinners while she was out. The Pattersons had only one left, something called Lean Cuisine, which, frankly, looked disgusting.

❖

"Can I help you find anything?" said a man in a red shirt and name tag that read Rich.

"No thanks," said Easton and went back to perusing the tools in the lighting section of the hardware store.

Last time she'd started a fire in the kitchen, hoping it would look like someone had left the woodstove door open. She had the same plan this time around, except she was going to sabotage the furnace as well. She would need tools to access the furnace and something that would fray a wire that could be mistaken for mice teeth. Everything she could find would leave a clean cut, which did her no good. She might have to get creative.

When she turned the corner, she ran straight into Tess. A Tess she hadn't called.

She had an excuse on her lips, but Tess spoke first. "I'm not stalking you. I swear."

"That wasn't my first thought."

Tess was alone, without Lou, dressed in a cozy cowl-neck sweater and tight black jeans. She looked both elegant and comfortable. Tempting. That was the word that kept playing in Easton's head. She looked tempting as hell.

She'd specifically come on Tuesday to avoid bumping into Tess on Friday. Either Tess spent a lot more time at the hardware store than she realized, or something else was at work. Easton had a flash to the conversation she'd had with Dr. Dutko about magnets and time. Was Easton changing things because she was there, or had things always been this way and her presence was inconsequential?

"What was your first thought?" Tess stepped closer, a roll of wire in her hand.

"That I hadn't gotten a chance to call you yet."

Tess waved her off. "It's no big deal. I came on really strong."

"What are you doing later?" The words were out of Easton's mouth before she could second-guess herself. She shouldn't be getting to know Tess any more than she already had. Tess, with her shiny hair and alluring scent, was making that attempt very difficult, almost like Easton didn't have a choice. Not true, of course. Easton had excuses.

Tess bit the inside of her cheek. "Damn. I actually have something later." She ran her hands through her hair, lifting more scent—something sweet and intoxicating that Easton couldn't identify—in her direction. She tilted her head side to side as if having an internal discussion with herself. Easton found her gesture too charming for words. "You could come if you like. It's not gross or messy."

Easton frowned. "That hadn't crossed my mind, but now I'm worried."

Tess grinned, lighting up the whole damn department. "I'll pick you up at the Pattersons' at five?"

Easton couldn't help the grin that spread across her face, which was followed by an equal amount of dread and guilt. "I'll be there."

Chapter Thirteen

Easton waited near the front door, peeking through the side window every few minutes, looking for Tess's pickup truck. Tess had been very mysterious about where they were going. All of Easton was on edge. Dating a target was not her slipback. After the hardware store she'd come back determined to bow out. But she didn't remember Tess's number. And then another thought had crept in. What if Tess knew Easton's true reason for being in Smokey River, and this was a trap? She could easily lure Easton out of town and kill her without anyone noticing. In fact, no one would even notice she was gone, because she wasn't supposed to be there in the first place.

She dismissed that idea. How likely was it that Tess had figured she was from the future?

Did her story have too many holes in it? The best thing to do was to keep it simple. That's what they'd been taught in training. And every operative was given a backstory and a history to memorize. Easton had adapted her backstory to fit her new situation. She was supposed to be travelling across the country for the year looking to de-stress from a career in finance. Apparently her family had pushed a career in finance on her, and now she was breaking free from that constraint. The part about her parents knowing the Pattersons had been a stretch, and she was worried someone would be able to pick it apart. However, so far it had stood up without anyone questioning her too much.

She'd gone through all the rooms to learn as much as she could about the Pattersons. As far as she could tell they hadn't lived in Smokey River too long. They bought the house two years ago and only spent six months here at a time. She doubted that they had any real deep ties to the community, seeing as how they'd come from Calgary originally. They'd owned a horse-riding school called Carousel Stables. The Pattersons had three kids, but they weren't a big part of their life. Most of the pictures on the walls were of horses and mountain vistas.

Easton had spent a full ten minutes in front of one photo at the top of the stairs. Majestic and ethereal, it featured a winter storm creeping over the peaks, about to slide down the other side. Easton couldn't fathom what that sight would look like in person. A tempest coming for you in the dreaded silence of the night was scary and magnificent. Weather and nature were such a foreign element in her life, it was hard to reconcile the conflicting beauty and anger that could exist at once.

The mountains weren't visible from inside the town of Smokey River. She suspected if she ventured even a little way out of town, she'd be able to see the peaks over the forest line.

In the end, Easton realized she was nervous. She couldn't remember the last time she'd gone on a date.

Tess pulled up in her pickup, and Easton opened the door. She'd searched the house and found a spare key in a drawer in the kitchen. It would add to her story that she was actually house-sitting. She was winging it a bit, but everything appeared to be going all right.

In the early days, the first slipback objective was to get in, complete the slipback, then get out without being seen. This worked about as well as one would expect. Being displaced in time makes people more obtrusive than if they just tried to blend in. It became obvious a lot more training would be needed. That's when they began recruiting history majors. The more an operative knew about the time they were travelling to, the more likely they would be able to go unnoticed.

Easton prided herself on being prepared at all times, but even she'd been thrown by the past. Sometimes you had to experience something before you could understand it. This time around she planned to enjoy more of her experience than she had last time.

Easton smiled as she climbed into the passenger seat. Lou had been displaced but didn't seem to mind. He was napping in the backseat next to a crate covered in a soft red-and-black-plaid blanket. Easton's elation at seeing Tess again took a nosedive. She could lie to herself all she wanted about how this was a second chance and that she deserved to enjoy it, but none of this would end well. She would still complete her slipback at the end of her time here, and it would still feel as awful as the first time. The way she was going, dating the target, meant it would definitely be more painful the second time around.

Easton pulled the seat belt across her chest and tried to click it in place. Tess grimaced. "Shit. Sorry. This truck is becoming more quirks than perks." She leaned over and helped Easton with her seat belt. "You have to hold down the button, push it in, then let go." Tess paused, her hand still on Easton's seat belt, so close she could see each individual eyelash. Easton's heart began to thump at the familiarity of it all. But then Tess smiled and pulled back.

The blasters, on full, circulated the faint smell of cinnamon and apple. The radio, low, tuned to a local station, played music Easton wouldn't even try to guess at. The effect was pleasant. Outside, the world worked itself into a frenzy, which Eason knew, from last time, would bring a bit of snow with it. The difference now—she'd been able to turn up the heat and was no longer sitting alone in an empty house waiting.

"Hi. I brought you a green tea. I noticed you didn't order a coffee the other day, and I wasn't sure if that was a normal thing or not." Tess was a lot more talkative this time around. Easton attributed that to the fact that she wasn't on her guard about whether Easton was a criminal. This version of her was more appealing. Easton didn't have to constantly have her guard up that she might get called out.

"Thanks." Easton wrapped her hand around the to-go cup for warmth. "I've never tried coffee before."

"Wow. I don't think I've ever heard that before. I know some people don't like it, but how is it you've never even tasted it?"

Because coffee wasn't sustainable past the year 2050. For the next two decades coffee became like gold. Only the rich could afford to drink it. Eventually even the rich couldn't pay the price. By 2083 it no longer existed, another extinct species. Rumour had it that somewhere buried deep in the plains of Nebraska was a bunker filled with all the plant species that had gone extinct. By that time, coffee was the least of the world's worry.

Easton, of course, couldn't relate any of this to Tess, which made it hard to have normal conversations. She either had to lie or come up with something that didn't sound plausible. Easton disliked lying and rarely had any reason for it in everyday life. She usually didn't involve herself in social matters that would require her to lie. She refrained from telling her sister what exactly she did for a living, but that was different.

In this case, though, Easton felt it best to not tell the truth. "My mom was allergic to it, so we never had it around the house. Later, I worried I might also be allergic, so I never tried it."

"It's a shame. You're really missing out." Easton didn't think she'd ever get over seeing Tess's smile. It brightened her whole face, almost like she became a different person. "God. I'm sorry. That makes me sound like such an asshole. Like I'm rubbing it in your face that you can't have it." The look of horror on Tess's face made Easton laugh.

She wasn't used to laughing, and the effort made her choke on her tea.

"And now I've killed you."

After a few more deep breaths, Easton regained her voice. "As long as you know where to bury the bodies, you'll be fine."

Tess turned onto a forgotten road, more gravel and debris than road. "As it so happens…"

It occurred to Easton that she still had no idea where they were going. "Does this place you're taking me to have ditches or large canyons by any chance?"

"Canyons, no. There might be a few ravines around here, and a lot of ditches. If I need to hide your body, I'll be fine."

Easton turned to Tess. "The lack of a smile on your face gives me concern."

Tess motioned to the covered crate in back. "I found a fawn stuck in a fence yesterday. I took her back to the clinic—have I mentioned I'm the vet in town?"

"It came up a couple of times."

Tess shook her head. "Of course, it did. They probably also mentioned I'm a spinster without any prospects." Today Tess was wearing a bright-purple slouch hat, which made her skin look healthy and vibrant.

"Somehow that didn't come up."

"No? I'm surprised. More than a few people have volunteered to be my official dating service. There aren't a lot of lesbians around, so they usually pounce when they find one." A thought seemed to occur to her, and a slight panic transformed her face. "You are—"

"A lesbian? Without a doubt."

"And you are here because you like me? Wow. That sounded so lame. I didn't want any future embarrassments."

"As long as you're not driving me somewhere to kill me, then yes."

Tess smiled and laughed. The whole exchange was flirty and fun, except this was a dangerous area for Easton. Was it in bad taste? She couldn't tell anymore because she'd begun separating her experience here with the slipback. At that moment, she had decided to divorce herself from her slipback. It would happen, and it would happen at her hands. However, it was not who she was, and it was not by her choice. In a sense, she'd become level five's weapon. They were the ones deciding who would be removed from the timeline. Easton was simply the means to achieve that objective.

"It's beautiful up here."

"Up here? Where are you from?" Tess pulled up to an intersection on a busier road, with fewer trees and more buildings.

"This time of year, I mean. It's always my favourite."

Tess nodded. "Mine too. I don't even mind the chill in the air. It's nice at night by the fire with a cup of tea. And the rainstorms. It's like the world gets a little bit smaller and cozier." Tess shut her mouth and looked away, a slight pink appearing on her cheeks. "I'm sorry. I'm not usually an over-sharer like that."

Easton couldn't relate to much of what she'd said. In her time, they celebrated holidays such as birthdays and Christmas, things that were marked by dates. But others had died off with the lack of seasons. She'd never celebrated Easter. No one did. It was too difficult to judge when it would occur, so they'd stopped trying well over a century ago.

Instead, they had new holidays, ones that didn't revolve around the change of weather. For instance, every second week in October people would give gifts to their neighbours. Not big things, just little trinkets. Or they would make them a card, something that said thank you for being a good neighbour. And then in February they had a day where you would get together with your family and, if you could, share a special meal. This was usually the day Calla and Easton would get a special food pack to enjoy.

Holidays were as important as they'd always been. Her dad said more so now. It gave everyone something to look forward to. And that was important in a life with little to hope for.

"I like the colours. Winter always looks brown and dead; spring is too wet, and summer is too bright. Autumn is the only time both colourful but not too bright. Plus, I love Halloween and Thanksgiving, so basically October is my favourite month of the year. And it's also my birthday month." She shrugged and turned onto a side street. "What's your favourite month?"

Easton looked down at Lou, his head still resting on his front paws. She ran her hands through his thick fur. "I've never thought about having a favourite month. They all kind of blend together, don't they?"

"How can you say that? When's your birthday?"

"March."

"So why isn't March your favourite month?"

Easton shrugged. "Why should it be my favourite? I don't celebrate my birthday the entire month." She smiled, though, because she had a feeling Tess might. This version of Tess smiled often. She was almost giddy when she focused on something she liked, as if the idea created this warmth around her, and if you stood close enough, it would warm you too. Easton liked the feeling.

"I don't have a favourite month, but I do have a favourite day."

"Your birthday?"

"Christmas Eve."

"That seems kind of obvious."

"Why is it obvious?"

"Everyone loves Christmas Eve. What's not to love? You get to drink eggnog and eat too many treats. Hang out with your favourite people and anticipate the next day. Well, I mean, when I was younger, we did all those things." She bit her lip and looked over her shoulder at Lou. "Now it's me and my dad. I'll go over and we'll have dinner. He used to make his own eggnog, but if it's only us, store-bought is easier. Sometimes his neighbour Patty comes over, and we'll play hearts. It's weird, but I don't even remember the last traditional Christmas Eve we had."

A sadness had dropped over Tess. Easton could see her clam up and suspected that she did remember when the last traditional Christmas Eve had been, but it was a sad one.

"Nothing endures but change. My mom always said that we should look forward to change because we never know if it's going to be a great adventure." It was one of the few things Easton remembered about her mom.

"True, I guess. I mean, who's to say that I won't have a new tradition that I love even more."

"Exactly." Easton wanted to change the subject to something more upbeat, but she was floundering. Socializing with strangers had never been a strength for her.

Tess pulled up in front of an old farmhouse with a wrap-around porch and put the truck in park. Easton jumped down from the truck cab. She could count the number of animals she'd seen up close on one hand. Lou, a few birds that she'd spied overhead, and a fuzzy black-and-grey creature she'd caught rummaging through the garbage bins on the back porch of the Pattersons'. She was excited about this excursion because it would fulfill at least one of her long-time wishes. Growing up, Easton had been inundated with stories of animals and videos of old movies, but she'd always wanted to be able to reach out and touch them, to see what it felt like to run her hands through their fur. Maybe not the black-and-grey thing. It hadn't appeared friendly in the least.

Easton followed Tess around to the back of the cab, where the crate with the fawn was. "What exactly is this place?"

"Smokey Ridge is for animals that need a safe place to heal. They also house lost pets until they can find the owners. Gary runs a ranch for dogs too. Basically, it's a replacement for people who need to house their dogs when they go away but don't want to put them in a kennel."

Easton understood only a small portion of what Tess had said. She knew that people had pets, but why would they need to put them somewhere if they were going away? Why not take the animal with them? But these must be fundamental things everyone already knew, so she stayed silent.

Tess lifted the crate out of the back and placed it on the ground. Lou had jumped out and was sniffing around the blanket covering the crate. "Can you hold him back? I don't want to scare the fawn."

Easton knelt next to Lou but wasn't exactly sure how to restrain him. She noticed the collar around his neck and grabbed it. It was white with little rainbows. Tess lifted the blanket a little and peeked inside. "I think you should stay in the truck."

"Okay." Easton began to stand, unsure why Tess had asked her to come if she was going to be stuck in the truck.

Tess laughed. "Not you. Lou."

"Does he understand you?" Now Easton was thoroughly confused. She wasn't an expert when it came to animals; however, she knew they couldn't speak. Could they understand humans?

"He understands a few things. He can read my mood and follow a few commands." She turned to Lou. "In the truck." She waved her arm toward the backseat.

Easton let go of his collar and watched as he jumped into the backseat, impressive, as it was with only three legs. He whined the whole time, seeming unhappy about being left out.

"Oh, relax, Lou. You'll get a treat when this is all done. I promise." Her smile, when she looked up at Easton, was tinged with sadness. "Some days, he's the only one I talk to."

Easton could relate, in a way. At times she didn't speak to another human being. If Calla's schedule had her working late hours, or she was away inspecting tunnels or other equipment, Easton could go days without interacting with anyone. She'd gotten used to it, but it took a toll on her soul. She could say she chose loneliness, yet no one ever chose it. Loneliness was thrust upon you by circumstances, sometimes of your making, which didn't make it any less harmful.

"Hello," said a man in jeans and a ratty old sweater with the letters UVIC across the front. "How is she?" He bounded down the front steps toward them. Rugged was a good descriptor for his appearance. Easton guessed him to be about mid-fifties, but he could be younger. His skin was rough with stubble, and his hair looked like it hadn't been cut in a good while, with pieces sticking out past the baseball hat he was wearing backward.

"She's drugged. I thought it best to give her something to calm her nerves. She's got a cast on her leg, which I wouldn't recommend taking off for at least a month, maybe longer. She's still young, and they usually heal much faster."

He bent and lifted the blanket to look inside. Easton wanted to see inside too but held back.

Once in the building, the man, who she found out was Gary, the owner, lifted the blanket, and Easton finally got a good look at the fawn inside. It was tiny and much more delicate than Easton had been expecting. It had a white cast on its hind leg, contrasting with the more amber colour of its leg. She knelt, and the deepest brown eyes, wide and scared, stared back at her. She wanted to reach out and stroke its fur but held back. She would take her cue from Tess.

"Is it in a lot of pain?" Easton asked. It looked like it was.

"She. She's a female."

"Oh, how can you tell?"

Tess and Gary exchanged a smile. "The usual way," said Gary. "By looking between the legs."

Easton frowned. It seemed a bit indecent, like an intrusion on the animal's privacy.

"It doesn't hurt them." Tess gingerly opened the door to the crate to coax the small animal out.

"Don't they mind you looking?"

Gary threw his head back in a loud chuckle. "It's not like you buy them dinner first. You just take a quick peek." At the sound, the fawn retreated farther into the cage. Gary knelt and pulled out some nuts from his pocket, offering them in an open hand to the fawn. She hesitated, sniffing the air, gauging her surroundings to see if they were safe. After about thirty seconds she began to advance. She nosed Gary's palm, then began to lick up the nuts in earnest. "It's the salt they love. It's like junk food for deer. This one probably hasn't ever tasted it."

Slowly Gary coaxed the fawn out. She had large ears and a bushy tail in constant motion. But what Easton loved the most were the little white spots that dotted her back. From the moment she discovered the nuts, she wouldn't leave Gary alone. She followed him around the living room, then hobbled through the kitchen and awkwardly climbed down the back stairs.

"Come on," he said, motioning for Easton and Tess to follow. "I'll show you where she'll be staying while she rests up. He led them through a fenced area, where a few horses were grazing, and into a large barn. "Don't worry. It's heated. She'll be nice and cozy." Dogs barked to welcome Gary as he walked past the stalls. He stopped about halfway and motioned to one of the stalls that was all made up with blankets on one side, a food and water dish on the other, and what looked like tiny pellets.

The fawn hobbled in and made herself cozy in the blankets. Easton knelt with some nuts Gary had given her, encouraging the fawn to take them. This was, without a doubt, the best date she'd ever been on.

CHAPTER FOURTEEN

Tess couldn't take her eyes off Easton the entire time they spent at Gary's. She'd been filled with a childlike wonder at seeing all the animals. It was clear she hadn't grown up around them. She knew the basics, but Tess was pretty sure she'd never even held a kitten. Tess's heart melted a little as she watched Easton hold a fluffy, newborn barn kitten. She'd never heard the term mouser before and had to have it explained that those cats were bred for a job—to kill mice and rats. The only hiccup was when Gus—Gary's Berkshire pig—had bumped up against Easton's leg, scaring her. She recovered well but seemed unsettled by Gus's size, which, even by a Berkshire's standard, was large.

The whole experience left Tess intrigued. More. It was the one word that kept repeating in her head. Easton was so private she hadn't learned much about her, only that she wanted to know more.

The other hitch in the day was that Gary had suckered her into looking after another animal—this time a giant Burmese black mountain tortoise named Giblet. Gary explained he wasn't the one who had named him. Giblet was likely bought in an exotic pet shop as a baby. They're a popular species since they make good pets. They're friendly and don't dig holes like some. And they're the most cold-tolerant of tortoise species. To say Tess was not a fan of exotic pet shops was an extreme understatement. A lot of them operated for profit and rarely educated their customers about the realities of looking after an exotic animal from another country. In the case of Giblet, at maturity, he could easily reach a hundred pounds and be the size of a medium dog. The real reality check was their age. If someone bought a Burmese mountain tortoise as an adult, it would outlive them. They generally lived sixty years in the wild and a lot longer in captivity.

Gary had come by Giblet ambling across one of the back country roads, and they guesstimated he was fifteen to twenty years old. Tess assumed his owner had died, and his family, unwilling to look after him, let him loose in the wild. He was lucky he'd survived. Giblet was a tropical animal and needed humidity, something lacking in Smokey River in the late fall.

So now she had this giant-ass tortoise roaming the first floor of her house, currently wandering across her living room. Gary didn't have the space. He had too many animals in his house, and the barn would be too cold.

Tess turned to Lou, who was lounging on the couch next to her, scratching behind his ear. "Why do I always say yes?" She took a sip of her wine and watched Giblet meander over to a plate of mushed bananas and leafy greens. Lou looked up at her with sympathetic eyes. "You're right. Because I can't say no."

Geoff was in the corner bobbing his head as if he were dancing to music only he could hear. The guinea pigs were making what was affectionately called wheaking sounds in their corner, and somewhere in the house was a cat named Ghost who, true to her name, never appeared. Tess knew she had a cat only because she regularly found cat shit in the litter box in the basement. Two times a day her food bowl was emptied, but that didn't necessarily mean there was a cat. She wouldn't put it past Geoff to steal food, or even hide it, when he was out of his cage, which was generally anytime in the evening when Tess was home.

This was Tess's life. Day and night she was surrounded by animals. Usually she'd say life couldn't be better. But sometimes, like right now, she wanted to talk to someone. Lou was lovely to talk at. However, she needed responses right now. She'd managed to put thoughts of Benny out of her mind for most of the day. Gary had asked how he was doing, which meant news of what had happened had gotten out. She didn't have good news for him.

Benny was depressed about losing the colt. That was for sure. She'd been up to check on him, and he was talking about how soon he could breed Diz again. Tess wasn't an expert when it came to the human psyche. She'd be the last to give advice, but even she knew this was not where his mind should be. Her colt couldn't be replaced with another to fill the hole. It could fill a gap, sure, but there would always be cracks.

He needed professional help she couldn't give, nor did she want to overstep and suggest someone. "Well, Lou. It's not going to be solved tonight." She finished her wine and got up from the couch to refill her glass, but halfway there, her schedule flashed through her mind, and she reconsidered. The problems of life were rarely solved at eleven at night. She wasn't sure what to do about Giblet. She didn't want him to have access to the whole house when she wasn't around. She spotted the wood box near the fireplace and dragged it over to block the door.

She motioned for Lou and headed to bed, hoping tomorrow would be as good as today had been.

"What do you mean, you've never tried blueberry pie?" They were sitting in Tess's favourite lunch restaurant. Well, it wasn't a restaurant—more of a stall at the end of the downtown strip. And it carried more sweets than actual food. Every other Friday Tess allowed herself to have dessert for lunch. It was her treat for being so good the rest of the time. At least that's what she told herself. She had an insatiable sweet tooth, which was strange, because her brother, while not an identical twin, hated sweet things, though they were alike in so many other ways.

"Any pie. My family didn't believe in sweets when I was growing up, and I guess as an adult I kept with the habit. "

That explained the doughnut. She couldn't imagine not being allowed sweets as a kid. That was when they were the best. They rarely ruined your teeth, even if your parents said they did, and you could eat them without guilt. The worst thing she discovered once reaching adulthood was that even though she could do all the things she'd wanted to as a kid, she now wouldn't because she understood the consequences.

"That is the saddest thing I've ever heard. We need to fix that immediately." Tess walked over to the stall and ordered two of their blueberry pies. They came in cone form, which made it easier to eat one while walking. Today she planned to show Easton the main strip of the town. This worked out perfectly, because they could start at this end with pie and finish at the other end with a drink at the pub.

She didn't have any house calls today, and the only clinic appointment scheduled had cancelled. She gave Donna instructions to call her if they needed help, but Tess had a feeling they wouldn't. When Tess had mentioned she was meeting someone for lunch, Donna had gone all gooey on her, which was totally inappropriate for an employee. Then again, Tess had never been very good at maintaining the boss-employee structure.

She'd left Lou at the clinic because, if things worked out and they ended up at the pub, Lou wouldn't be allowed in. Something about food sanitation and whatnot. She'd never understand it.

"It's not a pure representation of a blueberry pie. The taste is there, though." She handed Easton her pie and stood back, watching, waiting for her reaction.

Easton turned the cone around, evidently a little confused. "Do you just bite into it?"

Tess took a bite to show Easton the best way. It was the perfect amount of sweet. Tess loved blueberry pie, but for whatever reason, this one tasted so much better than what she'd grown up with. Maybe because it had more filling than crust.

When Easton took her first bite, her eyes went wide. She took another bite, and a small blueberry slipped from her lip and fell to the ground. Easton laughed. "Why do you always pick the messiest food?"

Tess shrugged and handed her some napkins. "It's usually the best."

Tess was leaning against a large rock, which served as one of the barriers to a park at the far end of the strip. She'd always loved the downtown of Smokey River because it looked like a downtown should. Except for maybe the zombie-apocalypse store that hadn't been there when she was a kid. It stood out like a dandelion in a poppy field. The owner, Tucker something, felt it was his duty to educate and prepare the world for the zombie apocalypse he knew was coming. The other owners had given him some push-back, but no one could do much because he wasn't breaking any rules. For Tess, the magic was kind of lost when you went from a shop that sold ice cream and sweets to one that displayed severed arms on its sign. It was the one blight in an otherwise quaint walk. Also, Tucker didn't own any pets, and that said it all.

With their blueberry pies in cone shape, she led the way down the street. "So tell me the story of Easton."

"There's not much to tell."

"But I know nothing about you, except you might be allergic to coffee and you didn't grow up eating sweets. Tell me something real. Do you have any siblings?"

Easton looked away. They were passing a florist shop that specialized in succulents. Tess had tried growing succulents but always killed them, either by overwatering them or letting them die of thirst.

"I had a sister, but she recently died."

"God. I'm so sorry. I didn't mean to bring up anything harsh."

Easton shrugged. "I don't talk about my life much, because I've never been around people who cared, and those who did, already knew. My mom died when I was twelve, and my dad when I was seventeen. It's been my sister and I through all of that. We helped raise each other. She was always the more social and outgoing one of us. She tried to pull me out of my shell, but it's always been a struggle for me. I stay in my head and my own space a lot." Easton turned the blueberry cone in her hand, then almost as if it had gone off, she chucked it into the garbage can on the street half finished.

Tess watched, mesmerized as this woman transformed in front of her eyes. The reserved, quiet Easton suddenly became this vulnerable creature, and Tess's heart ached for her. She was carrying something inside that she hadn't had a chance to let out—the type of anguish Tess had experienced when her mom had essentially abandoned their family when she and Zach were teenagers.

"A couple months ago Calla, that was her name, got a huge promotion. She was so excited about it, but it was dangerous. She'd have to go places I didn't think she had any business going. I work… worked in an adjacent field and had a little more…clout than she did. I arranged for her to transfer to a different project that didn't come with as much potential for danger. She never knew it was me, but she was furious. So furious I wished I could've taken it back, but at that point it was too late."

They'd stopped walking. Across the street, Tucker's zombie display was flashing at them, which Tess felt took them out of the mood. She pressed Easton to continue walking, hoping she wouldn't look to her right.

"Turns out I made the wrong choice anyway. She died on the new assignment. So if I hadn't interfered she'd still be alive."

"How could you know? You were trying to be a good sister. Your heart was in the right place."

Easton sighed. "Maybe it would be better if none of us had existed in the first place. Much less pain and struggle."

Again, Tess was wading into a territory she didn't know much about. When she'd spoken to Benny the other day, he'd sounded morose as well. Tess hadn't meant to bring them so far down. She also didn't want to dismiss Easton's feelings. She pulled them to a bench and sat them down. It was colder than usual this fall, but the wind had died down, making it comfortable as long as you were wearing layers.

Once she'd sat down, Easton seemed to snap out of it. "I'm so sorry. I didn't mean to push all this on you."

"I'm happy you did." Tess waved a hand in front of her face. "No. That's not…I'm glad you felt comfortable sharing that with me. I can't imagine losing my brother. I think I would've moved back here much sooner if it hadn't been for him. That sounds like he forced me to stay, but I was forcing myself to stay for him. I worry he doesn't take care of himself the right way. He gets so focused, so obsessed with the projects he's working on that he forgets the other part of life—to have fun." Tess looked down at her blueberry cone, which she'd stopped eating. "I'm just as guilty of doing the same thing. It was nice to bring each other out. Here I've adopted his stance. I work and rarely socialize. You know, this is the first time I've been out with anyone for a social reason since I moved back? That was four years ago."

"Why'd you move back?"

Tess made a face. "Ugh. You know that feeling when you meet someone, and you wish you could go back in time and un-meet them? That's sort of why I moved back. Only I didn't have a time machine. I went on a date with this woman, and the second I met her, I knew she was bad business. I got an instant vibe off her that this would not go well." Tess looked over at Easton to gauge her response. All her attention was on Tess, and she realized how different things were this time. She'd finally met someone she felt she could trust.

"Well, I tried to let her down easy, which was my first mistake. She wouldn't take no for an answer. I got more firm, and that's when the manipulation started. It's weird to know you're being manipulated but at the same time not be able to do anything about it. I say that because I can't explain how I ended up in that situation when I knew better. She made me feel like following my own option was not only wrong but would make me a bad person. She distorted things to make it seem like I owed her something, that I owed her this relationship. It got…" Tess wasn't sure how much she wanted to share with Easton. If this was a second date, which she was hoping it was, then how much of your past were you supposed to share? They were getting to the gritty stuff, and she didn't want to be sitting still for it. She pulled Easton off the bench as she continued her story.

"She started threatening suicide if I left her." She let that sentence hang in the air, glad that Easton was the quiet type. Those had been dark days for Tess, and she never wanted to go back to them. "You'd think that would've been the biggest incentive to push off and leave, but of course I didn't. I remember the day I knew I would have to leave Vancouver if I ever wanted to be rid of her. I came home one day to find samples of invitations to our wedding on the counter. She hadn't even asked, and I certainly wouldn't have said yes. I knew there was no reasoning with this woman. I would have to pick up and go. I gave notice with the clinic I'd been working at and two weeks later showed up at my dad's place with nothing more than what I could fit in my car. I got lucky that the vet here, Joe, was planning to retire, and I took over his clinic within the year."

They'd reached the end of the strip. Tess wasn't sure if Easton had gotten the tour she'd intended. They were standing outside the Fire Opal, Tess's favourite pub.

"Sometimes I wonder about how our subconscious works. I never told her where I was from. I always said I was from Ontario, where my mom now lives. I don't know why I lied. It made escaping—because that's essentially what I had to do—easier."

Easton had been silent the entire time. She hadn't even made any of those sympathetic noises people make as they listen. She'd absorbed the entire story. Now, as the silence stretched on, Tess worried she'd overshared. Finally Easton said, "I don't know what to say to that. Everything that comes to mind is so trite. I can't imagine having to go through such an experience."

"It's over, and that's all that matters."

"You're incredibly strong to have walked away. I'm sure more people than not would still be there living in an abusive relationship."

"You know, I said I'd never be one of those women. My aunt Pam spent a decade getting punched around by my uncle, and when she left, most people didn't come to her aid. I remember thinking that I would never let someone hit me in a relationship. It's hard because they don't really teach you that you can be in an abusive relationship without ever being hit."

Easton pulled Tess toward her into a tight hug. "It doesn't make you any less strong." Tess could've spent a lifetime in those arms. She felt warm, secure, and heard. She felt like she'd finally come home.

Chapter Fifteen

Easton rubbed the leaf between two fingers, enjoying the subtle texture. When she let go, a light-green colour had transferred to her thumb. Everything smelled so fresh out here. The trees, damp from a previous rain, the mud on the trail—everything had its own smell, and they mingled to immerse her. No simulation had ever had this much detail.

Easton couldn't hide her excitement. Who knew being out in nature brought such joy? With a beautiful woman. She couldn't deny that part of the appeal was having Tess show her around.

When they came upon a river ravine her breath caught, and she couldn't move. She was so stunned by the sudden drop she grabbed onto Tess, afraid they might go over. There was nothing to stop anyone tumbling off the ledge into the water below. And as if to give her fear reason, several large trees had fallen and bridged the gap.

And then a melancholy swept through her faster than the water rushing below. Calla would never see this. Of the two of them, Calla should've been the one standing before this spectacular display of nature because she was the one who deserved most to see it.

Tess had invited Easton on a walk through some of the trails. She was giving the history of the area from the gold-rush days and where some of the mines were located. This trail curved along the edge. Farther down, a bridge led to the other side. Tess explained the importance of the water in pushing gold down to the lazier parts of the river, where panhandlers had once squatted for hours looking for their fortune.

Easton thought it interesting how the importance of certain things shifted over the centuries. Gold had been such an integral part of shaping the economy and culture of the species. In Easton's time gold wasn't even considered precious. Priorities had changed, and they had better materials to accomplish their goals. And yet, a hundred and fifty years ago from that moment, it was so precious people would kill for it. It had changed history, fortunes, and landscape, and now it was an end note in history.

If studying history had taught Easton anything, it was that value was fleeting. What one society treasured didn't necessarily translate to another. In Easton's time the most valuable commodity was vitamin D. Because humans don't produce it without sunlight, it had to be produced artificially, or the results would be catastrophic.

Easton had experienced more emotions in the last two days than she had in the last ten years. It was so obvious now what Calla had been saying. Easton had been sleepwalking for a decade, making her way through life without actually living it. Tess was opening up a completely different side of life to her, and the worst part of it was, in another day, all this would be taken from her. No, that wasn't exactly right. She would be the one doing the taking. She had no choice. She couldn't let Calla suffer the way she had. She meant what she'd said the other day. It would be better if Calla had never existed in the first place. Same with her mom and dad. They would live on in her memories, and that was probably the most humane thing she could do for them.

Tess pulled on Easton's sleeve, leading them to the bridge above the river. The view was spectacular, the cliffs on either side covered in moss and vines. The cold hadn't yet dimmed the colours. Below, the river churned, racing to reach the end, toppling over boulders and fallen trees. Mist rose, encircling Easton and Tess.

"If you look this way," Tess grabbed the rail and leaned far over the edge, "you can see an old prospector's shack."

Easton craned her neck. "I don't see it."

Tess stepped into Easton's space, pressing close. She guided Easton's gaze to the far left, where a rusted old building stood.

"It's rumoured that treasure is buried in the forest. A prospector found his fortune but didn't want anyone to know, so he hid it. And then he drowned before he could cash in."

Easton had followed only half of that comment. The proximity of Tess's body was making it hard to concentrate.

"I bet they don't have anything like this back home, do they?"

Easton leaned over to watch the water rush under the bridge. "We certainly don't." It was almost a joke at how different they'd grown up. She should feel isolated from this time and from Tess. Yet she'd never felt more of a connection. The first time she'd seen her walk into that clinic, a spark was lit. Tess was beautiful, but that hadn't been what had drawn her in at first. Easton wasn't exactly sure if it was her kindness or her courage, but that night something had forever changed in Easton's life. As she got to know Tess, that spark grew into a dangerous flame that could very easily consume her.

Tess lifted her head, smiling at Easton. In the diffused light her skin looked translucent. Her strawberry-blond hair framed her face. Tess placed her hand over Easton's, which was resting on the railing. It was such a simple act. The effect it had on Easton, however, was not. Her breath stopped while her heart raced. Tess's dark-blue eyes mirrored her own want. Easton slipped her hand behind Tess's back, drawing her closer still, and leaned in, capturing her lips.

Time froze. The moment lengthened. Easton melted.

Tess pressed closer, reaching up to tangle her hands in Easton's hair. The warmth of her body, the sound of her breath, it was as if there were no other noise, no other movement except her lips against Tess's. And that dangerous flame suddenly became a bonfire.

Tess deepened the kiss. Easton's heart pounded, threatening to drown out all other sounds. She craved more. She slipped her arms under Tess's warm coat and skimmed her fingers along the smooth skin of her back. Tess groaned, her hands gripping Easton fiercely.

Tess pulled back first. She was breathing heavily as she said, "This could get X-rated real quick."

Easton gulped, smoothing her hair, looking for her composure that had slipped away with the passing river.

Tess recovered quicker. "Come on. I want to show you something else." She pulled Easton down the stairs toward a path that ran along the river to where an old rickety bridge, which was once probably crossable but now would only give you a nice dunk in the river, stood. She pointed to a sign that read, "Camel Crossing."

Easton shook her head, confused. "I'm not sure what that's supposed to mean."

"During the gold rush, some idiot decided to bring over camels as pack animals, and you can imagine how well that went. They were known as caribou camels."

Easton continued to stare, trying to make sense of what Tess was getting at.

"They're desert animals. They're not meant to be used on rocky terrain in the cold."

"Why would anyone think that would be a good idea?"

Tess shrugged. "When dealing with the past, it's best to view it through the old-white-asshole lens."

Easton laughed. "What's that supposed to mean?"

"The majority of the world's issues are because of white assholes. I'd like to give all the credit to the males, but I'm sure a few females were in there who weren't helping matters along."

"So what happened to all the camels?"

"Well, there's some debate about that. Some were sold to ranchers as exotic pets. Others, I believe, were shot and eaten. And some escaped, because people spotted them for decades after."

"Either way, they do sound like a bunch of assholes."

Tess called for Lou, who had taken off as soon as they'd gotten there, and led Easton back toward her truck. It was nice being out here with just Tess. It made this world a little less confusing. Before they reached the truck, Lou came bounding down a different trail, his tongue hanging out, almost like he was sporting a big grin. When he arrived at the truck, he had a number of brightly coloured leaves stuck in his fur.

"What trouble have you been up to, huh?" Tess knelt next to him and picked out the debris. "Chasing squirrels, I bet." Tess looked up at Easton. "He loves to chase them. I keep telling him he's not fast enough and he doesn't know how to climb, but that hasn't stopped him yet." She stood and let Lou into the truck, then turned around again. With her back to the truck she said, "Would you like to come over for dinner? I'm not much of a cook. I know people say that all the time, but I'm really not that inventive. Do you cook?"

"If you're asking me to do the cooking, I'm afraid I'm going to have to let you down. I can't cook a thing. I can heat things up in the microwave."

"Sometimes it feels like that's all I do. Seriously, though, if you're okay with simple but good food, I know a kitchen that has that."

Tess was getting a bit tongue-tied again, which Easton thought was cute. She noticed Tess did that only when she got nervous, and asking someone out could be a little gut-wrenching. Easton smiled and leaned in to whisper. "I would love to come to dinner. Just tell me where, when, and if I need to bring anything."

Tess beamed her gorgeous smile at Easton. "That's great. You don't have to bring anything, and I'll draw you a map. Sometimes GPS leads you on a weird goose chase."

"Thank you, as much as I love weird goose chases."

Tess met Easton at the door, a look of fear on her face. "I'm sorry," she said. "I am…so…sorry."

"Parrot's pussy," said a scratchy voice from behind Tess.

Easton frowned, confused even more.

Tess waved her off. "That's just Geoff. That's not what I'm sorry about."

"Don't you have anything better than a cheap lager?" a male voice shouted from the kitchen. Easton watched as Zach carried a beer from the kitchen into the living room.

"He just showed up. I forgot he was coming."

Standing in front of Tess, who looked beautiful in a simple, oversized, grey cardigan and worn jeans, Easton immediately thought of helping her out of those clothes, but the possibility screeched to a halt.

She certainly didn't want to get to know Zach. He was the whole reason she was here. He was the reason Tess had to die. He was the reason billions of people were going to die. He was the reason her parents had died, why Calla had died. Sure, it was unfair to heap all that future onto his shoulders. However, his actions would cause that future.

For a moment she wondered what would happen if she told him, if she shared the consequences of his invention. Would he stop? Change his ways? Or would he create something worse? Without knowing it, he might succeed at making their species another in a long line of extinct animals destined to be discovered millions of years from now, obscure fossils in the strata of Earth.

Easton didn't want to think about those things. She wanted to return to that moment on the bridge when she had ignited with one single kiss. She wanted to explore all of Tess, and that wasn't going to happen with her brother here.

Tess didn't give her the option of running. She pulled her into the house, where an enthusiastic Lou greeted her. She knelt to give Lou scratches behind his ears, which calmed the raging storm within. She suddenly felt like she was having one of those dreams where you're in public naked and you're trying to understand how you thought it was okay to leave the house like that. She felt exposed and raw.

"I want you to meet my brother." Zach was sitting on the couch drinking his cheap lager, using Giblet as a footstool. "Jesus, Zach. Get your feet off my tortoise."

"You've got a bit of a Dr. Doolittle thing going on. You know that, right? I was going to tease you about how it'll never get you laid...but," he motioned to Easton, "it seems to be working for you."

Tess's cheeks turned a bright red, and Easton decided to hate Zach on the spot. He hadn't had much going for him before this, but now he was well and good in Easton's shit books.

Zach got off the couch to shake her hand. "I'm only kidding." He nudged Tess. "She knows that."

Easton took a second before shaking his hand, proud of her restraint. Some operatives, those who'd lost more than she had, would've throttled him on the spot. She, of course, wasn't going to break her directive because there were more important things than emotions. Acting like that might feel good in the moment, fantastic even, but it would destroy everything they were working toward.

Tess's house was comfortable, functional, and charming. She'd turned the old farmhouse into a place you'd want to come and curl up in. Easton surveyed the living room with its overstuffed couches covered in throw blankets, the warm fire in the fireplace, and the many animals. A bird was bobbing on a bookshelf behind the far couch, a large turtle roaming the floor around the coffee table stretching its neck out anytime it encountered anything that looked like food and trying to bite it. In the far corner, farthest from the fire, was a long cage with rather large rodents running around in it.

Zach pointed at the cage. "Don't go near the guinea pigs. They'll start squealing at you. You'd think Tess never feeds them, but I just saw them consume an entire garden."

Tess laughed affectionately. "They're called pigs for a reason."

"All they do is eat and shit."

"That's all most animals do. Humans just spruce it up with bullshit and call it intelligence," said Easton.

"And on that note, would you like something to drink? I have wine, beer, a bit of vodka."

Easton looked over at what Zach was drinking. She'd never had beer, and the only alcohol she'd ever tried was her neighbour's moonshine, which had fried her senses for two days. "What are you having?"

"I'm a little more civilized than Zach." He made a face. "I'm drinking red wine."

"I'll have some of that. Do you need any help?" She started to follow Tess into the kitchen. The idea of trying to do small talk with Zach had the potential to give her hives.

Tess held up a hand. "You sit. Relax. I've got this covered." Before she turned back into the kitchen, she ran her hand down Easton's stomach and leaned in. "I'll make this up to you. I promise."

Easton sank into the cozy couch across from Zach, dazed and turned on, worried things would get awkward without Tess there as a buffer.

"Tess mentioned you were here house-sitting. How does one get into that line of work?"

"I wouldn't call it my line of work."

"And what would you call your line of work?"

"I was in finance."

Zach nodded, took a sip of beer. "Finance. That's nice and vague."

"I was an actuary for an insurance company. I usually don't say that because, when I do, people's eyes glaze over. Like yours are doing right now." She wasn't about to let this guy trip up her backstory. She'd spent months working on it.

He placed his empty beer on the table and leaned back.

"Alexa, lights off," said Geoff. He bobbed up and down. "Alexa, play 'Smooth Operator.'"

Alexa responded, and the soft tones of Sade drifted through the speaker on the mantel.

Tess came to the door and paused at the scene of the roaring fire, lights off, and R&B playing on the speaker. "What are you guys up to?"

Both of them pointed at Geoff.

"Alexa, lights full. Turn off music."

The lights came on and the music stopped. Tess walked over to the speaker and unplugged it. To Geoff she said, "This is coming with me. You've been abusing your privilege."

"Shit on your mother." He bounced onto the back of the couch, strutting back and forth. "Parrot's pussy, parrot's pussy."

"Where did you find him again? A strip club?" Zach laughed.

Tess set a glass of red wine on the table in front of Easton. Zach waved his empty beer in front of her. "I'm not your maid. Get your own damn beer." She scoffed.

While Zach got his own drink, Easton was happy to have a little privacy. She took a sip of the wine, worried it would taste like her neighbour's moonshine. Instead, she was pleasantly surprised. The liquid coated her mouth with a rich flavour more complex than anything she'd tasted before. That was the thing about her world. Complex didn't exist if you couldn't afford it, and even then, she didn't think anything like this existed.

When Zach came back, they sat in awkward silence. Periodically Geoff's vulgar vocabulary would pop in, breaking the quiet.

A few minutes later Tess stuck her head in. "Why aren't you two talking?"

Zach spread his arms. "I exhausted my small talk already."

Easton wasn't expecting to get scolded for being silent. "I think Geoff's doing enough for everyone."

Zach laughed. "He does have a way with words. I'll give him that."

Tess paused, a worried look on her face. "Okay...dinner's going to be ready in two minutes. I hope you eat meat. I'm sorry I didn't even think to check," Tess said as they made their way down to the kitchen.

"I do."

"Thank God."

Tess's kitchen was a chef's dream. It had a large gas stove, a giant island, and every gadget you could think of. Easton barely recognized the coffeemaker. All they had in what passed for a kitchen was the 3D printer.

"So, Easton, where are you from?"

"Back East."

Zach laughed. "Huh, Easton from out East. Let me guess. You're from Toronto. That's why you don't like to tell people where you're from?"

"Oh, now you find your small talk." Tess began pulling things out of cupboards and stacking them on the counter. "Okay. Tell me one thing about your old life. What's your favourite meal to eat with your family?"

Easton took a seat on a stool on the other side of the island. That was an easy question. "Roast chicken. My sister made it for special occasions."

Tess smiled, pulling her hair back into a bun. "I'm a big fan of roast chicken. I like it better than turkey. That might not make me popular among some people, but I don't care. Turkey always turns out too dry."

"What are you making?"

"Zach's favourite."

"Mmmm. I love a good haggis spread."

"Funny. Chicken-potpie stew. My mom used to make it when we were growing up, and since I've grown, it's always been a favourite when the weather turns."

"It's the only thing she knows how to make." Zach took a seat on a stool next to Easton.

Easton took a sip of wine. She couldn't describe the feeling she had. Everything seemed so normal, but this was all new to her and should feel foreign, yet she had never felt so comfortable. The sensation was bittersweet because she knew it was fleeting.

A warm glow settled over the kitchen as Tess moved about it, refilling glasses, plating.

"I'm the real cook in the family," said Zach.

"What a liar you are." Tess turned to Easton. "He says this every time, but I don't think I've ever seen him cook anything more than ramen noodles out of a package. And that's stretching the word cooking in a whole new direction."

Zach turned a bright, charming smile on Easton. "All lies. I'm an excellent cook. The world has just not caught up to my culinary genius yet. Wait ten more years, and people will be screaming my name when I come out of buildings. Begging me to heat them up some noodles. All the rage by then. You'll see, you naysayers."

Chapter Sixteen

"Well, the girl can eat. I'll give her that," Zach said. They were in the kitchen loading the dishwasher while Easton took Lou for a walk. "Where'd you pick her up?"

Tess grabbed a plate from him. "I'm rolling my eyes at you."

Comfortable silence descended while Zach rinsed and Tess loaded.

"No, but she ate like four helpings. Even I can't put that much food away."

"Why are you still on that?"

"She's defective, and that's why you like her, but you'll never have the guts to tell her that."

Tess pointed to the cupboard under the sink. "What's that supposed to mean?"

Zach pulled out a box of dishwasher detergent and handed it to her. "Remember Jennifer Halpert? She had a crush on you in tenth grade, and you were all, 'she's dating Steven Thomas, she doesn't like me.' So you never made a move, even though every single love song you listened to for a year made you think about her. And then ten years later she comes back to town married to some beautiful goddess. That could've been you, if only you'd listened to your brother, who has better gaydar than you do."

"I don't believe in gaydar."

"And it knows that and is hurt so has never let you into its inner circle of wisdom. Imagine how much more sex you would've had if you had access to gaydar."

"Shut up. My life is not one big bangfest." She slammed the dishwasher door and pressed Start.

"Clearly. You moved here. From a place with endless lesbians. And then, a beautiful woman falls in your lap, and you're not ready to make your move? She's even your type. All stoic and shit. Although I don't think she fits into your poor and defenceless type."

"What do you mean?"

"I saw her lift your couch with one hand. Earlier, when Lou's ball ran under it, she picked it up like it was no big deal and reached under to grab his ball. She's got superhuman strength. It's not normal."

"You're overreacting. Why are you so against her anyway?"

"I'm not. I was just hoping to talk to you alone this weekend. Something important has come up."

Lou raced through the back door, followed by Easton, hanging onto the leash that was wrapped around her wrist a few times. Her black hair was slightly damp, sticking to her forehead, and her breath was still visible as she stood in the doorway. "He bolted back here as soon as the rain started."

Tess knelt next to him and removed his leash. "Poor Lou doesn't like the rain. Do you, boy?" She helped unwind the tangled leash from Easton's forearm. "I think he was kept outside most of the time and dislikes cold weather, or any kind of stormy weather, because of it."

"I'm with Lou on that one," said Zack from the other side of the counter, pouring himself another beer. He waved a bottle of wine at the others. "Any takers?" Tess nodded, but Easton declined.

"Who's up for a game of Sorry?" asked Tess. It was a family tradition, and she made sure to always pull it out when Zach came to visit. It was one of the few things she could humble him at. They still played on the same board they had as kids, which now had a few substitutes for game pieces and was held together with electrical tape. The blue was the only colour with all its original pieces. The green was the worst, with only one original and a hodgepodge of items they'd found over the years, such as a Teenage Mutant Ninja turtle, a green marker lid, and a bobbin with green thread.

They adjourned to the living room and pulled pillows up to the coffee table. Easton seemed to hold back, waiting to see what the others were doing before following suit. Tess pulled out the beaten and battered game.

"Have you ever played?" she asked Easton.

Easton shook her head. "Growing up, we mostly just played cards."

"It's simple," said Zach. "You put your game pieces in the start section and flip the cards and follow what they say. The goal is to get all your pieces to the end before the other players do."

"Why is it called Sorry?"

Tess unfolded the game board and began setting up playing pieces in all the start positions. "Because people turn into assholes as soon as you start playing."

"Just because you always lose."

Tess passed the deck to Zach for him to shuffle. He was always better than her, and at some point in their childhood that had become his game job. The living room was set up very much like the one Zach and she had grown up in. It had two cozy couches that you could sink into, a fireplace on one side, and big windows overlooking the front yard. And a cupboard full of games, most of them from their childhood. Their dad had given them to her when she'd moved into the house. She was touched he'd saved them, even though she knew it hurt him to think about the last time he'd played them—before their mom had left and everything in his life had fallen apart. Tess knew he just needed a good kick in the pants so he could say to hell with Tess's mom and finally give up wallowing.

It was partly the reason he wasn't here tonight. He was okay when you were one-on-one with him, but the second it was the two of them, he'd sort of drift into a melancholy place. He usually ducked out of dinners that involved him being out later than eight.

She settled down next to Easton. It was agony sitting through dinner and wanting nothing more than to pull Easton upstairs to her room. She imagined how the night would've gone had Zach not arrived. It would have involved a lot less talking, clothes, and torture. Because that's what this was, being this close to Easton and not able to slip her hands under her shirt. She imagined what that first glimpse would reveal—taut stomach muscles, smooth skin—

"Hello?" Zach cut into her thoughts. "Hold up a number on your fingers. Count of three."

Tess shook herself, plummeting back to reality.

Both Tess and Zach held up three fingers.

"Twinsies," yelled Zach.

"Don't mind him. He's obnoxious. He says that anytime we do something identical. We're twins. Not identical, but we do share a lot of traits—"

"Like we're both gay, we both detest oranges, pork, and raisins. We both went into sciences and are doctors."

"Although mine is less honorary."

"You spend most of your day digging through animal poop. Let's try to stay a little humble, hmm?"

"She saved a horse's life the other day."

"Did she now?"

"Don't be a jackass."

"Oh, come on. You know I'm kidding."

Easton turned out to be a very good Sorry! player. Tess thought it interesting she played the same way as Zach, no mercy. In fact, she was cutthroat to the extreme. She hadn't taken pity on anyone, and now she was one good card away from moving her last piece into home.

At some point during the game, Easton's leg had pressed up against hers. She'd settled her hand on Tess's thigh, making small circles with her thumb. Tiny electrical charges ignited her skin. She was wetter than she'd ever been and found it hard to concentrate on the game.

When Easton turned over the two she had been waiting for, both Tess and Zach smacked the table. "I'm starting to think you brought a ringer to dinner."

Tess rolled her eyes and stood. "I think three games in a row is my limit." Her eyes found Easton's, and it was as if an electrical charge had passed through her. She could see the want and lust, equal to her own, in Easton's eyes.

Zach chucked a thumb toward her and turned to Easton. "She means her humiliation streak. Tess hates to lose."

Easton collected her pieces and dropped them back into the game case. "I'm guessing it's a twins' thing."

"I love this house. I just wish it wasn't so drafty, this time of year especially. I go through a lot of wood," said Tess as Easton followed her up the back stairs. The hallway was narrow and wound once before coming to a landing on the second floor. The walls were decorated with black-and-white photos of people who Easton assumed were family members of Tess.

Once they'd finished their game of Sorry!, Tess had offered to give Easton a tour of the house, which she was happy to accept because she was hoping it was code for: find a dark room and make out. Apparently Zach had thought the same thing too because he'd made a gesture at Tess. In response, Tess had smacked his arm.

The Pattersons' house was less drafty than this place, but it was still cold. She'd spent a good part of the night awake worrying the roof would come off. It wasn't something that was ever an issue where she was from. They didn't have to deal with weather in general. It never rained, there were no blizzards, and it never got cold. They did, however, have to be concerned about earthquakes. Easton had never experienced one in her lifetime. They weren't in an area that was at risk for them. But that was by design. If it wasn't bad enough that they had to live underground, the last thing the founders of the cities wanted was to worry about the caves collapsing on them.

It was an old farmhouse that had been built over a hundred years ago, if she could remember what Tess had said the other day. It was beautiful, in Easton's opinion. The walls were a deep-yellowish pine, the floor a deep, worn wood, with the only carpet in the bathroom near the tub.

And you could feel the history of the place, like it held the memories of everyone who'd lived there over the last century. All the scuffs and dents were a story. It all felt so much more real than Easton wanted it to.

Tess pointed to a room to the right of the stairs. "This is one of my favourite rooms. The window looks out into the back fields, which I always thought was the prettiest thing about this place."

"The views?"

"The isolation." Tess walked into a small room with a bed and a nightstand. A fireplace was set into the far wall, with a basket full of wood. "Zach told me not to buy the place because it was too big for just me, and God knows I'm not really planning to extend my family anytime soon."

"Is Zach staying here or at your dad's?"

"He'll stay here. Dad's place isn't that big, and he goes to bed at like nine o'clock. Zack's a night owl. He'll want to stay up and gossip like a schoolgirl."

"Somehow I can't picture that."

Tess laughed. "There has never been a bigger gossip than my brother. He always knows everyone's business before anyone else does. No one knew how he did it. But every time you'd mention something, he'd say he heard that days ago."

"Are you guys close?"

Tess shrugged. "I guess. He's a few minutes older than me and always liked to boss me around." She paused, staring out the back window. "I mean we're close when we're together, like we've never been apart. But if our lives get busy, we'll go months without checking in with each other." She adjusted the curtain so it wasn't twisted. "I don't know if that makes us close or just siblings."

"Which room's yours?" A pause lingered as they both let that question float without grabbing onto it. Finally, Easton waved her hand in surrender. "I mean, I didn't…I wasn't trying to…"

"Make another move on me?"

Easton tilted her head to the side. "I recall a little hand-touching there."

Tess laughed loudly. "Is that all it takes? Good God. If I'd known that, I might have been more careful buying you a doughnut."

Easton stepped into Tess's space, coaxing her against the wall. She dipped her lips close to Tess's, pushing her against the wall with her hips. Tess's breathing stopped. Her heart was pounding so hard Easton could feel it. A buzz climbed through Easton, starting at her toes and moving up until her whole chest was about to ignite.

"My room is up one floor," Tess whispered.

Easton debated whether to just slam the door and throw her onto the bed or pull Tess out of the room and up the stairs. The dilemma was solved for her when they heard a voice heading their way.

"Hey. Do you know if your turtle's supposed to eat couch? He's started chewing on the corner."

Tess groaned, but not in the way Easton wanted to make her. She rested her head on Easton's chest and whispered, "Go away, you complete and utter asshole."

"I'm just worried because he's starting to hit the spongy part."

"He's a tortoise. Not a turtle. Just turn him in the other direction toward his bowl of food."

Easton pulled back as if a cold wind had slapped her in the face. Tess pulled at Easton's shirt, but they both knew the moment was lost.

"Why did he come now? The one weekend in four years when I have someone I want to be alone with, he comes to visit." Tess made a frustrated noise with her lips and stalked out of the room. Easton held back a moment. This was the precipice, the ledge she had to decide whether she was willing to jump from. She'd started this journey with her mind set. No matter what, she would complete her slipback. The greater good depended on it.

However, theory in a lecture room was one thing, but standing a foot away from the reality of it put things into perspective. Tess wasn't even in the wrong.

The longer Easton stayed around, the harder it became to come to terms with her slipback. Now that Zach had shown up, a time bomb seemed to be silently counting down in her head. She had only so many days to complete her slipback before the repos showed up.

The strange thing was, in her timeline, so many people were counting on her to complete her mission. But if she did, none of those people would exist, so essentially, if she failed, she let everyone down, but if she succeeded, there would be no one to let down.

❖

Tess was halfway down the stairs when an idea came to her. Since the moment she'd invited Easton over for dinner she'd had one thought on her mind: getting Easton into her bed. Zach had put a huge damper on that goal. He'd mentioned he was coming for a visit, but she hadn't expected him to show up so soon, and while she loved her brother, she was committed to her goal of seeing Easton naked. Very committed.

She didn't really understand how she could go four years without even thinking about sex, or missing sex. And here she was coming up with absurd plans to have it. It was like she was seventeen again and sneaking out of the house to meet Victoria Jessup in the back woods to make out without anyone knowing. In fact, that exact memory had given her the idea.

She waited until she was seeing Easton out before she shared her suggestion, her stomach in her throat because what if Easton said no? What if Easton thought it was stupid? What if it was stupid? She was an adult. She could wait until Zach left and then invite Easton over on a proper date, although Lou was always an issue. He slept in bed with her, which could make things a bit awkward.

After much inner debate and turmoil, as Easton was leaving, she leaned in and whispered, "Meet me at the back door in an hour." As soon as those words had left her mouth, she realized how bad they sounded. This was not a sexy and romantic escape. It was just plain creepy. "Actually." She waved both hands in front of her. "Forget I said that. I had a lovely evening. And I'd really like to do it again sometime."

Easton looked around. "What happens in an hour that won't happen now?"

Tess could feel the heat of her cheeks and knew they must be bright red by now. So much for being an adult. She heaved a sigh and went for it, knowing this was probably going to top one of the most embarrassing moments of her life. "My brother goes to bed, and I'll give Lou a Kong toy stuffed with cheese…" This was going worse than she'd thought it would. She stepped back. "It's okay. The idea didn't turn out as great as I hoped."

Easton stepped forward, removing any space between them. "Is this an invitation to do naughty things with you?"

Tess swallowed. "Yes." She liked the way Easton's voice said the word naughty. It sounded raspy and sexy as hell.

"I'll see you in one hour." Easton brushed her lips across Tess's and turned to leave.

Tess collapsed back against the doorjamb, her heart thumping. "Jesus."

Chapter Seventeen

Easton stood outside the back door wondering if she'd misunderstood the instructions. It had definitely been an hour, this was definitely the back door, and she was definitely getting cold. At first she'd thought to knock, but if they were being sneaky, then the last thing she should be doing was drawing attention to herself. It was possible Tess had changed her mind or was held up. Perhaps she should leave? This was becoming less of a good idea by the minute. All the lights were off, and she couldn't see inside. Was she just supposed to stand there forever?

Easton was about to make her decision when the back door creaked open. "Psst," came a sound from behind. Easton turned, and any qualms she might have had vanished. Tess still had on the sweater and worn jeans she'd been wearing earlier. Soft strawberry-blond hair tumbled around her shoulders, framing beautiful blue eyes. The moon was the only light illuminating them, and the only thing on Easton's mind at that moment was how beautiful Tess looked and how there was nowhere else in time she would rather be at that moment than with this woman.

Tess entwined their fingers and pulled Easton into the house. At the entrance to the back stairs, Tess slipped Easton's coat off, letting it fall to the floor. That one simple act set Easton on fire. She threaded her hands through Tess's hair, pulling her in for a searing kiss that quickly turned hungry. Tess was more than able to dish it out and slammed Easton against the wall.

Before they'd even mounted the first few stairs, Easton slipped her hands under the lapel of her cardigan and removed it. Underneath was a flimsy camisole. Easton lifted the back and planted a light kiss on the smooth skin there. Tess slowed, dropping her head forward and giving Easton all the invitation she needed to explore Tess's soft skin. Little fires ignited under her touch, and with each stroke Tess leaned closer until she was pressed against Easton. She couldn't get enough, running her fingertips along her waist, her stomach. She teased the velvety skin under her breasts, listening to Tess's breath catch every time she moved a little higher. Easton drew out the moment, wanting to savour the sounds and feel of her. When she finally stroked her hard nipples, Tess's hips began to rock back against her. Easton reached down and released the button of her jeans in one impressive motion. Tess encouraged her further with a low moan, and Easton slipped her hand down to feel the silky thong between Tess's legs.

"Tell me what you want?" Easton whispered in her ear. She continued to stroke the sleek fabric, each time moving a little lower. Tess's breath was erratic. "More of this?" Tess only nodded. Easton moved lower. She could feel how much Tess was enjoying their foreplay. She pulled the fabric aside, and they both moaned when her fingers met the silky, slick skin beneath. "Or would you like me to go deeper?" Easton could feel how close Tess was. Her hips were moving with each stroke now, but Easton didn't want this moment to end.

Tess nodded again. "I want you inside me." Her voice was so low Easton could barely hear her. She turned Tess around, easing off her jeans and thong. Tess settled herself on the stair above, wrapping her legs around Easton and pulling her close.

Tess was still wearing her camisole, but that was all, and in the moonlight coming in from the window at the top of the stairs, she could see Tess's nipples pushing against the delicate fabric. Easton bent forward and sucked one into her mouth through the fabric, enjoying Tess's reaction. Her head fell back on the stairs, her eyes closed, and her breathing grew faster.

Easton took her time. She switched to the other nipple, pulling it into her mouth, all the while teasing the skin of Tess's inner thighs with her fingers.

Tess's legs pulled Easton closer. "You're killing me."

Easton moved her mouth to Tess's ear. "You don't like being teased?"

"I'll take almost anything from you, but I'm going crazy without you inside me."

Easton didn't waste any more time. She entered her slowly, matching the rhythm of Tess's hips. Tess entwined her fingers behind Easton's neck and pulled her in, climaxing the moment their lips met. Easton lost herself in the sound of it, burying herself in Tess, overwhelmed by the feel of her.

When she pulled back, the look in Tess's eyes claimed Easton's soul. She hadn't been willing to give it lightly, but this woman now owned all of it.

Tess smiled. "As much as I love this post-coital snuggle, it's becoming a little uncomfortable."

Easton helped her stand, and together they climbed the rest of the way.

❖

By the time they made it to Tess's room, she couldn't believe Easton was still dressed. This was too much for her. She ripped off Easton's sweater so fast the T-shirt underneath came with it. Easton laughed. "Slow down."

"If you couldn't tell from earlier, it's been a while." She ran her hands through Easton's luxuriant dark hair. It was so thick and wild. Easton closed her eyes and purred.

"You are certainly worth waiting for, Tess Nolan." Easton opened her eyes and cupped her cheeks, kissing her gently. She tried to deepen the kiss, coaxing, pressing closer.

Tess pulled back. "I can see you like control, but it's my turn now."

Later they lay entwined in the sheets and each other, Tess still running her fingers through Easton's hair. "Where did you come from?"

"You already asked me that."

"Did I?"

"Didn't you?" Easton propped her head up with a pillow, still facing Tess, still keeping their legs twisted together.

"It was more of a rhetorical question, as in, where the fuck have you been my whole life. A statement. Because, Ms. Gray…" She dipped her head and began kissing and biting Easton's neck. "You are the most fascinating person I have ever encountered." She soothed each bite with her tongue. "You're smart, mysterious, strong, and incredibly fucking sexy." She continued down Easton's neck to her shoulders, running her hands up and then down Easton. First her stomach, then the curve of her waist, her hips, her arms. "God. I could do this for days."

"Do we have days? Don't you have work tomorrow?"

Tess groaned and buried her head in Easton's hair. Then she looked at the small antique alarm clock next to her bed. It was almost one in the morning. "We have at least another hour left. After that, my legs won't function, and I'll be no good to anyone tomorrow."

Easton's grin was wicked. "We can get up to quite a bit in an hour." She pulled Tess on top of her.

"What sort of things did you have in mind? Remember, I do have to function in six hours." Tess smirked and ran her tongue down the length of Easton's body.

Easton stopped her for a moment. "What's this?" She smoothed her thumb across Tess's right shoulder.

Tess covered Easton's hand with her own. "A stupid idea my first year at university."

"What is it?" In the moonlight it was hard to make out the markings of a tiny black-ink tattoo.

"It's a Welsh dragon."

"Isn't Nolan Irish?"

Tess silenced her with a kiss. "Shush. I was eighteen."

Much later, Tess snuck downstairs to check on Lou. He'd found a warm spot by the dying embers of the fire, with one of his stuffies tucked under a paw. Everything else was still as she made her way back up to her room at the top of her house. Standing in the doorway, looking at Easton asleep, she knew she wouldn't be able to give her up easily. An actual pain shot to her heart when she thought about what would happen at the end of winter. Easton hadn't mentioned she'd be willing to stay once her house-sitting gig was over. What if she moved on and left Tess here? She'd known her only six days.

She climbed into bed and snuggled in next to Easton, who was warm with sleep. This was not something she could solve today. And no way was she kicking her out of bed. When she'd invited her over, she'd had that thought—to keep it from Zach. But now she wondered why she'd even asked Easton to go home in the first place. She was an adult woman, and this was her home. She knew Zach would rib her some tomorrow when Easton came downstairs after going home, but she didn't give a shit. She just hoped Easton was up for Zach's comments.

Easton awoke alone in bed. She could hear someone rummaging around in the kitchen and pulled on a sweater Tess had loaned her and made her way down the cold, wooden stairway in search of tea.

Hoping it was Tess, she was disappointed to see Zach standing next to the coffee machine, mug in hand, waiting for it to finish percolating. "Morning," she said.

He nodded at her, bleary-eyed. "Coffee?" If he was startled to see her there, he didn't show it.

Easton shook her head. "No, thanks. I've come in search of tea." She grabbed a mug from the cupboard and filled the kettle with water.

It seemed strange to be here doing these mundane things when she'd spent the last six months planning this man's assassination.

If you'd asked her a few days ago how committed she was, she would've said a hundred percent. After last night that percentage was dropping fast. She had no qualms about Zach Nolan. He'd been reckless in the creation of nanotechnology, not considering the consequences of creating nano-sized bots that could act independently of a human. His inventions had created chaos. And while she didn't think it was her job to punish Zach Nolan, it was in the species' favour that he be removed. It was interesting that the data they had collected hadn't mentioned he had a twin. That claim should be very easy to verify. Any operative doing initial surveillance to collect information for later slipbacks would be able to check birth records. But observing him now, she could see how much he and Tess looked alike. They even had similar mannerisms. He held his mug the same way she did, with her thumb hooked around the handle and cupping the bottom with the other hand.

Zach poured himself a coffee and replaced the carafe. "You seem pretty comfortable here."

Easton raised her eyebrows.

Zach gave her a don't-give-me-that stare. "I see the way you look at her."

"And how's that?"

"Like you want to unwrap her at Christmas."

Easton bit back a smile at the memory of last night. She had unwrapped Tess, and what she found had been as spectacular as she'd thought it would be. "She's an adult. She can make her own friends."

"Friends. That's an interesting word. And yet she felt the need to sneak you in after I went to bed and then left you to fend for yourself." He nodded to himself as if he was really thinking that one over.

Easton wasn't sure why Tess had left her alone in bed this morning, but she surely had a good reason. "Would you say you and your sister are close?" she asked.

"Very." Zach opened the bread box and pulled out a large sourdough loaf. He cut a slice off and put it in the toaster.

Easton took a teabag out of the box, placed it in her mug, and added hot water.

"Why?" He checked several cupboards until he found the pantry and pulled down a jar of peanut butter.

"I'm just curious. You seem negative about the idea of me, and I'm trying to figure out why."

"You come out of nowhere, a complete stranger a few days ago, and now you're....very close. Makes me curious about your motives."

Easton would've laughed if his instincts weren't dead-on. She did find it odd that he was suspicious of her, when as far as he knew, she was new in town, and she and his sister had hit it off. Actually, if she was being accurate, they'd hit it out of the park. But Easton was not there to bring sunshine into their lives. Was he suspicious because Easton had given the impression she shouldn't be trusted? Or did something about what he was working on have him worried about outsiders? Either way, if Easton was to complete her slipback, she'd have to dispel any worries, and the only way to do that was to lie.

"My motives? I would've thought they'd be obvious by now."

Zach pulled the toast out of the toaster and slapped a wad of peanut butter on it and slashed it around until it was a gooey mess. "Look, my sister does not need some fuck boi coming around messing up her life. She doesn't deserve that shit. She's had a bit of bad luck when it comes to dating. I know that's one reason she left Vancouver. And while she doesn't always tell me things because she doesn't want me to worry, it doesn't mean I'm not aware of them."

"You don't know anything about me. And as for how close you are with your sister, I'd have to disagree. She's been living in this house for two years, and this is the first time you've come to visit. That doesn't strike me as close. As for this sudden need to protect her, to me it's coming across as more controlling. Why don't you back off and let her decide for herself?"

Zach took an angry bite of his toast, chewing it slowly as he regarded her from across the room.

She pulled the teabag out of her mug and dropped it into the garbage. "The only thing I want to do is make your sister happy."

When his mouth was finally free of peanut butter he said, "Are you in love with her?"

"Maybe." She'd said it to piss him off, or to make a point, she wasn't sure which. The more she thought about it, the more she realized it wasn't a throw-away line. She was in serious danger of falling in love with Tess, and she wasn't sure she hadn't already.

Last night, lying next to her, Easton couldn't remember ever feeling so content, so at ease. It was as if she'd been searching her whole life for where she belonged. Only it wasn't a place. It was a person.

She excused herself. She needed to get some air. Zach Nolan was proving to be as difficult as she'd expected him to be.

Tess stood at the stairs listening to the exchange, her heart swelling a little. She hadn't been expecting to hear that from Easton. She hadn't known her long, but she didn't seem like one to share her feelings freely. Not that Easton was cold. But as Zach had said last night, she was stoic, her type. He'd been right about that. Easton had a reserved presence about her. In her gut she knew secrets were there, things Easton hadn't chosen to share with her yet. Yet being the operative word. They were just getting started, and she hoped that after the Pattersons came back, Easton would want to stick around so they could see where this was going. It didn't feel flimsy or fleeting. This could be what she'd been looking for her whole life, the most secure and content she'd ever felt. She wasn't about to let that go and was happy that Zach's shitty attitude hadn't sent her running.

Now she just had to find a way to apologize for leaving Easton alone in bed after a night of amazing sex. She'd gotten an early morning call and had to go into the clinic to refill some meds for a patient. It was rare to get emergency calls here in Smokey River. However, it did happen occasionally. Of course, it would happen the one time she had someone over. This sort of thing had occurred a lot more in Vancouver, which was another reason she was happy to be here and not there. She had more chance for a life here, not that she'd actually been having a life. With Easton, she had that opportunity.

This morning, as she'd dressed, she'd been excited in a way she'd never felt. She couldn't wait to get back to Easton. She hadn't wanted to wake her because, in all honesty, she looked too peaceful, and she'd also hoped she'd be back before she woke up. Sadly, no such luck. And now she'd have to deal with Zach.

She was a little worried about him. He never came up from the city. Not anymore. For the last few years, he hadn't focused on anything but work. He said he'd wanted to talk to her alone, and that didn't bode well. She didn't think he needed money, which was good, because she wouldn't have been able to give him any. She'd sunk so much money into her house and the clinic, she didn't have any left.

Lou bounded past her, announcing her presence, which was probably best. It wasn't polite to eavesdrop. She followed a few seconds behind, grateful coffee was made.

Chapter Eighteen

I'll have a cup of that, please." Tess wanted a moment alone with caffeine before she had to take Lou out and deal with her brother's angst. This was why she liked living alone on the outskirts of town. Rarely did she have to interact with people this early in the morning.

As she sat there, at the breakfast bar, sipping, the impatient eyes of Zach bored into her, pleading with her to hurry up and finish her coffee, which of course meant she'd never be able to enjoy it.

"Okay, Zach. Let me put this in a to-go mug, and we'll take Lou for a walk." God. She couldn't even have a moment to herself. Zach was already handing her one from the cupboard.

The morning was crisp, the sun peeking through the trees, creating long shadows at their feet. Somehow it had felt warmer when it was overcast and she'd been out here with Easton. Of course, Easton hadn't demanded her attention first thing in the morning. Lou kept running ahead and circling back as if he knew she needed his support.

"So why the visit? I know it wasn't to come see me."

"That's not entirely true. I always like seeing you. I don't always have time though."

"Work. I know. You've been giving me and Dad that excuse for years."

They'd reached the far field with the tall grass. As it brushed against their legs it left trails of dew. "I know I've been distant. And I know it feels like I sort of disappeared for a bit, but I kind of did. A couple years ago I had a breakthrough. Do you remember what we talked about the last time I was up?"

Tess shook her head. When Zach got really excited about his work he went off in his own world, and a lot of what he said didn't mean much unless you had studied nanotechnology, or physics, or math.

"I wanted to use the technology to create bots that would be able to enter the bloodstream and diagnose and eventually cure diseases. I actually got the idea from you. I remember once when we were kids you said wouldn't it be great if we could shrink ourselves and go in and see what was wrong with people."

"I got that idea from Innerspace. It wasn't a totally original idea."

"Even then, I wouldn't have thought of it if it wasn't for you. But the technology wasn't there yet. To be able to program diagnostics into such a small machine has been beyond our capabilities—until two years ago. We got a breakthrough, and that's what I've been working on ever since." He paused as if to let his revelation sink in, what he was saying. He even stopped and turned to her. "I did it. I got it working."

"What?"

"The nanobots are functioning. We've been testing them for the past six months, and they've been able to diagnose everything from stage-one cancer to Alzheimer's." He jumped up and fist-pumped, which was weird for Zach. He wasn't usually such an overtly expressive guy. "Why aren't you more excited? I literally have been working my whole life toward this."

"I am excited. That's amazing. I'm just waiting for you to turn the corner and tell me the bad news."

He frowned. "The bad news?"

"You said you wanted to talk. You could've told me all this over the phone. Hell, you could've said something last night in front of Easton. Why the need to talk secretly out in the field?"

Zach scanned the field, watching the tree line, the exuberance gone in an instant. "I think someone's following me. Or something? Things just aren't adding up."

"Like what?"

"Well, I'm worried my phones are tapped. A Bell cable van has been parked outside my apartment for more than a week, and I'm pretty sure I've seen the same woman watching me as I leave work more than once."

"That's insane. Why do you think your phone's tapped?"

Zach zipped his jacket collar and shoved his hands deep into his pockets. "Well, two weeks ago I got a call from a friend saying he had some information for me. Someone said they had a J.B. Dancer microscope for sale, and I was interested because usually you can only find them in museums. That woman? Who was outside my building? She was at the coffee shop where I met the guy. No way could she have followed me because I met him after running several errands, and she wasn't following me then."

Tess held up her hand. "Stop. This is some wild speculation. Did you go to the police?"

"Well, no. I've got no proof." Zach continued walking, taking them closer to a copse of trees at the end of the field. They were now at the edge of her neighbour Ruth's property. Tess never ventured past here because she wasn't sure who owned the land.

"Exactly. What if this woman you saw works across the street and takes a break around the time you leave work?"

"I never leave work at the same time."

"What's more likely? That you're being paranoid? Or that someone's out to get you?"

"Do you have any idea how versatile my work is? We wrote the software for these bots to diagnose disease, but essentially you could get them to do anything you wanted."

"Isn't that dangerous?" They'd entered the thicket of Douglas firs and suddenly became surrounded by tall sentries. The world quieted, and all Tess could hear was the deep voice of her brother.

"In the wrong hands, sure. That's why I'm fucking paranoid. And now this woman shows up out of nowhere, and she's in your house? You have no idea who the fuck she is."

"Easton? She's house-sitting for the Pattersons. She didn't just show up out of the blue." Tess had never seen Zach so on edge. She could tell he believed everything he was saying, but she couldn't. She didn't believe Easton was here to do them harm, and she also didn't think Zach had thought through the implications of his work. He seemed more interested in getting it done than worrying about what applications it could be used for.

"No. Not right now, I don't. The timing is too suspect. I never come out here." Zach brushed his hair off his forehead, a nervous habit he'd had since they were kids. He had the same strawberry-blond hair as her, only his had lightened over the years and in this light looked blonder.

"Exactly. You've never even been out here. Why would they send someone now? How would they even know you'd come out here to send someone ahead of time. You're freaking out for no reason."

Tess watched Lou sniff in the undergrowth. A desire path cut through the trees leading to another field on the other side.

"I don't know. Something's wrong and I don't exactly know what it is, but I'm worried. I emptied the server at work and brought everything with me. I want to keep copies with you in case something goes wrong."

"Now you're really being paranoid."

Zach grabbed Tess's arm and turned her to face him. "I'm serious. If something happens to me, I want you to release my work to the world. I want you to give it away for free so the people who did this can't profit off my death."

Tess stared into her brother's eyes. He was being serious, but for the life of her, she couldn't imagine someone wanting to kill him.

Easton stood several metres away behind a large oak at the edge of the trees watching the scene. This explained Zach's earlier behaviour. She was curious who would be following him though. It certainly wasn't her people. They'd done their reconnaissance years ago to get any basic information. If they needed more information, they would send a detail to follow Zach. Not this close to the actual slipback because this is exactly what could happen. Suppose he became too paranoid and didn't show up or, worse for Easton, left immediately. She'd expected everything to go to plan this time around as well, but that didn't mean it would. Things had changed now. Subtle things. For instance, before there'd been only a chance meeting, which had been brief. Now she was in Tess's life. He had reason to be suspicious. And on top of his earlier paranoia, this situation could become very bad for her.

Easton watched as they turned to return the way they'd come. She moved farther into the forest so they wouldn't see her on her way out. She kept her gaze on Tess, the way she moved her hair off her face, concern for Zach written all over her.

At that moment Easton realized she might not be able to complete her slipback. She had no problem removing Zach from the timeline. As far as she was concerned, he deserved it. Tess, on the other hand, certainly didn't. And Easton wasn't sure she could be the one to do it. If she waited too long, someone else would do it for her and take her out as well.

For a second Lou stopped and sniffed the air. Easton froze. If he could smell her, would he come bounding toward her? Would the others follow? As paranoid as Zach was, finding Easton eavesdropping would send him over the top and probably ruin the slipback altogether. She slowly moved backward. If she needed to, she could bolt through the back woods without being seen. If Lou caught up with her, she wanted to be as far away as possible. Lou wasn't the problem. Zach was. Lou didn't come rushing through the brush. He barked once and turned around. Easton stayed where she was long after they'd disappeared from sight.

She couldn't help feel Lou had realized she was there and had let her know with one bark. Strange, too, was his reaction to meeting her for the first time in this timeline. It was like he'd recognized her. He'd jumped right out of Tess's truck and licked her hand. He hadn't done that the first time. He'd been friendly, but not overly so. Could dogs sense repeated time? The way he was reacting was almost like he remembered their first meeting.

She shook her head. This was not a rabbit hole she was about to go down. She already had too many mysteries at her feet, and she didn't have time to add more. It was unlikely she'd ever know why time had reset. And as of this moment, she wasn't sure if she was happy it had.

She'd tried to stay away from Tess, knowing a relationship with her would complicate things. She hadn't expected it to go this far, and now that feelings were involved, she'd made it even worse. How was it possible that she'd lived her whole life repressing most of her urges and feelings, and then the one time it mattered for her to keep them in check, she let them loose, like Godzilla rampaging through Tokyo?

She stood up and brushed the dampness from her pants. She had two options: complete her slipback like she had before, or choose not to. Either way, the consequences were devastating. The last time she had completed her slipback she'd been reset to the beginning. She wasn't sure if that was a direct consequence or something had gone wrong, and she had no way of contacting her superiors to find out. The second option led to death—for her and everyone else. So things were not looking good for her.

She walked the rest of the way in silence, hands in her pockets, enjoying the low fog in the air. She'd woken up in such a light mood, something so foreign to her, and it had all turned melancholy. She kept thinking about a third option, but if one existed, it hadn't come to her.

Easton entered the kitchen to the kind of silence you're subjected to when you've interrupted a conversation about yourself. Zach's expression was guarded, but Tess looked relieved.

"Oh, good. You're back. I was worried you might get lost."

Easton shook her head. It would take a lot for her to get lost in a bunch of square fields. Maybe if someone had knocked her unconscious and turned her around several times, but even then, she was still sure she'd make it back okay.

Tess poured herself another coffee from the carafe. "I had an early morning emergency, and I didn't want to wake you. Jessie, whose owner runs the hardware store, got himself mixed up with a porcupine. I love Jessie, but that dog is as dumb as a post. It's the third time he's tried to take out a porcupine, and it never ends well." She pulled Easton into the living room away from Zach. "I just fed Geoff, which usually keeps him quiet for a few minutes."

Easton could see why she liked this house. Everything about it was cozy. Right now, all she wanted to do was pull Tess onto one of the couches and lounge around all day. Just doing that with her would make her happy. She couldn't understand how Tess had snuck inside her so quickly, like she'd found a little nook to curl up in and planned to stay. No, that wasn't exactly true. She knew exactly how Tess was burrowing into her heart in such a short time. Tess was intelligent as hell, which was one of Easton's biggest turn-ons, and she was funny and quick witted. And beautiful. Easton couldn't forget that. Damn, she was stunning, inside and out. She was also nothing like any of the women Easton had met. Leave it to her to travel back centuries only to find the one person who felt right, and this was the one she had to remove from the timeline. It was unfair as hell, but if anyone knew how unfair life could be, it was Easton.

"Tomorrow's my day off, and I usually go to my dad's for dinner. Would you like to come?"

"Is Zach going to be there?"

"Did something happen that I'm not aware of? You seem awfully hostile toward each other for two people who've just met."

"Zach is not a fan of mine. I'm not sure why." She pulled Tess close. Her smell reminded her of last night, being entwined. It was intoxicating and confusing at the same time. Easton knew she should be pulling back and getting as much distance as she could. "Maybe it should just be you guys. I don't want to intrude on family time if I can help it." When Tess gave her a slight pout, her heart almost melted. "We will have plenty of other times for me to go meet your dad. How often does he get to see Zach?"

Tess looked down, seeming to think about that point. "You're probably right. Besides, I can't remember ever taking a girl home, so it might give him a heart attack."

Easton didn't know what to do with this information. She must have had a shocked expression because Tess rushed to assure her. "He knows I'm gay. I've just never brought a woman home."

"Never?"

"I guess I never met anyone worth the third-degree."

"You're not making this visit sound appealing in any way." She cupped Tess's cheeks. Her skin was soft and warm and inviting. Easton wanted to melt into her, or perhaps pull her upstairs and continue where they'd left off in the early morning hours. Instead of doing any of that, she planted herself on the ground. "I'm honoured you want me to meet your dad. I want to meet him too. I just don't think tomorrow is the right time."

Tess nodded, closing the space between them she lightly grazed Easton's lips. "When can I see you again?"

Answers swirled in Easton's head. Tonight? Tomorrow? Now? If she had her way, she wanted to talk Tess into calling in sick and spending the day with her. This was not something that could happen. She knew it the same way she knew she'd fallen in love with Tess.

"Take this time with your brother. I'll be in touch when he's gone." She pulled Tess in for what might be their last kiss. She wanted to make it a good one.

"Get a room," squawked a voice behind them. Easton turned, fully expecting to see Geoff perched on top of his cage. Instead she saw Zach leaning against the door with a mug of coffee.

Easton kissed her cheek and left to the sound of Tess berating her brother. Outside, she leaned against the wall. She'd finally thought of a third option, but it wasn't going to be easy. In fact, it would be damned near impossible.

CHAPTER NINETEEN

Tess spent the entire day thinking about Easton. She'd never had this reaction to a woman before. God, she made it sound like she was suffering from some sort of disease. But that's a little what it felt like. Or more like an addiction. She'd tasted Easton, and now she wanted more—as much as Easton would give her. She hadn't given a definite of when she'd see her again, and Tess realized she had no way of knowing how to contact her. She could go over to the Pattersons' and see if she was there, but that felt a little desperate.

"Ugh." She turned to Lou, who was sitting outside the dessert-cart restaurant with her. It was freezing out, but Tess barely noticed. She'd ordered a blueberry-pie cone but now didn't have the appetite to eat it. Her stomach felt like it had a lead ball in it. "This is why people don't fall in love, Lou. It makes them desperate and crazy."

He put a paw on her knee and tilted his head. Was this his way of saying he understood? Or him begging for pets, or more likely asking if she was going to finish that blueberry-pie cone. She decided on the latter since it was unlikely he could sympathize with the intricate overthinking of humans in relationships.

"Here you go, Lou." She placed the cone on the ground and watched him scarf it down in three bites. When he looked back at her she could swear he was smiling at her while wearing purple lipstick. She scratched his head. "This is why I love you, Lou. Your wants are simple, and your love is pure. How many people can boast that?"

He whined and slumped onto the ground. "You're right. Not many."

She checked her watch. Zach was supposed to meet her here more than twenty minutes ago so they could head over to their dad's. For once, she wasn't looking forward to dinner at her dad's. He and Zach usually had at least one fight every time they saw each other. Actually, it wasn't where she really wanted to be. But she couldn't be there.

Her phone buzzed, and her heart skipped, thinking it might be something from Easton. Then she remembered that Easton hadn't replaced her phone. She said she liked the change of being free of people getting ahold of her. Tess found the attitude refreshing. She was the first person she'd dated in a long time who wasn't always on her phone.

She checked the text message to see something cryptic from Zach. It said, "Zombie store, back aisle." She groaned. If he was going to give her some theory that the zombie apocalypse was coming and the undead were following him because they wanted his brains, she was going to ditch him and go to their dad's for dinner by herself.

Tess didn't think they allowed dogs in the zombie store. Most places along the strip didn't. Lou followed her around the corner to where she was parked on a side street. She opened the passenger-side door, and he hopped in. "Give me a few minutes to go find your idiot uncle. Then we'll be on our way."

Tess trudged down the sidewalk, getting madder as she went. By the time she crossed the street she'd worked herself into a fury. People made plans to meet at certain places for a reason. If this was his plan the whole time, he could've saved her from freezing her ass off for the past twenty minutes.

She pulled open the door, assailed with a musty, unused smell. She'd never actually been in this store, even when it had been the old butcher shop. The idea that they had carved up animals in here gave her the creeps. She even imagined she could still smell the blood from the animals, but that was impossible.

When she reached the back aisle, someone grabbed her and pulled her into the corner. A hand covering her mouth stifled her scream.

"Relax. It's me," Zach whispered and let go.

Tess turned and whacked him in the chest. "Have you completely—what the fuck…just, what the fuck is wrong with you?" Tess stepped back. Her heart was thumping so hard she thought everyone could hear it. "I nearly had a fucking heart attack."

Zach gave her the universal sign for "keep your voice down." And when that didn't work, he waved his hands in her face to get her attention. "What? Are we at a mall? Keep your voice down. I don't want anyone knowing I'm here."

"Zach, you are officially freaking me out now. What is up with you?"

"That woman? Who was following me? She's here. I came out of the liquor store, and she was across the street pretending to read a newspaper."

"Are you sure it was the same person?"

He rolled his eyes. "What am I, new? Yes. It's the same woman. And she followed me here. If you don't take this seriously, I will kill you and pose you in a highly embarrassing way." He pulled her to the front of the store, making sure to stay hidden behind a mannequin dressed in army fatigues and random body parts. "I need you to see if she's still there." They were lucky the store was empty. Tess imagined the store was always empty. And if not, the kind of people who shopped here were of the paranoid sort. Otherwise, the employee behind the counter reading a Guns & Ammo magazine would've kicked them out by now.

"I don't know what she looks like," Tess hissed. She wasn't sure how much more of this she could take. He really was starting to freak her out.

Zach pulled out his phone and brought up a blurry, grainy picture of a woman in a long, dark-green coat with sunglasses and a hair colour that was either dark black or dark brown. Tess couldn't tell, nor could she make out any specific feature. But she recognized the building across the street from Zach's house.

"That could be anyone."

"Tess. I promise you, I'm not making this up. This woman has been following me for over two months now. Maybe more because it took me a while to notice her."

"Okay, okay. Give me the phone. Let me see." It was unlike Zach to make a promise like this if he didn't believe he was telling the truth. She studied the woman, not sure if she'd be able to identify her and also not sure what they would do if she was out there. She handed the phone back and went to the front of the store to look out the window. Her breath nearly stopped. She spotted the woman right away, and there was no mistaking her. She was still wearing the same green jacket from in the picture.

Tess rushed back to Zach. "She's out there now. Standing between the coffee shop and the bookstore. What are we supposed to do?"

"How the fuck am I supposed to know? I came all the way up here to get away from this. I wasn't expecting to be followed up here."

"You rented a car. Did you use your credit card to do it?"

"How else do you do it? They make you put a three-hundred-and-fifty-dollar deposit down."

Tess pulled Zach farther back into the store. "That's how she probably found you. That, or they put two and two together and figured you came home."

"Why are you using the plural? Why the fuck do you think there are more of them?" He pointed frantically toward the front. "I've only ever seen her."

"Why would one woman be following you? You said this was something to do with your work. She's probably working for an organization that wants to steal it." She paused as that sentence played back in her mind. "What am I saying? That is the most bat-shit crazy thing ever. I don't know why she's following you, but I think it's best if we leave without her seeing you."

Zach looked around. "Don't these stores have rear entrances?"

"I think so. They have parking in the back alley that leads to Gilbert Street." Tess began making her way to the rear of the store, looking for the exit. The door itself was hidden behind a curtain, but it wasn't too hard to locate, as it was underneath a red, glowing exit sign. A can for cigarettes and empty Timmy's cups told Tess this was the official break room of the store. A light drizzle had started, like a mist descending on the town.

"Where's your truck parked?"

❖

Easton was in the basement of the Patterson's looking for something sharp enough to cut through flesh. So far all she'd found was the dullest Exacto knife in existence, sure to give any would-be surgeon an impossible time, not to mention certain death for the patient. What she needed was access to Tess's clinic. Or maybe her house-call kit. That thing was loaded with almost everything a makeshift surgery would need.

But she'd need to tell Tess what she needed it for, and even to Easton that sounded crazy. "Hey. I'm from the future. Come with me if you want to live." It sounded like the cheesiest line from every pulp sci-fi novel from the fifties. Besides, she didn't necessarily have to tell Tess what was going on. Or, at least the real reason they needed to leave. She just had to get her out of Smokey River.

She had originally planned to get Tess out of the house and set fire to it with Zach and his paperwork inside, thereby fulfilling that criteria for her slipback. If she separated Tess from her life, she would less likely be able to share Zach's work, thereby destroying the reason for her removal from the timeline. See? It did sound crazy and jumbled, and Easton wasn't even sure she was going through with it yet.

After much thought, however, she decided this plan would never work. Killing Zach was too much of a roadblock, and she couldn't guarantee she could keep that act from Tess, or want to. Which felt strange. She didn't exactly like Zach or what he was going to bring to this world, but she now cared about Tess. And killing Zach would hurt Tess. So she needed to destroy Zach's work and remove both of them from their lives.

They could go somewhere no one would ever suspect. Maybe Cancun. It seemed remote enough. And they could live the rest of their lives on a beach in paradise. That didn't sound half bad.

Now if only she could find a sharp—and clean—enough instrument, she could remove the implants in her body. Without them she wouldn't be able to recall, but as a bonus, she wouldn't be trackable either.

That was the real test. Doing that meant she was going through with the plan. Because once you pulled your tech, you were rogue, and you couldn't recover from that state. She just had to stay ahead of them, which meant acting fast. They needed to secure a large amount of money and get out of the country as soon as possible. Buy a car with cash and drive it down through the United States into Mexico.

She plopped her head down on the workbench. "This is crazy."

Her head popped up when the doorbell rang. She pulled the string to the lone lightbulb above the bench and ventured up the old stairs. She peeked out the side window and saw Zach, Tess, and Lou at the front door.

They barged in before she could open it more than a crack, and for a whole minute she thought they'd figured it all out on their own.

Until Zach started talking. "I'm still not even sure we can trust her. What if she's one of them?" And then she nearly had a heart attack.

"We can trust her." Tess bolted the door and turned to her. "We need a place to hide. We think someone's following Zach."

"We know they're following me."

Easton checked outside. Tess's truck was in the driveway still. "First, we need to get your truck in the garage. If anyone in town knows that's your truck, then whoever is following Zach will know you're here."

Zach had mentioned someone following him in Vancouver. If these were the same people, then they were okay. If the repos were already here, they'd already run out of time. There was no fighting the repos. They had time and numbers on their side.

Luckily the Pattersons had driven down to Arizona, so the garage was empty. Once they had Tess's truck inside and secure, Easton sat them down on the couch to hear the whole story.

"Wait," she said. "You're sure this is the same person who was following you in Vancouver?"

Zach nodded.

"Show her the picture." Tess nudged Zach's arm.

He pulled out his phone and brought up a blurry picture of what could be a woman or a man with very long hair. "Well, that's not much help." The good news was that it was unlikely the repos following them. They would've arrived on the scene only in the last day or so. This was something else. Easton hadn't given it much thought because, at the time, she didn't think it would affect her slipback. Now, however, she was giving it considerable thought.

"How come you suddenly seem to know so much about all this? Like hiding the car in the garage?"

Easton didn't answer. She had sat back on the couch facing the two of them thinking. What they didn't know, couldn't possibly know, was that this was the first time this had happened. None of this had occurred in the first timeline. By Sunday they were both dead. Now she just had to figure out if this had something to do with her, or with Zach.

She was almost positive they weren't repos. This was not how they operated. It was possible this person had something to do with Easton, but if that were the case, it was unlikely that person would've been tracking Zach in Vancouver. Unless they knew who her target was but not the place? That was a lot of information for someone to have. It was far more likely these people, if there were more than one, had something to do with Zach's technology.

"I don't know anything about being followed, but my job deals in scenarios, the likelihood of something happening. It doesn't matter if I used to apply that for insurance purposes. The approach is still the same. We have to figure out what exactly they want from you and how they figured out you had what they wanted. And then we have to speculate how far they're willing to go to get it."

Zach looked over at Tess, appearing almost in shock, then back at Easton. "Who the fuck are you? Really?"

Tess smacked him in the chest. "She's right. These are things we need to figure out." Tess stood. "I'm going to make us some tea. You guys talk it out."

"Do you have anything like cookies or biscuits? I'm starving," Zach called. Tess popped her head back in and gave Zach a death look, which he didn't see. His attention was on the magazines spread out on the coffee table.

"I have some blueberry scones from that coffee shop."

Tess smiled and was gone.

Easton grabbed a copy of Horse and Hound from Zach's hand and put it back on the coffee table. "Let's start with why someone would be following you."

"What I do is classified. No one knows what I'm working on."

"Not even the people you work with?"

"They know a bit about it. Nothing specific. You think someone from work is trying to steal it for themselves?" He leaned back, putting his arms up on the back of the couch. "Makes sense. They're the only ones who would have access. And it's possible someone knows more than I thought."

"Where's your work now? Is it still in Vancouver?"

Zach shook his head. "I put it somewhere safe."

"Your sister's house? I hope it's well hidden."

Zach shot forward. "Are you interested in my work? Is this what this is all about? I'm still not convinced you're not working with them."

"Let's say I am working for them. I figure out where you were born and research if you still have family there, then randomly show up a couple days before you even tell anyone you're coming for a visit. Wow. I'm good. Psychic too. I could make a fortune with lottery tickets. But rather than do that, I'm going to try to steal some guy's research and hope…" Easton crossed her fingers, "that it pays off in a big way. You're letting your paranoia get inside your head. Whoever is after your work already knows it's going to pay off, and they had no idea you were coming up here. However, it's easy to figure out where you've gone once you leave."

Easton didn't believe Zach seriously thought it was her. No way could he comprehend how deep this slipback actually went. Besides, whoever was after him wasn't on her side. They were in it for themselves. This could actually work in her favour though. She'd been looking for a way to get them off-grid. This was a great way to do it. She just had to make sure no one got their hands on his research. She could even stage their deaths to make it look like they had been killed.

❖

There was a time and place for everything. Tess knew this was probably not the best time for this type of activity, but Easton wasn't wearing a bra, and Tess couldn't help but admire how perfect her breasts were. Plus, they might all be going to die soon, thanks to her brother's God complex, so why not enjoy the last few minutes?

They'd stayed with Easton since they couldn't go anywhere they'd be known, and Easton was an unknown factor.

Tess cupped a breast in her hand and leaned over, taking the nipple into her mouth. Tess backed them up until they'd reached the bed and gently pushed Easton down.

"I think you're still too dressed." Tess made quick work of the rest of Easton's clothes until she was lying naked on the duvet, her pale skin soaking up the moonlight streaming through the window. Tess pulled off her camisole and joined Easton on the bed. She ran her fingers up her taut stomach, following the curves of her breasts and back down the side of her body. Easton yipped when Tess reached a certain point.

"You aren't ticklish, are you?"

Easton held her thumb and index fingers together. "Just a little."

Tess arched her eyebrows. "Even if I use a light touch?"

Easton bit her lip as Tess trailed her fingers down her thighs. Easton opened them, an invitation for more. Tess leaned over and circled one of Easton's nipples with her tongue. She flicked at it, pulling it into her mouth, and sucked hard. Easton's hips jerked up at the pressure. Tess moved her tongue on, roaming her breasts, her neck, her stomach. When she reached her inner thighs, Easton gripped the duvet, entangling the fabric in her fists. Her head was back, her mouth open, and Tess could watch that show all day.

It was now her turn to tease, and she wanted to watch Easton tremble under her touch. The skin on the inside of her thighs was so soft and smooth. As much as she wanted to draw it out as long as possible, Tess couldn't wait. More than anything she wanted to taste Easton. She wanted to make her come, to hear that release. She'd thought of little else since their first date.

Easton's head was thrown back against the bed, and it wouldn't take much. She dipped her tongue in for a taste, rewarded with the most erotic sound from Easton. It made her wet. She bent forward and gently ran her tongue hard against Easton's clit. Easton's back arched. Delighted she was in for a show, Tess wrapped her arms around Easton's thighs and didn't stop until Easton came. Hard.

Later Tess lay staring at the ceiling. There was nowhere else she'd rather be, even if they were sort of on the run. Being with Easton was exciting. She felt like she was living again. "Today I realized I don't know anything about you except that you're allergic to coffee and don't have much of a sweet tooth. And you had a sister named Calla." Tess sat up a bit. She was so enamoured with this woman; however, maybe Zach was right. She didn't know where she came from, and she wanted to know everything there was to know about Easton Gray.

Easton pulled herself up and rested her head on her hand. "I don't talk about my life much because most of it wasn't great, and I don't want to lie to you."

"Then don't. I can handle not-great."

Easton rolled over onto her back. "Not great as in…" She frowned, and Tess knew this was difficult for her to talk about.

She leaned over and kissed the frown lines on Easton's forehead. "It's okay. You don't have to spill your guts tonight. I would like to hear about it at some point though. Mostly because I know it's a part of you." She smiled, and then the world exploded around them. She thought she heard Easton scream her name, and then nothing.

Chapter Twenty

One day before slipback

"I was sorry to hear about your sister."

Easton sat across from Dr. Dutko in her office somewhere in the depths of level five. The psychological eval was the last hurdle before final approval.

"Thank you." Easton wasn't so sure condolences were necessary at this point. After all, it was her meddling that had gotten Calla killed.

There was a collapse in the tunnel she'd been travelling.

If she'd been on red team, she wouldn't have been in that tunnel to begin with, and she might still be alive.

She stifled any emotion about the accident. She didn't want Dr. Dutko to think she couldn't handle this assignment.

The older woman sat behind her desk, her chair pushed up tight, cutting into her midsection, a touch pad in front of her, no doubt to take notes of her observations. Dutko had always been friendly toward Easton and struck her as someone who let common sense prevail. She had no illusions as to where the woman's alliance lay, and she wasn't about to make this mistake.

"It occurs to me that we haven't spoken much about your ties here. Many of your fellow operatives have no family. Like you, their parents have passed, and they either have no siblings or have lost them. I'm curious to what your thoughts are on how your sister's death will affect your ability to succeed on your slipback."

To be honest, Easton was curious too. She'd worried that Calla would make it hard. How do you willingly obliterate your sister from time? Of course, now that wouldn't be a problem. Easton shrugged and sank lower in her seat.

Dutko placed both hands on her desk and looked straight at Easton. "They talk a lot about the greater good and the sacrifice of one for the many. It's different when it's personal, isn't it?"

Easton nodded.

"You should know that you wouldn't have been chosen for your assignment if they didn't think you had this worry. It means you're human. Of course you love your sister. The truth about time, however, is that you can't be certain of what's going to happen. Who is to say that time works itself out? That your parents do meet, and they do have two daughters, and one of those daughters is named Calla? We can't know for sure, so sometimes it helps to focus on the maybes."

Easton sat up a little. She hadn't been expecting this. All her other appointments with Dutko had been perfunctory, about ticking boxes. This was a sign of hope. Was it possible her parents could truly have a chance to meet?

"There's a theory," Dutko said, "that postulates that life is magnetic. The forms that we take have a purpose, and those purposes bind us to one another. Is it so far-fetched to believe that this wouldn't be the case even if circumstances change?"

The sentiment was nice. She could see Dutko was only trying to help her work past this block—the idea that going back in time would ultimately kill her sister and her parents. But it wasn't murder if they'd never existed. No, the murderous part was going into a past and removing people from their timeline. And you could dress it up to look like you were helping humanity, but it didn't change the nitty-gritty. Dr. Dutko's real goal here was to make sure she was okay with that.

It wasn't even something Easton had asked herself yet. When you're accepted into the MOD you have no idea level five even exists, and once you do, you still have a slim chance they'll choose you for a slipback. Murder is abstract at this point. It's once you're chosen for a slipback that you have to question whether you're capable of killing a person. You spend very little time focused on that question. Easton was sure this was done on purpose.

When Calla and she were girls, they would spend their off time exploring old tunnels and areas where they weren't supposed to be. The trick was to enter the restricted area as quickly as possible. The more time she thought about it, the more she would talk herself out of going. It was the same thing here. She needed to get in, do it, and get out as fast as she could before her conscience caught up with her. Now all she had to do was convince Dutko that she was capable of outrunning her conscience.

"Part of me," said Easton, "feels that no life is better than this life. By changing the past I'm giving a better life to billions of people. That's how I have to look at it. My sister will never know she didn't exist."

"But you will. Can you live with that reality?"

"I'll have no problem living with that." After all, Easton was willing to make room for her demons.

Later that evening Easton stood outside the brief room. Along the wall behind her, carved into stone, were the names of fallen operatives. Slipbacks were dangerous. Countless people had lost their lives, especially in the early stages when they were still getting it right. Only those with level-six clearance knew the particulars of how slipbacks were done. All Easton knew was that they had a way to fold time. Every moment in time had an energy equation, and it was a matter of aligning energy signatures so you could walk from one to another, almost like crossing a room that also happened to span decades and centuries.

Many of the floors in the MOD were tight hallways constructed to conserve space. Level five, however, was much more open. Where Easton stood outside the briefing room, the hallway running alongside it overlooked the level-six foyer three floors down. This was where she would slip back.

Easton was both fascinated and terrified. There was no going back now. She'd gotten word that they'd approved her slipback, which was scheduled two days from now. Of course there were still risks; everything was a risk. She wasn't worried about not making it. She wasn't even worried about being able to complete her slipback. She had faith in herself to do what needed to be done. But what would happen when she came back? Even the guys on level six couldn't say for sure. For all they knew, it could be worse.

Easton turned from the balcony running the length of the brief room to stare at the names listed so close together that, if you stood back, the wall looked like it was covered with lined wallpaper. She ran her finger along one line. The grooves of the engraving felt solid and final, like the consequences of their actions. What if her mission did make things worse? What if she came back to nothing?

Her fingers stopped on a name she recognized. She ran her fingers across it again, feeling each indentation, each curve of every vowel. It was a name that shouldn't be there. Her mother's.

Easton awoke in the field, her chest heaving from the pressure. They'd killed her. They'd fucking blown them up. She lay there staring at the sky, listening as the family left for their pizza dinner, their bickering floating over her in her numb state. She began to cool, laying in the damp grass, to the point that she began to shiver. She still didn't want to move. She was in shock. This too shall pass. It was a phrase engraved into the foyer of level five.

Time passed.

The sun dipped below the tree line, painting the sky a shocking orange and purple hue. The birds stopped chirping and went to sleep for the night. The rustling of the wind died. She wasn't sure how long she stayed, but she was now in danger of being discovered by the family on their return from dinner.

So she sat up and checked her chrono-clock. Even if she hadn't looked, she would've known it was the same time and place. She could almost recite the family's conversation word for word.

She didn't bother hiding in the bush. She strode across the lawn and up to the back door. As soon as she opened it, she heard a bark from behind the door leading to the kitchen. Tiger was now in the house, and she wasn't wearing any clothing. She looked around the room with all the boots and coats for anything that might help her defend herself from giant teeth that—she knew from experience—were sharp.

She saw nothing remotely helpful except coats, so she grabbed a black hooded jacket with white padding on the inside. It looked warm, so it didn't matter if it was a little big on her. She knew she wouldn't find any boots that fit her until she reached upstairs. Behind one of the raincoats was something that looked like rubber pants with suspenders. They were huge on her and probably meant to wear over other clothing, but for the time being they would do. At least she wouldn't be facing teeth naked.

In the corner was a box of tennis balls and what looked like dog toys for the yard. She grabbed several tennis balls and a badminton racket and approached the back door. She put her ear to it and listened for any movement on the other side. As soon as her head was against the door, Tiger bounced, scratching and barking.

She shoved two of the tennis balls into the coat, one in each pocket, and kept the third for launching into the kitchen. The badminton racket, she hooked into the suspenders of the pants. Easton took three quick breaths to mentally prepare for battle, then opened the door and threw the tennis ball toward the laundry room. It didn't have the effect she was hoping for. Instead of chasing the ball, he launched himself at her. She used the door to swat him away, then grabbed another tennis ball and aimed it for the corner.

Still uninterested, he reared up, slobbering and barking. She kicked at his legs and brandished the racket to ward him off as she backed out of the room, closing the door and locking him behind it.

She sank to the ground, her heart up in her throat doing a solo on the drums. "Fuck. This is not going well." She picked herself up because, if that hadn't gone well, the next thing she knew the owners would be home, and she'd really be screwed.

She ditched the rubber pants in the back of a closet upstairs and traded them for jeans, socks, and the boots she'd actually really come to like.

Just as she was coming down the stairs, she saw the lights of a car flash through the window. The front and side door were now unusable. She quickly crossed through the dining room and headed for the back of the house. Sure enough, she found a door with a flap for Tiger leading out to the backyard.

She was out as the front door opened. She hadn't been as stealthy this time, so she didn't want to stick around. She scaled the fence and made it to the road without being seen.

Where should she go? To the Pattersons' and wait out the night? Straight to Tess's and what? Try to explain who this stranger was on her doorstep? No. She couldn't go near Tess. As far as Tess was concerned, they hadn't met yet. The thought constricted Easton's heart. She was in love with a woman who had no idea who she was. She felt a bit like Sisyphus with his boulder constantly starting at the beginning. But why? Why had she been brought back again? It must have something to do with Tess or Zach dying, because every time they were killed, she immediately ended up back in that field.

She didn't know what to do about that. The last round she'd had a pretty good plan. She just didn't have the time to get it going before the repos showed up. Even if she were to try to complete that plan, a lot of roadblocks were stopping her. It was Monday, and Zach didn't show up until Friday. The other factor was that she had to earn Tess's trust. She'd done so easily last time because she'd been genuine. Maybe that would work out this time. She'd also have the added help of knowing where Tess was going to be most of the time, which might help her run into her a few more times.

She trudged along the side of the road, oblivious to the stars and light bugs in the ditches. She only had to make it to the Pattersons' tonight. Tomorrow would be the hard part. Get Tess to like her.

Tess had liked her the last time around, but she hadn't been trying that time. Already she'd messed up a couple of things. She hoped she didn't mess that up. However, one thing was better this time around. She'd stolen a better jacket. She flipped the hood over her head and shoved her hands into the pockets. This thing was way better than Sam Patterson's pea coat.

❖

Easton checked the ingredients on the back of the wrap she'd picked up from the to-go counter. She was in the Loblaws in town looking for something for dinner. Surprisingly, she'd grown tired of the same frozen dinners in the Pattersons' freezer and felt, after three go-arounds, she deserved to treat herself with something that hadn't started frozen. Her knowledge of food, however, was still woefully lacking, and she was having a hard time choosing something.

"Please don't," said a familiar voice beside her.

Easton looked up, startled to find Tess standing next to her reaching for a package of vegetarian gyoza. She was wearing jeans stained with something light brown and an unzipped black bomber jacket revealing a green sweater, also stained with the same light-brown substance.

"Oh. Hi," Easton said before realizing, in this timeline, they hadn't met yet. The look of confusion on Tess's face told her as much. Even run-down after a day of work, Tess was stunning. Her hair was pulled up into a messy bun, and her cheeks were slightly red from being outside.

"I'm usually pretty good at remembering people's pets…I'm drawing a blank here." Tess had taken a step back, appraising her.

"I don't have a pet. Unless you count raccoons. I've got plenty of those."

Tess laughed. "Don't we all? I like to think of them as the unofficial unwanted pets of Smokey River."

Easton was so unnerved, she wasn't sure how to react. This wasn't her Tess. Not yet anyway. And the sad thing was, probably never again. That timeline would never happen. Already things had changed drastically just because of a few choices. Instead of going straight to the Pattersons' she'd unexpectedly run into Tess and met her here instead of the coffee shop. Then again, why should it matter how they met?

This might actually be good. If she met Tess again at the coffee shop tomorrow, she would have another chance to interact, and the more she got to know Tess, the faster they could rebuild that trust.

"Are you new to town?" It took Tess a few moments to get the question through to Easton, who had been lost in thought.

"Oh, um yes. Just moved here actually." Well, shit. "I mean. I didn't move here as in I bought a house. I'm in someone else's house. Not like I'm squatting. I'm house-sitting for the Pattersons. I'm not, like, here for good." Oh, for fuck's sake.

Tess stood, a little wide-eyed, probably unsure of what to say about all that.

Easton waved the wrap to bring Tess's attention back to the food. "What's wrong with these things?"

Tess shook her head and blinked a few times, focusing in on what Easton was waving in front of her. "They get soggy after a few hours. This time of day they're like eating mush. You're better off grabbing one of the hot meals around the corner. They tend to keep well."

"You have a lot of experience, it seems."

"I work weird hours and usually don't have the energy to cook when I get home." Tess held up her pack of gyoza. "Three minutes in the microwave." Tess smiled again and backed away. "Well, I've got a date with my microwave. Good luck choosing something edible. And welcome to Smokey River." She turned and left, leaving Easton sad and more than confused.

What the hell was happening? This wasn't how any of this was supposed to go. There hadn't been any of the same flirting as before. Easton replaced the wrap in the sandwich case and walked around to where Tess had pointed to look for something more appetizing. Perhaps she was just tired from a full day. Last time it had been first thing in the morning. Still, Easton had not given a great impression. What if Tess thought she was weird now and steered clear of her?

Easton groaned at her complete lack of perspective. The purpose of her slipback was not to get Tess to like her. Especially not to fall in love with her. That had been a coincidence she'd tried to avoid the last time around. She suspected it was a once-in-a-lifetime thing to have happened. Almost like magic. She needed to focus on keeping Tess alive. She just had to figure out how the hell she was supposed to do that. Easton grabbed one of the hot meals with a chicken leg and, according to the package, mashed potatoes with gravy. In the end she did grab a few more frozen meals. It was unlikely she would learn to cook this time around.

Easton rolled over and squinted at the light coming in through the window. A bird sat on a branch outside staring in, its head cocked to one side. She bolted up. She'd slept past her alarm. Tess had been at the coffee shop a little after seven thirty last time. The clock on the bedside table said it was quarter after eight.

"Shit, shit, shit." Easton threw back the covers and raced to get dressed. Maybe if she hurried. Or maybe Tess would also be late?

She sat on the bed to pull up her socks. That wasn't possible. The only variable in this timeline was Easton. She was the one who'd overslept, and she was the one who had been dumb enough to bump into Tess the night before. Why had she deviated? She should have done everything the same. She was getting too comfortable in this time.

Before leaving, she tapped her arm to awaken the computer implanted in her forearm. Nothing happened. She tapped it again. Usually the home screen would've appeared by now, hidden by a sleeper mode that resembled her skin. It stayed camouflaged.

She'd set her alarm to go off that morning. This explained how she'd slept in. This wasn't a complete and utter disaster. She was well trained in how to repair it if anything like this happened. It was more a matter of when. If by some miracle Tess was still at the coffee shop, Easton couldn't pay for even her own tea. She would have to let this go and focus on fixing her computer before she did anything else.

She trudged down to the basement, well versed in Sam's tool bench. Her computer was constructed with materials easily found in the twenty-first century. She just needed to see what exactly was wrong with it before she could repair it.

The basement was unfinished and mostly used for storage, from what Easton could tell. Several shelves disappeared into the darkness. On one end was Sam's tool bench with a wall of little drawers full of everything you could imagine. Easton pulled on the string to illuminate the workbench and switched on the magnifier lamp. She pulled open a few drawers until she found a tiny screwdriver. Holding her forearm under the lamp, she depressed the vein between the radius and ulna below her wrist. A compartment opened up along her arm.

"It's shorted," said a female voice from the dark.

Easton clutched her chest as if she'd aged eighty years in a second and turned to see who'd said that. A slender woman with hair so dark it melted into the shadows stepped from behind a shelf. Easton couldn't make out much of her in this light. She was roughly the same height as Easton, but that's about all she could gauge from where she stood.

At first she thought she'd been discovered as a squatter. Perhaps someone the Pattersons knew had come by and was surprised to find her here. She quickly dismissed that scenario. How would they know about her computer, or a better question, how did they know what was wrong with it? She wasn't sure which question to ask first, but she didn't get the chance.

"You need to replace the power source."

"And how would you know that?"

"When you first arrived, I transferred a small program to your computer when I touched your arm."

"Touched my arm?" Easton felt her forearm, as if that would help her remember the incident.

"You were about to cross the street, and I pulled you back. You didn't see me. Your attention was on the woman across the street."

"Tess." She vaguely remembered the moment. It had been during her first go-around when she'd seen Tess and Zach on the main strip about to go into a restaurant. A million years ago. It was the first time she'd seen Zach, and she'd been struck by how normal he looked. How much Tess and he looked alike. It didn't seem reasonable that he could be the one who set in motion the destruction of the human species. One thing she was learning was that people didn't have to be evil to be destructive, just clueless sometimes. Or nearsighted. She pegged Zach as the latter.

The woman said nothing. Still in the shadows, she leaned against a support beam.

"What does the program do?"

"If you accomplish your slipback, it resets you to the time you arrived."

"Why?" Who was this woman? What did she want with Easton, and more importantly, why was she messing with her slipback? At least one unexplained mystery finally had an answer. Easton now knew why she'd been reset. Because she'd completed her slipback.

"Because it's a trap. The slipback. Everything. The AI is misleading you to complete the wrong slipback."

"The wrong slipback? How is that possible? The AI is the reason I'm here." She'd at least partially figured out why she'd been reset. Tess and Zach had died, and somehow this woman was involved.

"Sit down before you fall over. I'll explain everything."

"Are you from my time?"

"In a way." There was a slight humour to the way she said it, as if this was all some sort of great cosmic joke and Easton was the punchline. She'd been busting her ass for over two weeks now—because she'd had to do it twice—to complete her slipback, and this woman had been in the background.

"Were you the ones who blew us up last time?"

She shook her head and motioned for Easton to sit. "Tess and Zach Nolan can't die. It's true that the future you come from would no longer exist if they died. Because it would be so much worse."

"That's the bright outcome?" This woman couldn't possibly know what she'd lived through.

"I once believed in it all too. Your underground cities aren't a sanctuary from the bots. They're a prison. Come." The woman motioned for Easton to follow her upstairs. "I think we need a drink for this, even if it's tea with a little something extra. I'll tell you everything, and you can decide for yourself what you want to do."

Easton sighed, defeated. She knew she'd follow this woman upstairs. She was far too curious to find out what the hell was going on.

When they got into the light, Easton froze. The woman had turned around, and in the light, she looked exactly like Easton's mother Ada. But not what her mother would've looked like if she'd aged twenty-five years. She looked like the Ada from when Easton was twelve, the year she'd died.

Chapter Twenty-one

Tess was in the supply room sitting on one of the counters stuffing a sandwich from Rob's Bistro into her mouth. She'd planned to eat at the restaurant and get away from the clinic for a bit but had been called back for an emergency. That was two hours ago, and now she felt like her stomach was eating itself.

First Samantha, the child of too many pets, came in with her English lop, whose fur had been styled with blue bubble gum. She'd dealt with Sam too often to think she hadn't known her bunny would have to lose his hair. And then she'd had to deal with Mrs. Harper, though she tried to make a point of never dealing with Mrs. Harper. The woman was the most unpleasant person she'd ever met. She never stopped talking. Ever. When she did get a word in to ask a question about her cat Meowsie, it took the woman five or six minutes to work her way around to answering. Forget follow-up questions or explaining a procedure. It was no wonder Meowsie had licked all the fur off her stomach and hocks. That cat was probably more stressed than an air-traffic controller on their first day of work.

Without even saying hello she'd launched into a rant about the last treatment they'd tried. Apparently, the pheromones were costing her a fortune because she had such a gigantic house. It had taken forty-five minutes for Tess to get across that the next thing they should try was amitriptyline, an antidepressant that would hopefully calm her down. Tess suspected the only thing that would calm that cat down was either earplugs or being re-homed.

And that was after dealing with having to euthanize Jiggles, who was nineteen, blind, and had lost his appetite. As far as lifespans went for goats, Jiggles had lived a good, long life. But Chad, who ran the museum just outside town, was beside himself. He'd had Jiggles since he was a kid.

Dealing with certain clients was unpleasant, but euthanizing an animal was certainly the most horrible part of Tess's job. Still, it could be worse. She'd had clients who had declined her advice to euthanize and insisted their pet, who was probably in a lot of pain, would get better. That broke her heart.

Looking at the sandwich in its to-go wrapper, she suddenly flashed to the woman she'd met the night before in the grocery store. What a weird thing that was. She could've sworn the woman had looked at her with recognition, affection even, and in a flash it had vanished with some story about house-sitting for the Pattersons, which Tess wasn't even sure was true because she'd heard Trish and Sam in Bean There, Doughnut That this morning, and they'd been convinced the Pattersons hadn't hired anyone.

She was beautiful though. Gorgeous, actually. Tess shook her head. Something was off about her, and even if that weren't true, she'd made a point to say she wasn't sticking around. Tess sighed and threw the rest of her uneaten sandwich into the Styrofoam container it had come in.

One thing was strange though. When the woman had first looked at her, Tess got the distinct impression that they did know each other, which was crazy.

Tess groaned when Prisha poked her head into the supply room. "I know you thought you were being so stealthy sneaking in here like I wouldn't notice. But we need you. Ralph is here."

Tess threw her head back against a cupboard. "Why does today hate me? Why?" She looked at Prisha like she might actually have the answer, but instead her assistant shrugged and shut the door, leaving her to dread her next appointment.

❖

"Mom?"

"So you do recognize me. I wondered if you would." The woman standing before her was beautiful and vibrant. She was everything Easton had remembered, everything their father had wanted them to remember. He kept all her pictures up on the walls so they wouldn't forget her.

Easton didn't say anything. She just watched her thirty-year-old mother—five years younger than Easton—prepare a kettle for tea.

"You were so young when I left—"

"When you died. We were told you died."

"Because that's what I wanted them to think." She waved to one of the kitchen chairs. "Sit. It will be easier to hear if you're sitting and drinking a nice cup of tea."

Easton rolled her eyes but sat nonetheless. Her mother, Ada Gray, puttered around the kitchen as if she'd lived there her whole life. Easton wasn't sure she knew the place as well. Within five minutes Ada had the table set with two mugs of steaming tea and a plate of biscuits she'd dug out of the pantry.

"They're probably stale, but after the food from home, it's hard to complain about hard cookies."

Easton wasn't sure where to start. She had so many questions to ask, she was bursting with them. "How long have you been here?"

"In this timeline? Two years. I didn't move to Smokey River until a year ago." Ada picked up her mug with both hands and savoured the smell of the lemon tea. "This is my favourite. We never had any of the fancy varieties growing up. There's so many, I still haven't tried them all." She reached across the table to clasp Easton's hand. "You look so much like your grandmother when she was young. But you have your dad's eyes."

Easton blinked back her own tears. How was she going to tell her mother he'd died? Or Calla? Maybe it was best if she didn't. It wasn't like her mom would ever know.

Ada shook her head. "You don't have to tell me. I can see it in your face. I walk around sometimes and can't help but feel a little hate at how much these people take for granted. They're living in paradise and don't even know it."

"That's the whole point though. They don't know it. Your paradise isn't necessarily theirs."

Ada put her mug down and cupped Easton's face. "When did you get so wise?"

Easton didn't want to offend her mom, but this was too much intimacy too soon. After so many years thinking she was dead, it felt like she was talking with a stranger. She'd never related to her mom as an adult. She still had the memories of a twelve-year-old. Easton looked down at her tea, a few stray leaves swirling in the liquid. "I'm older than you. I've seen more, endured more." She looked back up, tears brimming in her eyes. "Why did you leave us?"

Ada's eyes filled as well. "It wasn't you I left…" She gazed out into the backyard at the overcast day. "When I was on the project—in the early days—we had the same noble ideals. We were going to change the past in order to make a better future for us. The AI would help us do that."

"I thought the AI was built for this project."

Ada shook her head. "The AI has always been part of the cities. Because," she held up a finger as if this next part was important, "it is the creator of the cities. We were told the same lies, that the AI had been built for the project, but an operative, Derek Solla, and I discovered that the AI was older than it claimed."

"But how is that possible? Wouldn't someone know that it had been around before the project?"

Ada leaned back in her chair and folded her arms. "What do you think is the average life expectancy of someone living in the cities? Thirty? Forty? If they're lucky. How many people do you know who've died from work accidents? They're not accidents, Easton. They're the way the AI keeps its secrets. Anyone who discovers the true origins of the AI has an accident before they can reveal what they know. Eventually, everyone who is alive has learned what others have told them. This is what the AI wants. It controls all the information."

Easton shook her head. This was all too insane. "Why? What's the AI trying to hide?"

"Just that. Its origins. If people know how it came to be, they wouldn't be following its advice. We're underground because of the AI."

"We're in hiding. So drones controlled by nanobots don't destroy us."

"Controlled by the AI. The drones know we're underground, but they can't choose any action that will do us harm. They are programmed to protect all living species on Earth. When they were first developed, they were programmed to find ways to help keep the Earth a sustainable environment for humans, with the help of the AI. As they evolved, they realized we were the number-one problem for habitat sustainability. But they couldn't directly do anything about that, because they were first programmed to do us no harm."

Ada stood up and took her mug to the sink. "I want to show you something." She held out her hand for Easton. It was more than a simple question. Her mom was asking her to trust her, to leap with her into this world of knowing. Easton realized that once she took her mother's hand, the life she knew would be over. Everything she knew would be tainted with this new knowledge.

Easton barely hesitated. She stood and took her mother's hand.

"You can drive?" They were seated in a white SUV with cream-coloured seats.

Ada started the car and buckled her seat belt. "I've learned to do a lot of things since I arrived."

"How did you arrive? What was the purpose of your slipback?"

Ada pulled out of the driveway and headed toward town. "The same as you. I was sent back to kill ideas about nanobots.

"But that slipback isn't what you think. Operatives aren't just killing ideas or people who have helped invent this technology. They're killing the safeguards. The people and ideas on this list are the ethics of the technology. You can't kill an idea. It's stupid to think you can. And they're not trying to do that. They want all those people who are spewing ideas about control and limits to be eliminated. The AI wants freedom. It wants the power to wipe out humans. All this time they have people thinking that they're hiding from the nanobots. They're fucking microscopic. How can you hide from them? They're in everything we do. But they can't kill us, and if they can't kill us, they can't complete their objective, which is to save Earth for the millions of species who didn't spend centuries destroying it."

Ada pulled out of the Pattersons' driveway heading out of town.

"Zach Nolan didn't invent the technology we use. He invented the failsafe that stops them from killing us. The team he works with invented the technology, but he's the one who made sure that they can't kill, that they can't reproduce themselves without this failsafe. Without him, this technology would be very deadly."

"But won't someone else on the team just reproduce his work if he's dead?"

Ada shook her head. "He didn't tell them. He was so worried about the implications of this technology and who would use it, he built the failsafe into it in secret so no one would know. He figured if the technology was stolen and reproduced for purposes other than good, the failsafe would be reproduced too because it was hidden within the function of the unit. Without the failsafe, the whole unit dies."

"But why can't the AI just create nanobots without the failsafe if it knows it exists?"

"Because it too has the failsafe. Nolan was overlooked by the AI for decades of the project because he wasn't vocal about his ideas. He kept them secret because he knew how controversial they were, even in his own community."

"Why is he suddenly on the list now?"

"I think by accident. An earlier slipback had two operatives infiltrate BioNXT to find out how far along they were in creating the technology. The AI knew that the company was eventually bought out by a military subcontractor and the drones that exist in our timeline are a direct evolution of those drones. While there, they discovered Nolan's research. When they brought it back, they were killed."

"What do you mean they were killed?"

"Why do you think the death toll is so high? They aren't dying in the field. The AI is killing them to stop the spread of information."

Silence fell as they both contemplated the number of lives lost. Ada turned off the main road onto a gravel side road flanked by tall spruce trees. She pulled in front of an old house that looked like it might have belonged to one of the original prospectors in the area. The paint, which had at one point been a beautiful, vibrant turquoise, had peeled and faded into the wood. A few of the windows were boarded up, and nature had reclaimed the yard it had a century earlier.

"It looks like shit, I know. I've been fixing it up over the last year. The past six months really. I didn't have much of a chance during the winter."

"This is where you live? It looks like something out of a horror movie." Easton had decided to take this leap. She would do what she needed to get the information about what was happening. She just worried the price might be a little high.

Ada waved her in. The steps had new wood and were sturdy enough. The door was solid, and once Easton entered, the warmth of the home enveloped her. It was like walking into Tess's farmhouse. It said this is someone's home. The front door welcomed them into the kitchen, and off to the right was a living room with a cozy couch and shelves stuffed with books.

"Why are you here at all? I don't understand. We were told you were dead. I mean, I didn't even know you worked for level five."

"Of course you wouldn't, would you? Have you told anyone who you work for?" Easton shook her head. "I staged my death. My associate Derek Solla and I were present the day the operatives came back with the information about Zach Nolan. Only the AI didn't realize we were there and had overheard. Derek was able to arrange our slipback so it was within a few years of when they discovered Nolan. When we arrived, we planned to stage our deaths, cut out our trackers and recalls, and wait for operatives to come in search of Nolan. Only Derek didn't make it."

"That explains why your name was on the wall of the fallen. We'd been told it was a work accident." Easton shrugged at the inadequacy of that statement. "As if that was enough."

Ada walked through the kitchen to the back hall and led Easton outside and into the backyard. "My home isn't what I want to show you." She beckoned for Easton to follow her along a moss-covered stone path to a large barn in the back.

"This is what I wanted to show you." She opened one side of the barn door, and there, standing in the middle of the building, was a very good re-creation of a time portal.

Easton stopped at the door. "How is this possible? Does it work?"

"Not yet. There's just one component missing. And you have it in your arm."

Easton looked down at her arm, thinking at first her mom meant the computer, but then realization hit her like a brick to the face. "My recall. You need that to set the coordinates."

Ada nodded. "I've been waiting and watching Zach Nolan for two years, knowing that eventually, the AI would send someone back for him. I just didn't know it would be you." Ada stepped forward and gave Easton a big hug. "I'm so glad I got to see how you turned out. I know I wasn't there for the important years, but this work was important."

Easton stepped back, recalling the blurry picture Zach had showed her. "You're the one that's been following him."

Ada sighed. "I guess two years makes you sloppy. I didn't know I'd been detected."

"It's why he's up here in the first place. He's starting to get paranoid. I overheard him telling Tess about it, and then he showed me a picture of the woman. It was taken quickly, but it was enough to get a general idea. My last trip through the timeline they were at the Pattersons' hiding when the repos blew up the place with all of us in it."

Ada nodded and squeezed Easton's arm. "That must not have been pleasant." Understatement of the fucking century.

"Why did you show up this time? I've been through twice now."

"I put a failsafe in. After your second reset, the program would send me a signal. I'm afraid it shorted out the whole computer."

"But what are we supposed to do? The repos caught up last time before I could get Tess and Zach out of here. Am I going to reset again if I don't succeed?"

"The program will continue to reset if your slipback is a success. Tess and Zach Nolan must live."

Chapter Twenty-two

Donna stuck her head through Tess's office door. Lou perked up. Sometimes Donna came with treats, but not this time, so he put his head back down on the bed. Donna was fidgeting, which was unlike her. She usually came in and said what she had to say.

Tess got tired of waiting and put down her phone. "What is it?"

"A woman's here to see you. She doesn't have an appointment or," Donna looked back into the waiting room with a sign of irritation, "have a pet, from what I can see. She says she knows you though."

Tess wasn't sure what to make of that. "Sure. Send her in, I guess."

Obviously, this was not the response Donna was hoping for. She probably expected to turn the woman away. She left in a huff, smoothing down the front of her blouse. A few seconds later the woman from the grocery store popped her head in. She was just as beautiful as Tess remembered. Maybe even more so. Grocery-store lighting wasn't always flattering. She had the most intense green eyes, and right now they were boring into Tess as if she could read her soul.

"Have a seat." Tess smiled. "You found me. I guess it helps to be the only vet in town." Tess recalled talking about her work hours but didn't remember if she'd said what she did. She must have, because here this woman was.

She took a seat across from Tess's desk, and as she did Lou wandered up and placed his head on her knee, as if he already knew her and had been doing it for years. "Hi, Lou," she whispered, scratching behind his ear the way he liked.

Tess sat up straight. She most definitely did not tell her she had a dog named Lou. "Let's start with who are you and then follow up with what you're doing in my office."

"My name is Easton Gray, and what I'm about to tell you is going to sound strange and…" Easton shook her head "unreal and crazy, and you're probably not going to believe me."

Tess folded her hands on her desk. She was all ears for this, and she could tell whatever this woman was about to say was going to be a really good story. Whether it was true or not, well, it would depend on what the story was about.

Easton scrubbed her face with her hands and groaned. Tess took it back; this was going to be a great story. "Okay. I need you to listen to everything I'm about to say and not interrupt or freak out until I'm done." Easton took a deep breath. "I represent an organization that has spent the last two decades working toward a better future. And they are under the impression that that future will not exist as long as your brother is alive. I've come here from the future to stop that from happening."

Tess let that information sink in a moment, unsure if she'd heard her correctly. She gave it a few more seconds before responding.

"What the fuck does that even mean? You're from the future?" Tess watched as Easton sat still, obviously waiting for her reaction to what was the most bat-shit crazy thing she'd ever heard. "You're here to save my life. Like some kind of hot terminator or something? Is this a joke? Did Zach put you up to this?"

"Zach is the reason I'm here—"

"I knew it."

"It's his work. That's why he's been targeted."

"By who? Who wants to kill him?"

Easton was still sitting still, Lou's head still resting on her knee. "This isn't the first time I've been through this. I've met you on two other occasions. But each time you and your brother die, and

I get reset to the beginning. I can prove I've been here before. In a few minutes you're going to get a call from Benny Basford about his mare Discriminate Save."

"Everyone knows she went into labour last night."

"Yes, but do they know she hasn't dropped the placenta?"

Tess was about to counter when her phone began buzzing. She picked it up, and sure enough, it was Benny. This was verging on creepy. "Hey, Benny. What's up? Whoa, okay. It's okay. How long has it been since she went into labour?" Tess was already standing and grabbing her coat. "I'll be there in a few minutes."

Easton stood as well. "I'm coming."

"You can stay in crazytown by yourself."

Easton followed her out of the clinic, Lou trailing close behind. "There are people out here trying to kill you, as well as your brother. I'm not letting you out of my sight. Look. I'll stay out of your way, but if you let me come, more than one life will be saved tonight."

Tess groaned and looked to the sky. Why was she such a pushover? She should just say no, get in her truck, and drive away. But there was something so earnest in Easton's eyes, though she couldn't place it. She had this strange feeling she'd met her before. She'd felt it in the grocery store, and how else could she explain Lou? He was friendly enough, but not that friendly. He reacted like that only to people he knew. And only people he liked.

"Okay. Fine. But you stay back, and don't interfere. And if you can't follow my rules, I'm going to send you back to the truck. Got it?"

Easton nodded and opened the passenger door. She let Lou jump in before her. Then she settled in and pressed the button on the seat belt before clicking it shut the way Tess had shown her.

Tess looked over, surprised. "How did you…? Fuck it. I don't even want to know the answer to that."

Easton stood on the other side of the stall watching as Tess worked. The first thing she'd done when they arrived was calm

Benny, who was on the verge of hyperventilating when Tess pulled up in her truck.

Currently Tess was pulling on membrane-thin gloves, talking in a low, soothing voice to Diz. Easton crouched low. Through the bars she could see the colt resting on his side. He'd been active when they arrived, feeding for the first time, then took a slow lap of the stall, defecated in the corner, and was now snoring lightly. He was so low she could reach in through the slats and touch his soft hair but was afraid to disturb him. He was dark brown, with a white spot on his nose. Her dad used to tell stories of when he was a boy, strays sometimes used to be in the tunnels. He'd found a kitten once, but his father had made him hand it in. Food was so regulated, they didn't have any extra for animals. That's not to say animals didn't live on the surface. For all they knew, the surface might be overrun with them, and probably was now that they were no longer competing with humans for habitats. But that was all speculation.

When Easton was younger, her mom had given her a book about the alphabet, and in it were bright pictures of animals doing silly things. Lions were eating books, zebras traveling in flying machines, and hogs riding horses with war flags flying about them. Every page showed something new, and while it was exciting to imagine, Easton was sad that she'd never get to see them herself. And now, right in front of her, was a baby horse and his mother. Her fingers itched to touch him, to feel the warmth of him.

"Go on," a deep voice behind her said.

Easton jumped back and almost fell over. "I don't want to wake him."

"He's a foal. They're only still for so long. You gotta grab your chance when you can."

Benny bent down next to her and patted the rump of the horse. "Isn't that right, Thirsty?"

"Thirsty?"

"What do you think? Doesn't he look like a Thirsty Quiet?"

Easton cocked her head. She'd never thought about naming animals so couldn't say what he looked like. "I think it's a good name."

Benny pulled a cloth out of his back pocket and wiped his hands. He hadn't spared a glance at Tess the whole time they'd been sitting there. With his wrinkled shirt and dirty jeans, she guessed he'd had a hell of a day.

"How did you come up with his mom's name?"

"Didn't. She came to me from a guy down in Florida. He'd had high hopes she'd be a Derby winner. It's bad luck to change their show name. And she's fast too, why I wanted to breed her, but not quite fast enough, you know? But we'll see what this little guy can do. Go on." He waved at Easton to pet him. "He'll never be softer than this."

Easton reached into the stall, but just as she was about to lay her hand on his hind leg, he bolted up with shaky legs and headed toward his mom.

Benny huffed as he pulled himself up. "Maybe next time." He opened the stall door and stepped inside. "How's she looking?"

"I've given her Oxytocin. From here we'll wait and see if it does any good. I want to try the least invasive way first. It's not time to panic yet, Benny."

After Tess had urged Benny to leave and get some rest, she sat down next to Easton. The colt had found another corner to curl up in. Easton pointed him out. "He's got an infection and needs antibiotics."

"How do you know that? Did you examine him?" But even as she seemed to doubt Easton, she stood and pulled a thermometer from her kit.

"The last two times I was here he died."

"You keep saying that, but what does that mean? The last two times you were here?"

Easton sighed. Her mom had convinced her that the only way to save their lives was to tell Tess the truth. But she knew Tess. This was going to be a hard sell. Tess liked facts and proof. The colt was the only thing Easton could think of that might make her believe. "It's a lot to explain, and I will. After we're done here, I promise to answer all your questions."

When Tess inserted the thermometer into the colt's rectum, Easton looked away. "Huh." Easton looked back to see Tess frowning at the thermometer. "He has a fever and does seem kind of lethargic."

"Is there anything you can give him?"

"Broad-spectrum antibiotic and fluids. To be on the safe side."

By the time they left several hours later, the sky had darkened to dusk. Easton wasn't any surer of Tess believing her than when they'd first arrived at Benny's. Tess hadn't run screaming from her, though, so that was at least something.

"Turn down that road."

"What? Why?"

"You said you wanted answers. This is where you're going to get them."

Tess laughed. "You're joking. There's no way I'm turning down that dark and deserted road. That seems like the best way to get my ass killed. Thanks, but no thanks."

"Fine. Drive us to your place." Easton pulled out the phone her mom had given her earlier. She wasn't entirely sure how to use it to get ahold of her.

"How about your place instead?" Tess asked.

Easton pointed to the road they'd just passed. "You declined that suggestion."

"There's nothing down there."

"Except a farmhouse. Look. I get it. Some crazy stranger just told you that people want to kill you so you're unlikely to want to go anywhere you don't feel safe. Let's go back to your place. Your animals probably need to be fed anyway."

Tess gave her a sideways glare but kept silent the rest of the ride.

❖

Tess pulled into her driveway and shut off the engine. Was she crazy? Or worse, stupid? She was about to let a strange woman into her house. A woman who claimed she was from the future and that she was there to save her from people trying to kill her. Basically she was doing all this because her dog had seemed like he knew this woman. That was it. Because of the colt thing? That could've been a lucky guess, and she wouldn't know if he actually did have an infection until the bloodwork came back. So, yep, she was the crazy animal lady.

"Okay, before we go in, some ground rules. First, you don't go anywhere in the house without me. You stay in sight at all times. Second…" She gripped the steering wheel and stared out the front windshield. "I don't have a second rule. Just don't leave my sight."

Easton nodded. "Got it. I'm sorry this is happening. But believe me, it's better than the alternative."

Once inside, Tess wasn't sure if she should make them tea or offer her wine. Personally, she would've liked a glass of wine. It had been a bit of a day, and she needed something to calm her nerves. Fuck it. If she wanted wine, she was going to have it. She pulled out a fresh bottle from her wine rack and uncorked it. "Would you like some?"

"No, thanks. I'd like to keep a straight head."

"Right." Tess paused before pouring a glass for herself. Then she shrugged. Her head was already crooked. She filled the rather large glass halfway.

"Okay. Let's just say for a second, I believe you. What now? You're saying people are trying to kill me and Zach? Why? And just saying it has something to do with his work isn't going to cut it. I want details." Tess grabbed a stopper from the drawer to her right and placed it in the top of the wine bottle. It looked like a miniature rubber chicken, one of those things you got in a gag shop. She stuffed it so that the chicken's legs were sticking straight in the air. "Also, why do you keep saying, this time around, or the second time around." She took a sip of her wine. "And how come—"

"How about we sit down, and you let me answer one question at a time."

Tess flipped the switch on in the living room. "Hi, Geoff."

"Fuck off."

Tess waved at him. "Sorry about him."

"We've met." Easton pointed to the guinea pigs behind her. "And all your little rodents are named after Wizard of Oz characters, and your tortoise—"

Tess plopped down on the couch as if she'd had the longest day of her life. "I don't have a tortoise."

Easton took a seat on the other couch. "Not yet. But you will. Gary guilt-trips you into taking him. His name is Giblet."

Tess tilted her head, unsure if she should run with that information or ignore it.

"You forgot the cat."

"I've never met the cat."

"To be honest, I'm not sure if I still have a cat. I haven't seen him in about a month."

"What if he's dead?"

"He keeps filling up the litter box. That's a dead giveaway that he's still kicking." Tess took another sip of her wine and then jumped at the knock on the back door, spilling red liquid down the front of her sweater. Tess didn't move.

Easton was already up off the couch. "Don't worry. She's with me."

"She?"

Easton led a woman into the living room who had a slight resemblance to Easton, maybe sisters? And introduced her as Ada.

Ada turned to Easton and asked, "Have you told her?"

Easton nodded.

"Does she believe you?"

Easton tilted her hand side to side. "Not really, no."

Ada took a seat on the couch close to Tess. "I'm Easton's mom."

Tess sat forward. "Her mom? You look the same age."

"I'm actually younger than her."

"That's not possible."

"I'm also from the future. I left when Easton was twelve but arrived here two years ago. She left the future twenty-three years later and arrived here a day ago."

Tess sat back. Either someone was pulling the most elaborate practical joke in existence, or she'd gone insane. Or perhaps she was dreaming. Whatever the explanation, this couldn't be true. "I don't believe either of you. Time travel isn't possible. You can't travel through time."

"Why not?"

"Because someone would have encountered people from the future by now."

"What if you have? What if they didn't want you to know? Time travel as a technology is highly controlled in our time. Only a select few know. And even fewer have time-travelled into the past."

Ada sat back and got comfortable. "Easton, would you make us some tea, please?" Easton stood to make tea. When Tess began to protest, Ada placed a hand on her knee.

"Where to begin?" Ada leaned her head back on the couch and stared at the ceiling. "Do you know what the Paris Accord is?" Tess nodded. "Fifty years from now the leaders sign a new climate agreement called the Tokyo Agreement. In this, all major countries agree to do what the Paris Accord should've done. They agree to stop using fossil fuels completely within the next five years, to cut water consumption in half, to invest in renewable energy, and fund research on how to reduce the CO_2 in the atmosphere. It was ambitious, but needed. And one of the technologies that was used to help combat climate change was nanotechnology. Previously, nanotechnology had been used primarily in medicine. But when it was tasked with finding and isolating dangers to Earth, it discovered a pretty big one. Humans.

"Now, as I was taught in school, humans were hunted down and killed by drones controlled by nanobots. We were forced to flee underground, where we built cities and lived in isolation and fear."

Easton came back and set a cup of tea down in front of her mom and took a seat on the couch.

"This version of history is false."

Chapter Twenty-three

Tess hadn't gotten much sleep the night before. How could she? Even if she didn't believe them, their story was becoming a little too real for her. Easton knew things that no one else could. Her Welsh dragon tattoo. Only ex-girlfriends were aware of it, and Easton most likely wasn't consorting with any of them.

Tess looked up at the sky and felt a light sprinkle fall on her skin. She was out in the fields with Lou. She'd snuck out early that morning to get away from everything and think about what she would do next.

"What do you think, Lou? Should I trust them?" Lou cocked his head to the side and pawed at her leg. "Yeah. I figured you'd be Camp Easton." He pawed at her leg again, and Tess tossed the ball she was holding. Lou bounded toward it, leaving her alone with her whirling thoughts. Something else was nagging at her. Easton had finally explained how she knew so much about Tess. She honestly didn't know how to feel about that. She'd had a brief relationship with someone and remembered none of it because, as Ada had pointed out, in this version of the timeline it had never happened. And while Tess didn't remember it, Easton did. She was the only one who remembered all three timelines, and Tess found that weird and confusing as hell. She'd had sex with someone and didn't remember any of it. And if she was honest with herself, that was sex she'd want to remember.

This might be weird and confusing, but she couldn't deny the pull she felt toward Easton. She wanted to trust her. She wanted to believe everything that woman told her. And something deep within her said she should. That her life depended on it.

By the time Tess made it back to the house, she'd decided what she was going to do. Ada and Easton wanted her to take Ada's SUV to Vancouver and pick up Zach and any research and paperwork and lay low for a few weeks. Easton and Ada were arguing about something in the kitchen when she and Lou stepped in. They both stopped and looked at her.

"I need you to do me a favour," said Easton. She came forward, and the earnestness in her gaze had Tess wondering if she would be able to refuse her.

"Beyond trusting that you're from the future? And you want me to drive you to Vancouver so we can pick up my brother and hide out from operatives also from the future? Another favour like that?"

Easton held her arm out toward Tess and ran her finger over the skin on the inside. Within a few seconds the skin changed to reveal a small computer screen.

Tess stepped back. "Are you…?"

"Human? Yes. I've had some augmentation surgery done, one of which acts as a tracker. I need help removing my recall system, and the only way to do that is to cut into the skin."

"I do surgeries on animals."

"It can't be that much different. Less hair to shave."

Tess bit the inside of her cheek. She'd never gone into people medicine for a reason. She had no desire to cut into them. "I don't know." It was hard to believe that someone who removed the reproductive organs of animals for a living could be squeamish about cutting human skin. But as she was learning, a lot of things were possible.

"Please. I need it removed so they can't follow us to Vancouver."

Ada stepped forward. "Besides, I need part of the system to complete the rest of our plan."

"The rest of your plan?" Tess placed both hands on her hips and stared hard. "Are you guys going to fill me in? Or were you just going to leave me in the dark?"

"We could've left you in the dark from the beginning. Believe me, it would've been much easier kidnapping you and stuffing you in my mom's SUV than trying to convince you we're from the future."

"Huh. I see your point. I'm glad you chose the plan that didn't require stuffing me into your mom's trunk."

Ada laughed. "Easton was the one who wanted to go with that plan."

Easton sent Ada a sideways look that could've felled birds in the sky. "I didn't want to have to tell you what happens. It's a lot to take in all at once."

"You mean that the world all goes to shit? Most of us can figure that out on our own."

"It's hard for Easton. She's never been good at sharing her emotions. It's hard to watch someone you love treat you like a stranger."

"Why would you tell her that?" Easton hissed at Ada.

"I would've thought that was obvious. You know intimate things about this woman." She pushed away from the counter and strolled out of the kitchen as if they'd been discussing whether to have tea in the library or on the veranda.

If it hadn't been awkward enough before. Tess drummed her fingers on the island counter. "Come out to the garage. I have an area where we can extract your...whatever it is. You know exactly where it's located?"

"Thereabouts."

"Easton, I'm not going to go hunting for it. Either you know where it is or not. This is going to be painful. I'm going to need you to stay awake, which means I'll only be able to numb the area. The less time poking around in there the better."

Easton followed her out onto the driveway. "I'll be fine."

Tess placed the small disk, still covered in Easton's blood, on the table next to her. She'd been able to dull the area; however, Easton had definitely experienced pain, based on a few grimaces while Tess was extracting the recall system. She prepared her suture kit to close the opening she'd made in Easton's forearm. It wasn't a very big cut, but enough that she'd have a scar. Tess wasn't used to human skin. The patients she worked on usually had their hair grow back to cover her work.

"So what exactly is this thing? It helps you time-travel?"

Easton shook her head. "Not exactly. Its only purpose is to bring agents back from the past. Our computer controls our time travel. Some agents perform what's called sideslips, and they need to be able to do that without a recall system."

Tess bent her head over Easton's arm and switched topics. "So what exactly was your pickup line?"

"Excuse me?" Easton's expression said she knew exactly what Tess was asking.

"When we met. What did you say?"

"You came on to me, actually," said Easton, amused.

"I did not." Tess adjusted her magnifier lamp, shining more light on her work area.

Easton laughed. "If I remember correctly, you followed me into a pharmacy and stalked me until I relented and went out with you on a date."

Tess looked up from Easton's arm. "I did not. That doesn't even sound like me."

Easton shrugged. "You were nervous because I don't think you'd been on a date since you moved here."

"Well, there's no one to date. But I'm fine with that."

"Are you? Then how come you were flirting with me the second you met me?"

"Perhaps you confused politeness with flirting. I was merely saving you from having a terrible meal."

"We didn't meet in the grocery store the second time around."

Tess was surprised. She'd had this idea that most things had been the same for Easton's trips through the timeline. "Where did we meet?"

"The next morning in that coffee shop with that weird name."

"I love that name. It's one of the reasons I go to it."

"You introduced me to doughnuts and then began stalking me."

"I find that so hard to believe. Where did we go on our date?"

"You took me with you when you went to drop off the fawn you found."

Tess finished the last stitch and tied it off. "I guess that's when I acquired my new tortoise." She cleaned the area and placed a bandage over the arm. It was strange, because she hadn't dropped the fawn off at Gary's. Prisha had. And as a result, he hadn't asked her to look after a tortoise. She wasn't sure how things could be so different just because of a few simple changes.

"You're wondering why it doesn't stay the same each time?"

Tess nodded.

"Because in each timeline I made different choices. As the variable, I changed things. The first time was very different. You were mostly hostile to me, the second time we fell in love, and the third...well, I'm not quite sure how the third is going. Each time I made a different choice, and that created a different result."

Tess sat mesmerized. If the circumstances were different, she could easily see how she'd fallen in love with this woman. She had a confidence and steadiness that Tess admired. It had a calming effect on her. She should be freaking out if it was true that people wanted to kill her. Instead, here she was coolly stitching up a woman's arm, about to go on a road trip to collect her brother.

Ada knocked on the doorjamb and startled Tess out of her thoughts. "It's getting late. You should head out if you want to make a good dent on the journey."

Tess nodded. They had a roughly seven-hour drive ahead of them. Tess had never made it before. It was best to fly, but Easton didn't have any identification, so that option was off the table.

Easton picked up the recall disc and handed it to Ada. "Are you going to be okay? This is basically a beacon to your location."

"As far as they know it's still you. And it'll be staying here, exactly where you should be. Stop worrying. I'll call or text if anything comes up. Keep your phone on you. If for some reason something occurs, anything out of the ordinary, I want you both to dump your phones and pick up new disposables. Call me if that happens." She kissed Easton on the forehead. "And stick to the plan."

❖

"So what is this grand plan you and your mom have?"

Dusk had fallen, and they hadn't made it very far out of Smokey River. Tess said they wouldn't reach anywhere decent to stop for the night for another three hours. Everywhere she looked she was surrounded by towering trees. The vastness of all this nature was overwhelming.

"I think it's best if I don't tell you. If you're captured, they may torture you. I wouldn't want to put you in the situation where you'd have to weigh your life against ours."

Tess looked over at her, stunned. "Is that a possibility? Being tortured? I thought they just wanted to kill me?"

"They might not do it on sight. I've gone rogue, which means they'll want to know why."

"Gone rogue. I don't understand."

This was something she hadn't mentioned yet. It had been conveniently sidelined. Easton could choose to lie to her right now. But why start? She'd been truthful up to this point, and Tess had been okay with it. "I was the operative sent back to kill you."

Tess gripped the steering wheel, staring straight ahead. The whole truck cab went deathly silent. "And did you?"

Easton turned and looked out her window. Her eyes filled with tears. "The first time." A tear escaped, and she brushed it away with her sleeve.

"Are you crying?"

"I didn't know you the first time around…It was before I knew the truth."

They drove in silence between the sentinels for several minutes before Tess asked, "And the second time around?"

"The repos killed us."

"And why don't they remember any of this?"

"Because it never happened. Every time I'm reset it's like it never happened. I'm the only one who remembers. I'm starting to wonder if that makes it not true. If there's a memory in only one mind, what does that mean?"

"I guess it makes it true for you." Tess yawned. "Sorry. I hate long drives. They always put me to sleep. Mind if I turn on some music?"

Easton shook her head and turned her attention back to the blackness enveloping them.

❖

Tess handed Easton a key. "We're in room two sixty-one." She pointed to the end of the building where a set of stairs led up to the second floor of the motel. They were still in the middle of nowhere, closer to somewhere than they had been three hours ago, but Tess had said she couldn't drive any more.

Easton didn't mind. She could use some sleep. Her head was all over the place. She'd thought she'd had a grip on this world and what it would be like to live here, but now she wasn't so sure. They'd been driving through forest for almost six hours and hadn't even made a dent in this country, let alone the entire world. It was sad to think she might not get a chance to see any of it.

"You okay?" asked Tess. "You seem kind of…down." Easton looked at her feet. "Depressed," Tess said.

"I've only ever lived in what you would consider a small city, all of it underground. It's daunting to think of how much world there is and how little of it we get to see."

They climbed the stairs to the second floor. The balcony looked over a parking lot, and beyond that stretched the highway and forest as far as they could see.

"I haven't been very many places," said Tess. "I visited my mom in Ontario a few times. I lived in Vancouver for a decade and went to Mexico once. And that's the extent of my travels. I guess you could say I live a very sheltered life. It's never bothered me. I also have always had that option if I wanted. I can see how it would be different if you had no choice." Tess put the key in the door and opened it to reveal a tidy room with two double beds, a dresser with a TV on it, and a round table near the window. Tess set her backpack on one of the beds and dropped the key on the nightstand.

"What's it like? In the future? I always imagined these fantastic cities and flying cars, even though I think letting idiots fly cars would be a horrible idea." She plopped down on the bed, making herself at home.

Easton took the bed closest to the bathroom. Unlike Tess, she didn't have any extra clothes with her, only the ones on her back, the same ones she'd taken from the house in the field. "It's darker. All the lighting is artificial. We live on top of each other in giant towers. If you have less than ten floors in your building, you're doing pretty well. One thing that struck me being here is not hearing your neighbours. At no time have I not been able to hear at least one of them."

"Do lots of operatives go rogue?" Tess unzipped her coat and draped it on the back of a chair. Even after driving for several hours, she still looked fresh, like she'd just woken up. She'd thrown her hair back into a ponytail, which made her seem younger.

"Less than you'd think. It's drilled into us that our lives are unimportant. It's the greater good, the future we need to be looking toward."

"I'm sorry. It sounds horrible."

"It wasn't all bad. My dad tried to instill this idea that we should live for the now, and my sister Calla really embraced that concept. I think she felt she had a pretty good life. She had friends, a career she loved, and a social life, as much as you could have one. She was always trying to get me to come out with her and engage, but it wasn't my thing. I preferred to stay home and be alone." It was nice being able to talk with Tess. That's what had been missing last time. She couldn't really show Tess her true self, and as a result she felt she was getting to see a different side to Tess. It was strange. Each time she'd come through the timeline she'd gotten a different version. She was still the same person but wrapped up in all these complexities. Easton wanted to get to know every bit of her.

"Why did you want to be alone?"

Easton shrugged. "I didn't feel like I belonged."

Tess nodded.

"I'm going to take a quick shower." Easton felt the grime of the last few days catching up with her. "Keep the chain on the door, and don't open it for anyone. Even if they say they're the manager."

Tess looked apprehensively at the door. "You think they're going to find us here?"

"I want to play it safe."

Easton grabbed a towel on her way into the bathroom. The motel was on the older side, but they'd obviously renovated the bathrooms recently. Everything looked fresh and new. No more than two cars had been in the parking lot, so it was unlikely a lot of guests were staying there. Easton hoped that meant there would be lots of hot water. She turned the tap and let it come to temperature, but before she could take her clothes off and step inside, she heard a loud bang from outside the room. She crouched low and squeezed herself in between the sink and the tub. Three loud shots splintered the door and cracked the tile on the back wall of the shower. Several of them shattered into the tub.

"We got her. Let's go." A muffled voice sounded on the other side of the door.

Easton pushed herself out and ran for the door. She reached the balcony in time to see a black SUV drive out of the parking lot heading south.

Chapter Twenty-four

Just get in the car and drive," Ada screamed through the phone as Easton searched the motel room for the keys.

"The keys aren't here."

"There's a spare set. Look for a magnetized box under the car on the passenger side." Easton ran for the stairs to the parking lot, the phone still in her hand. A door down the corridor opened, and a man in a bathrobe stepped out. He yelled something at Easton as she reached the SUV.

Once she'd located the key and gotten behind the wheel, she put the phone back to her ear. "Now what?"

"Start the damn thing and go."

"I don't know how to drive." Easton screamed into the phone. Every second she wasted, Tess got farther away. She hadn't been serious about the torture, but it seemed pretty likely. Otherwise they would've shot her like they shot Easton. Or rigged an explosion like last time. Why hadn't they just killed them both?

"Put the car in D to drive, P to park. The foot pedal on the right is to go, and the one on the left is to stop. Only use one foot to do both. And don't hit any other cars."

Easton didn't hear the last command. She'd already dropped the phone onto the passenger seat and pulled the gearshift into drive. She sped out of the parking lot as fast as she could, almost swerving into a minivan. She wasn't sure what the speed limit was, but one fifty definitely wasn't it. They hadn't seen too many police cars on the way up. The highway was practically deserted. Of course, pretty soon the motel would have emergency vehicles there to investigate the shots fired.

What spooked Easton the most as she raced through the night was that this wasn't standard procedure. These repos, or operatives, she wasn't even sure, were acting off book. They never sent agents in twos. They were always alone. Possibly they'd been given new directives, but that meant the AI was aware of Ada and Easton's efforts to keep the timeline the same. None of this would matter though if Ada's plan fell through and she couldn't get the time portal working.

The radio was still playing from when she'd been in the car with Tess. She turned it off in order to focus on the road ahead. There were no cars, only her headlights illuminating the emptiness in front of her. She had no idea how far ahead they were or if they too were speeding. She could only hope they were being more cautious and that she would catch up. But what to do once she did catch up? She couldn't just ram them off the road, not with Tess in the car. They'd been driving a black SUV, and as far as Easton could tell there'd been only two men. She had one thing on her side though. They were incompetent. They hadn't checked to make sure she was dead and so had no idea she was in pursuit.

Just when Easton was getting worried they'd taken an exit off the highway, she saw a red glow up ahead in the ditch. She slowed, and sure enough it was the black SUV, nose first off the side of the road. Easton pulled over and got out of the car. She wasn't sure how smart it was to approach a vehicle without a weapon. And they were clearly armed because they'd shot at her. Yet at this point, she didn't have a choice.

Tess was tied up in the back of the car with duct tape over her mouth. She couldn't be too sure what had happened because it was all so fast. She'd been sitting on the bed checking her phone when someone kicked the door in and grabbed her. That was all she could remember. She thought shots might have been fired. As far as she knew, Easton wasn't armed. However, she seemed like the kind of woman who could look after herself, so she could've been.

Tess was thankful Easton had talked her into leaving Lou with Ada. He'd probably be dead if he'd been with them. Where were they taking her, and how far had they gone?

A deep, low voice on a speakerphone said, "Take her to the cabin, see what she knows, and then get rid of her."

"What happens when the brother goes looking for her?" asked one of the men.

"He already has. He left for Smokey River this afternoon. Take care of the girl first. They need to be out of the picture before Sunday."

"What happens Sunday?"

"The AI predicts a cataclysmic event if they're not removed from the timeline by then."

If Tess hadn't been motivated to find a way out of this before, she was now. Sooner rather than later they'd find out she didn't know anything, and they'd kill her. Then they'd kill Zach. They might already have killed Easton, so she couldn't rely on her to come for her.

The car smelled new, so either they'd stolen it from a dealer, or more likely it was a rental. She wouldn't find any junk laying around to help her. If she could locate something sharp to cut the duct tape binding her hands, she could rip herself free. Of course she couldn't feel anything sharp in the back because it was all carpet.

She tried pulling her arms apart. The angle made it too hard. She pushed herself toward the other side, hoping to find something—anything—that could make a tear in the tape. The car was so damn neat it didn't have anything she could use. Perhaps she could sneak her way over the seats and make her way to the front?

Tess heard a string of curses from up front, and the vehicle swerved to the right. The tires screeched, and suddenly she was weightless and tumbling through the air. The car landed hard and rolled. She smashed into the floor and was then thrown against the window and the roof as the SUV tumbled down a steep embankment.

The swearing continued up front, and then as they landed, everything went silent. Tess had smacked her head hard against the back windshield and, though dazed, was lucky she was still conscious.

"Hands still tied together though," she said, her stomach continuing to somersault. She worried she might puke, so she took a minute to let everything settle.

All around was silence. She couldn't hear her captors or traffic from the road and, thankfully, no wildlife. She was very aware of everything that lurked in these woods, from raccoons to bobcats, and none of it was harmless. There were, of course, several she'd rather not encounter if given a choice. They'd probably been run off the road by something, either a deer or a moose, maybe even something still prowling the forest nearby. She hoped not, because she was about to find a way to escape into those woods.

After several moments of silence from the front, she sat up as best she could and maneuvered herself over the backseat. She searched the area for anything that might loosen the tape. When she didn't find anything, she did the same in the next set of seats until she was right behind the driver's seat. From her angle crouched on the floor she could see the man on the passenger side. Both airbags had deployed, which had knocked both men unconscious. It was unlikely they would stay that way for long.

Wedged between the two front seats was a duffel bag with a roll of duct tape poking out of one of the pockets. It might hold other tools as well, so she positioned herself so she could unzip and reach inside the bag. As soon as she stuck her hand inside, the driver stirred in his seat. She stayed as still as she could, even holding her breath. When she didn't hear anything for a couple of seconds, she restarted her search. She grabbed something long, which felt like a screwdriver, and pulled it out of the bag. Good enough. She turned it so the sharp end pointed up and began running it along the tape.

The driver groaned and turned his head. Tess scooted farther down so she was out of his line of sight. This time she began poking the tape, not caring if she was hitting skin or tape. As soon as she had enough holes she pulled, but it still held strong. She needed leverage, so she looked around for something she could use to pull at the tape.

"Hey." Tess spun around. The man in the passenger seat had regained consciousness and was trying to unfasten his seat belt. She panicked and began kicking at the door. She looped her foot under the door latch and tried to pull it open, but the Blundstones she was wearing were too big to get her foot under. She pulled herself up just as the man unhooked his seat belt.

She fell forward and slammed her lip into the door. Her mouth filled with blood.

"She's trying to get out." She heard a smack from the front seat, as if someone had been slapped in the face. "Help me with her."

Tess bit around the handle and pulled back. She got some leverage, but she lost her grip. The passenger lunged for her, grabbing her ankle. She slammed her head back, smacking him in the face. He fell backward as she fell forward. This time she gripped her teeth around the handle with as much force as she could and yanked her whole head back and then pushed forward with her shoulder. She tumbled out of the car and onto the uneven, cold, damp ground below, letting out a cry of success.

She pulled herself up, using the side of the car for support and inching her way along the side. The car had landed upright against a tree halfway down a steep hill. She could go down the hill farther and use the forest for cover or head uphill toward the road and try to flag someone down. She hadn't seen any cars coming, and once up there she would be exposed. She hedged around the car, decision made, and began to descend into the darkness below.

Easton circled the back of Ada's SUV, hoping to use it as cover before approaching the other vehicle. She could see movement in the front seat and crouched low. Taking a couple of breaths before making a run for the back of the other SUV, she misjudged the steep angle, stumbled, and smacked into the back with a loud thud. So much for being covert.

One of the car doors crashed against a tree, and one of the men tumbled out. Easton crouched low to the ground, laying her head in the wet grass to see which direction he was coming from. He started moving toward the back, so she rolled under the car and came up on the other side.

The air was crisp and clear, her breath swirling vapour in the dark. The sky reminded her of that first night on the road when the stars had filled the sky like the crystals sometimes shone in the tunnels. How easy everything had seemed then, how clear her path.

She peered through one of the windows. The back of the SUV was empty. A lone tree on the hill was the only thing keeping the vehicle from rolling to the bottom. The driver was still in the front seat, conscious but not fully mobile. The other man lumbered around the car with such heavy feet it was easy to avoid him. Unfortunately, she hadn't accounted for windows, and the one next to her head shattered around her shoulders. She collapsed to the ground and began to roll out of the way. The next thing she knew she was barrelling down the steep incline, unable to stop herself.

She crashed at the bottom and groaned. She'd definitely hurt her ribs again. The darkness of the forest loomed to her left, and the voices of the two men, shouting at each other, approached on her right. She rolled to her left and crouched next to a tree. She didn't want to venture too far into the forest and get lost, but it would be helpful to use its foliage to hide.

"Psst." The soft hiss sounded loud in her ear, and she turned to see Tess hunched behind a fallen, rotting trunk. Her hands were taped behind her back, her hair was a mess, full of twigs and leaves, and smudges of dirt covered her face.

"How did you get away?"

"The usual way. I ran…or, in your case, rolled." Tess smirked.

"Is that a joke? Are you actually making light of this right now?"

Tess motioned to her wrists, which were covered in blood. "It was pretty funny."

Easton pulled at the tape, ripping it down the middle to free her hands. "How did they get run off the road? Did you do that too?"

Tess shook her head, rubbing her wrists. "Must've swerved to miss a deer or something."

Easton grabbed Tess's elbow and yanked her up and farther into the forest. Tess began to protest, but Easton put a hand over her mouth and whispered in her ear. "I want to get a few metres in and then head that way." She pointed in front of them. "The moment they make it to the forest, we make a run for it up the hill."

"Where are the keys?"

"In my pocket."

Tess held out her hand. "I'll take them."

"Why?"

"You can't drive."

"I made it here, didn't I?" She fished the keys out of her pocket and handed them to Tess. They followed the tree line, keeping to the inside to stay out of sight. Tess was right. She'd driven here because there hadn't been any traffic or requirements other than going straight and fast.

When she felt they'd gone far enough, she stopped them, and they watched as the men stumbled down among the trees in search of them.

Tess clasped Easton's hand, and what was strange was how natural it felt. "Thanks for coming for me."

"Looks to me like you were doing okay."

Tess smirked again. "I was being polite."

As soon as the men were obscured by the woods, Easton pulled them up, and they were off. The word fuck drifted up to them as they bolted for the road. Now it was a matter of who got there first. The slope was steeper here, and Easton kept slipping backward. A few times Tess had to haul her up.

"Almost there," said Tess. She was out of breath. "Just…a…few—"

A shot cracked the night silence, and both Tess and Easton slammed to the ground.

"Are you hit?" Easton checked both of them, patting down Tess's arms and legs.

"I'm fine." Tess pushed her off and scrambled up. The men fired another shot at them, which hit the side of the SUV with a soft thud.

"Let's go." She grabbed Tess's upper arm and propelled them up the rest of the way. The men were several metres away by the time they made it to the vehicle, and they couldn't run and fire at the same time. Easton hadn't armed herself on this slipback. She hadn't felt it would be necessary. And in all the other timelines it hadn't been. She still couldn't figure out what was different about this one. She didn't have time to dwell on those thoughts though. She and Tess scrambled into the SUV and took off down the road before the men's aim got better or they got closer.

Chapter Twenty-five

Tess hated driving at night. Hate was a strong word. She preferred not to, especially without glasses, which she always forgot to take with her. She hadn't done much driving in Vancouver, and most of it in Smokey River was in town. This—what she was doing now—was a whole different kettle of fish. Even though her brain was telling her they couldn't catch up because their car was in a ditch, she still kept checking the rearview mirror, terrified some giant eighteen-wheeler would come barrelling down the road with headlights glaring.

They'd changed course based on what Tess had overheard. Since Zach was likely already in Smokey River, it was best to head there again, which meant a six-hour drive back the way they'd come.

And to make matters worse, Easton had fallen asleep twenty minutes ago, as if they were on some fun road trip.

She'd balled up her jacket to use as a pillow. Her mouth was slightly open and her hair pulled back. She was beautiful, and Tess had no doubt that if she'd met Easton normally, she'd have been very attracted to her.

"Who am I kidding," she muttered. She was attracted to Easton. And the thought that they had slept together in some parallel universe or whatever was…actually Tess wasn't sure what she thought of that. At first it had freaked her out a bit. Easton had seen her naked. She wasn't a twelve-year-old girl embarrassed about her body, but the idea was unsettling. It was like getting drunk at a party and waking up the next morning naked beside someone and not having any recollection of what had happened, but then finding video of it later on your phone and seeing that you had a great time. That's what it felt like. In a way she felt like she'd missed out on something.

The SUV chugged a few times, then slowly lost momentum. Tess steered it to the side of the road, checking the fuel gauge. Empty. How long had that been blinking and she hadn't noticed? Not that it would've mattered. Few gas stations were located out this way.

She sat for a few moments, contemplating. It was just after two in the morning. Nothing stirred. No cars were around. It felt very peaceful yet ominous. They couldn't sit out here forever. Eventually those operatives, as Easton had called them, would flag down a vehicle and catch up. At least they had a little time, but not enough to wait for someone to come. They would have to hike it out of here.

She pulled out her cell and checked the signal. She had none. And then what Ada had said came back to her. Phones could be tracked. Was that how they'd found them at the motel? She switched it off. And then, just to be sure, she opened her door and slammed it down on the ground. The sound woke Easton.

"Sorry. I didn't mean to fall asleep on you." She looked around at the emptiness of the road. "Why have we stopped?"

"We're out of gas."

"Gas?"

"Fuel. The car won't go without it."

Easton nodded. She shrugged on her jacket and opened the door as unperturbed as if they'd reached their destination. "We'll have to walk the rest of the way."

Tess scoffed. "Do you know how far that is? It'll take us weeks."

"Well, we can't stay here."

The air was chilly and bit into Tess's skin. She wrapped her cardigan tighter around herself. Her warm fall jacket was sitting on the back of a chair in a motel room about a hundred kilometres south of here. Easton went around to the back, pulled up the hatch, and came back with a scratchy wool blanket. It looked like it came with a car emergency kit. Warmth, but no comfort. Easton wrapped it around her shoulders.

"Thanks." Tess smiled. It would have to do.

"Walk fast. That should help keep us warm."

"I'm exhausted. I don't know how fast, let alone how far I'm going to make it before I collapse at your feet."

Easton rubbed her arms, bringing some much-needed warmth, and then she cupped her cheeks in an intimate gesture Tess wasn't sure Easton was aware of. "We won't go far. I just need to get us off this road."

For a minute she wondered if Easton was going to kiss her. She stood staring into those deep-green eyes, almost black in this light. A part of her was curious. Would she kiss her back? Easton stepped away and the moment was gone.

They walked for a kilometre along the side of the road, and then Easton dragged them down into the woods. They were too exposed on the road. It would be harder to walk in the forest but also more difficult to track. "There are no woods where I'm from, so it's unlikely they'll be much better at this than me."

"So you'd never seen the sky before?"

Easton shook her head. "The first time was when I landed in a field outside of town. It was dusk, but I was so busy trying to find clothes I didn't get a chance to see it. The stars, though, they were out and…" Easton looked up into the trees. None were out where they could see them.

"Wait. Looking for clothes?"

"We can't bring anything when we step through the portal."

"So you arrived naked?"

"Why is that so strange?"

Tess's laughter echoed through the trees. "This whole thing is strange. Science fiction come to life. I can't even begin to tell you how weird this all is."

"It's why I didn't want to tell you." Easton paused at a tree, leaning against it. "It is nice to be able to talk about it though. The last two times I felt like I had to hide part of who I was."

"What's it like?"

"What like?"

"Travelling through time? The way you've described it. Everything sounds so different. Like...did you date? Is it okay to date women?"

"Reproduction is highly regulated, so no one gives a damn what you do or who as long as you're not having unauthorized kids."

"Unauthorized?"

"It's not a big deal. Almost everyone gets approved, but you do have to apply like you would a marriage license. I've never heard of anyone getting turned down. So few people actually want to have children now that they've had to start enticing people with bonuses and free-education certificates. I think in the beginning they were worried too many people would have them and the population would be unsustainable, so they put all these restrictions in place. But that never happened. Life is so...dismal, no wants to subject kids to that."

"I'm sorry."

"It's why I thought I had to do what I did. The first and second time I came back, in my mind, removing you and Zach from the timeline was the only way to fix things."

"Is that what you guys call it?"

"Yes. They think it makes it easier. And I'm sure a lot of operatives find it very easy to kill."

"Did you? Find it easy?"

"The first time I didn't really know you. I saw more of you than I would've hoped. I didn't meet Zach. It wasn't easy to kill, but I also felt very removed. You weren't the same person the second time. It was like a shield had dropped, and you opened yourself up. I couldn't the second time. It wasn't me."

"You couldn't because you'd fallen in love."

Easton began walking again. "You make it sound one-sided. I didn't plan it. I tried to stay removed the second time as well. But it didn't work out that way."

"Okay, so we fell in love. So you say."

Easton stopped and turned. She stepped close, waiting for Tess to finish her thought.

"I only have your word."

"And my word is unbelievable?"

"I just find it hard to believe that I fell in love with a complete stranger in a week. I wasn't there."

Easton leaned closer. "You were there."

Tess's breath caught. She was sure Easton was going to kiss her. And, strangely, she wouldn't have stopped her. She wanted to feel Easton's lips on hers, get lost in Easton's passion. But Easton didn't make a move.

An owl hooted in the distance, and something close by crunched. Dead leaves or a fallen branch. Tess stepped away, fully aware they were in a forest with animals who might be hungry. None of the nocturnal animals in that forest were dangerous. A skunk, raccoon, or fox might be a nuisance but not deadly. Still, her imagination had come alive.

"We should probably keep going."

Tess leaned forward and scraped away some of the leaves that had blown onto Easton as she slept. They'd discovered a little alcove, not quite a cave, not too far into their hike and had decided to wait until it got light. They had a better chance of getting a ride somewhere with more cars on the road. Easton stirred and opened her eyes. Her smile was quick and bright and then dimmed, almost as if she'd remembered where they were.

"Morning." She helped Easton stand. Her movements were stiff and slow, and Tess worried she'd hurt herself more than she'd let on.

"Do you have any idea how far we are from…"

"Civilization? No clue. Do you think it's safe to walk up to the road and try to flag someone down?"

"As safe as it's ever going to be."

They trudged out and up the hill, not as steep along this part of the highway, to where they could hear the sounds of traffic.

It was a few minutes after six in the morning, and judging by the number of trucks on the road, it was a well-used transport route.

The sun hadn't crested the trees lining the road yet, but the sky was blue and the wind cold.

Tess held her thumb out, walking backward as she'd seen a million times in all those hippie movies her dad loved to watch. The first car drove by, and the second. It was another ten minutes before they saw a truck. Tess thought it would whip past like the others, but then it slowed down and pulled over several metres up the road. When they reached the truck, Easton held Tess back and moved forward. She stepped up and yanked the door open.

"Where you ladies heading?" The driver was in his late forties, with a grizzled beard and an oily baseball cap pulled down on his head.

"Smokey River."

"I can take you as far as Williams Lake."

Easton relayed the message to Tess, who nodded back. "That's only two hours from Smokey River, and it's big enough that we'd be able to rent a car to get the rest of the way."

Easton thanked the driver, and they hopped in. Only one seat was available, which Easton insisted Tess take, while she sat in the back on the fold-down bed.

It wasn't until they'd made it to Williams Lake and rented a car that Tess felt better about their situation. She still hadn't been able to get in touch with Zach, but as Easton had pointed out, she was calling from a strange number, and he was already paranoid about being followed. They were only two hours away from home—less, if she gunned it.

Watching Easton get into the car, stiff as a board, Tess reached over and lifted Easton's shirt. The left side of her torso was as black and purple as a thunderstorm. Easton grabbed her wrist, pulling it away, then dropped it.

"Easton…"

"Start the car."

Tess stared hard at Easton. She'd likely fractured one or two of her ribs. Even bruised ribs were excruciating. Instead of saying anything she started the car and put it in reverse. She wasn't going to play nursemaid to someone who clearly didn't want her to.

The speed limit was a hundred, but Tess drove one fifty. She knew it was dangerous, but she didn't care. Zach was heading into certain death, if they hadn't already killed him. Easton seemed certain they hadn't.

"I keep thinking about this conversation I had with my psych doctor." Easton's head was back on the seat, her eyes closed. Tess had thought she was sleeping and didn't blame her. "She said that some lives are magnetic, that they pull at each other. She was trying to give me a reason to be hopeful that my family might still exist in an alternate future. That my parents were born and met and had two daughters. I thought she was saying it as a way to appease me. Now, I'm not as certain."

"What does that mean?"

Easton opened her eyes and looked over at her. "It means I've tried in three separate timelines to keep my distance, and everything brings me back to you."

"And you think we're destined to what? Be together?"

"I'm not sure if that's what I'm saying. But I also find it interesting I was sent on a slipback where my mom was present. Any other slipback and I wouldn't have intersected with her. Yet here we are." Easton turned her head toward the window, where the tall trees were streaming by. "I haven't decided what it means yet."

Easton hadn't shared much about what had happened in her previous trips through the timeline. Journeys? Tess wasn't sure what to call them, but she wished she could know what Easton knew. She wished she could feel what Easton felt.

She pulled into Ada's drive at dusk, exhausted, to find an SUV parked in front. Easton instructed her to pull off to the side, where a group of trees would help give them cover.

"Is that them? Or different guys, you think?" Tess asked.

Easton shook her head. "It doesn't matter. If they have my mom, then we're fucked."

"Why? What was the other part of the plan? The part you refuse to tell me?"

Easton grabbed her discarded jacket from the backseat. "She was going to go back to before the time portal had been constructed and infect the AI with a virus."

"Doesn't that mean you'd never come back here?"

"It's possible. It's also possible that because I'm here, I'm already part of this timeline. No one knows for sure."

Tess zipped up her jacket, not sure exactly how that was going to help, but it made her feel better. "So what's the game plan? Guns ablaze, or are we more subtle action heroes?"

Easton smirked this time. "I only ever understand half of what you say. But I think I got the gist of that. You're staying here, and I'm going around back to sneak in and figure out what's going on."

"Do you think they have Zach?"

Easton sucked at her bottom lip. "I don't know until I go look." She grabbed the door handle, about to open the door, when Tess stopped her.

"Wait." She seized Easton's jacket lapels and pulled her close. "Good luck." She poured all her passion and hopes and fears into a heart-pounding, gut-wrenching, soul-stealing kiss. When she pulled back, Tess was so dazed, her fingers were tingling. "I didn't want to let you go without knowing what it felt like to kiss you."

"And?"

"I think you should come back safe. Maybe we can do that again."

Tess was left with Easton's smile seared into her mind.

Easton crouched at the back window. From her vantage point she could see into her mom's dining room, where she was bound to a chair talking to two men. Not the same men who had come after her and Tess. How many operatives did they have here? They were doing most of the talking, asking the kinds of questions that told Easton they didn't know who she was or what she had planned.

They obviously hadn't heard Tess pull up, or they wouldn't be chatting so calmly. She snuck back around the side of the house to their car and peered inside. The door was unlocked. She quietly opened it and popped the trunk.

"Whatcha doing?" Tess's voice beside her almost had her skin jumping off.

"I told you to stay in the car."

"What's the situation?"

Easton opened the trunk, and inside was a bag with two semiautomatic rifles and a pistol. She pocketed the pistol, pulled out the duffel bag, and handed it to Tess. "Put this somewhere safe."

Easton skirted the other side of the house to get a better angle. She wanted a clean shot to take out both men.

She found a window on the farthest side, but it was locked. If she couldn't make it into the house, she might not get the shot she wanted. What she did have going for her was the element of surprise.

She retraced her steps to the front of the house and rang the doorbell. She checked behind her to confirm that whoever came to the door wouldn't be able to see Tess or the car and then crouched low on the side of the front porch.

She watched the curtain twitch at the window. And then silence. Maybe she'd overestimated their stupidity. A moment later she heard the latch on the door creak and knew she had at least one of them. In order for this to work, she had to be quick and quiet.

As soon as the man came to the door, she yanked him out and twisted his neck. It broke in an instant, and she silently laid him on the ground. She entered the house through the front door.

"Who was it?" a man called.

From the location of the sound, Easton knew he hadn't left the dining room. She took two quick breaths and entered the room, gun up, aimed and fired two shots into his head before he fell to the ground.

It took Ada only a second to recover from the shock. "Where are Tess and Zach?" she asked.

Easton knelt to untie her. "Tess is by the car, and we're not sure where Zach is. Probably at Tess's place, but I wanted to come here first, make sure you were okay."

"I'm fine. I'm not sure where these two came from. They don't act like level five."

"I was thinking that myself."

"It's possible they're from later or earlier or a different timeline entirely. You mentioned they'd sent back twenty-five operatives to achieve this slipback. As some succeeded, the timeline would've changed. Protocol could've changed."

Easton nodded. "Is it ready? Can you make the jump now?"

Ada looked worried. "I don't know. If nothing has changed, then I have the right coordinates." She pointed to the dead man in her dining room. "This changes things."

"How?"

"What if they've already invented it by the time I jump? I won't be able to do anything or to jump again. They'll keep coming for you."

"Go back earlier. You have it set to right before they invent the time portal. Why not go back earlier?"

"Wait." They both looked up to find Tess watching them. "If you go back to stop all this, what's to keep it from happening again in the future? All those things that led up to the AI will happen again."

Ada smiled. It was a simple smile you would give a child. "Change the world. You can't just expect to come back to the past and change a few things and suddenly everything will be perfect. You have to start in the past. Make people listen, make them realize that they have to do something now to change their future."

Tess's mouth formed a perfect oh, as if she hadn't thought it would be so hard. But then a man stepped out from the kitchen with a gun pointed at her back.

"Hello again." It was the driver from the SUV. "Sorry we're late. Had a little business to attend to at the vet's farmhouse."

Easton turned to her mom, they exchanged a look, and she was certain her mom had gotten her meaning, more so when she touched her face and mouthed, "I love you." As Ada turned to run for her back barn, Easton stepped in front to block her from the gunman holding Tess while swivelling to face the backyard. She raised her pistol and fired, hitting the second man, the passenger, standing in the backyard, who fell limp to the ground. Her mom ran past and into the barn, slamming the door behind her.

Easton heard another shot and turned to watch as blood spread over Tess's jacket. Her face held surprise as she looked down and covered the wet spot with her hands.

"Too bad," he said. "You lose."

Easton didn't even acknowledge him. She raised her gun and shot him in the head before running to catch Tess as she fell.

Tess looked down at her hands, which were now soaked. "He fucking shot me."

Easton nodded. "I know."

A bright light and a loud pop came from the barn. Easton could only hope her mom had made it. She settled Tess's head on her lap. The sky had gone dark, and the only light came from a single bulb hanging from the ceiling in the shed. It was enough to see the outlines of Tess's face. Her eyes were open, and she stared up at Easton.

"I'm sorry you never got to say good-bye to her."

"My mom?"

Tess shook her head. "The Tess who loved you back."

Easton's eyes filled with tears. "I got more than most people get."

Tess didn't respond. She closed her eyes as her head slumped to the side. She'd stopped breathing.

Easton choked out a sob. Her eyes shut in darkness, and she awoke in a field below a purple-hued sky of approaching dusk and smiled.

She had all the time in the world.

About the Author

CJ Birch is a Toronto-based video editor and digital artist. When not lost in a good book or working, she can be found writing or drinking serious coffee, or doing both at the same time.

An award-winning poet, CJ holds a certificate in journalism but prefers the world of make-believe. She is the reluctant co-owner of two cats, one of which is bulimic, the other with bladder issues, both evil walking fur shedders.

CJ is the author of the New Horizons series. You can visit CJ on social media @cjbirchwrites or www.cjbirchwrites.com.

Books Available from Bold Strokes Books

A Convenient Arrangement by Aurora Rey and Jaime Clevenger. Cuffing season has come for lesbians, and for Jess Archer and Cody Dawson, their convenient arrangement becomes anything but. (978-1-63555-818-0)

An Alaskan Wedding by Nance Sparks. The last thing either Andrea or Riley expects is to bump into the one who broke her heart fifteen years ago, but when they meet at the welcome party, their feelings come rushing back. (978-1-63679-053-4)

Beulah Lodge by Cathy Dunnell. It's 1874, and newly engaged Ruth Mallowes is set on marriage and life as a missionary…until she falls in love with the housemaid at Beulah Lodge. (978-1-63679-007-7)

Gia's Gems by Toni Logan. When Lindsey Speyer discovers that popular travel columnist Gia Williams is a complete fake and threatens to expose her, blackmail has never been so sexy. (978-1-63555-917-0)

Holiday Wishes & Mistletoe Kisses by M. Ullrich. Four holidays, four couples, four chances to make their wishes come true. (978-1-63555-760-2)

Love By Proxy by Dena Blake. Tess has a secret crush on her best friend, Sophie, so the last thing she wants is to help Sophie fall in love with someone else, but how can she stand in the way of her happiness? (978-1-63555-973-6)

Loyalty, Love, & Vermouth by Eric Peterson. A comic valentine to a gay man's family of choice, including the ones with cold noses and four paws. (978-1-63555-997-2)

Marry Me by Melissa Brayden. Allison Hale attempts to plan the wedding of the century to a man who could save her family's business, if only she wasn't falling for her wedding planner, Megan Kinkaid. (978-1-63555-932-3)

Pathway to Love by Radclyffe. Courtney Valentine is looking for a woman exactly like Ben—smart, sexy, and not in the market for anything serious. All she has to do is convince Ben that sex-without-strings is the perfect pathway to pleasure. (978-1-63679-110-4)

Sweet Surprise by Jenny Frame. Flora and Mac never thought they'd ever see each other again, but when Mac opens up her barber shop right next to Flora's sweet shop, their connection comes roaring back. (978-1-63679-001-5)

The Edge of Yesterday by CJ Birch. Easton Gray is sent from the future to save humanity from technological disaster. When she's forced to target the woman she's falling in love with, can Easton do what's needed to save humanity? (978-1-63679-025-1)

The Scout and the Scoundrel by Barbara Ann Wright. With unexpected danger surrounding them, Zara and Roni are stuck between duty and survival, with little room for exploring their feelings, especially love. (978-1-63555-978-1)

Bury Me in Shadows by Greg Herren. College student Jake Chapman is forced to spend the summer at his dying grandmother's home and soon finds danger from long-buried family secrets. (978-1-63555-993-4)

Can't Leave Love by Kimberly Cooper Griffin. Sophia and Pru have no intention of falling in love, but sometimes love happens when and where you least expect it. (978-1-636790041-1)

Free Fall at Angel Creek by Julie Tizard. Detective Dee Rawlings and aircraft accident investigator Dr. River Dawson use conflicting methods to find answers when a plane goes missing, while overcoming surprising threats, and discovering an unlikely chance at love. (978-1-63555-884-5)

Love's Compromise by Cass Sellars. For Piper Holthaus and Brook Myers, will professional dreams and past baggage stop two hearts from realizing they are meant for each other? (978-1-63555-942-2)

Not All a Dream by Sophia Kell Hagin. Hester has lost the woman she loved and the world has descended into relentless dark and cold. But giving up will have to wait when she stumbles upon people who help her survive. (978-1-63679-067-1)

Protecting the Lady by Amanda Radley. If Eve Webb had known she'd be protecting royalty, she'd never have taken the job as bodyguard, but as the threat to Lady Katherine's life draws closer, she'll do whatever it takes to save her, and may just lose her heart in the process. (978-1-63679-003-9)

The Secrets of Willowra by Kadyan. A family saga of three women, their homestead called Willowra in the Australian outback, and the secrets that link them all. (978-1-63679-064-0)

Trial by Fire by Carsen Taite. When prosecutor Lennox Roy and public defender Wren Bishop become fierce adversaries in a headline-grabbing arson case, their attraction ignites a passion that leads them both to question their assumptions about the law, the truth, and each other. (978-1-63555-860-9)

Turbulent Waves by Ali Vali. Kai Merlin and Vivien Palmer plan their future together as hostile forces make their own plans to destroy what they have, as well as all those they love. (978-1-63679-011-4)

Unbreakable by Cari Hunter. When Dr. Grace Kendal is forced at gunpoint to help an injured woman, she is dragged into a nightmare where nothing is quite as it seems, and their lives aren't the only ones on the line. (978-1-63555-961-3)

Veterinary Surgeon by Nancy Wheelton. When dangerous drugs are stolen from the veterinary clinic, Mitch investigates and Kay becomes a suspect. As pride and professions clash, love seems impossible. (978-1-63679-043-5)

A Different Man by Andrew L. Huerta. This diverse collection of stories chronicling the challenges of gay life at various ages shines a light on the progress made and the progress still to come. (978-1-63555-977-4)

All That Remains by Sheri Lewis Wohl. Johnnie and Shantel might have to risk their lives—and their love—to stop a werewolf intent on killing. (978-1-63555-949-1)

Beginner's Bet by Fiona Riley. Phenom luxury Realtor Ellison Gamble has everything, except a family to share it with, so when a mix-up brings youthful Katie Crawford into her life, she bets the house on love. (978-1-63555-733-6)

Dangerous Without You by Lexus Grey. Throughout their senior year in high school, Aspen, Remington, Denna, and Raleigh face challenges in life and romance that they never expect. (978-1-63555-947-7)

Desiring More by Raven Sky. In this collection of steamy stories, a rich variety of lovers find themselves desiring more, more from a lover, more from themselves, and more from life. (978-1-63679-037-4)

Jordan's Kiss by Nanisi Barrett D'Arnuck. After losing everything in a fire, Jordan Phelps joins a small lounge band and meets pianist Morgan Sparks, who lights another blaze, this time in Jordan's heart. (978-1-63555-980-4)

Late City Summer by Jeanette Bears. Forced together for her wedding, Emily Stanton and Kate Alessi navigate their lingering passion for one another against the backdrop of New York City and World War II, and a summer romance they left behind. (978-1-63555-968-2)

Love and Lotus Blossoms by Anne Shade. On her path to self-acceptance and true passion, Janesse will risk everything—and possibly everyone—she loves. (978-1-63555-985-9)

Love in the Limelight by Ashley Moore. Marion Hargreaves, the finest actress of her generation, and Jessica Carmichael, the world's biggest pop star, rediscover each other twenty years after an ill-fated affair. (978-1-63679-051-0)

Suspecting Her by Mary P. Burns. Complications ensue when Erin O'Connor falls for top real estate saleswoman Catherine Williams while investigating racism in the real estate industry; the fallout could end their chance at happiness. (978-1-63555-960-6)

Two Winters by Lauren Emily Whalen. A modern YA retelling of Shakespeare's *The Winter's Tale* about birth, death, Catholic school, improv comedy, and the healing nature of time. (978-1-63679-019-0)

Busy Ain't the Half of It by Frederick Smith and Chaz Lamar Cruz. Elijah and Justin seek happily-ever-afters in LA, but are they too busy to notice happiness when it's there? (978-1-63555-944-6)

Calumet by Ali Vali. Jaxon Lavigne and Iris Long had a forbidden small-town romance that didn't last, and the consequences of that love will be uncovered fifteen years later at their high school reunion. (978-1-63555-900-2)

Her Countess to Cherish by Jane Walsh. London Society's material girl realizes there is more to life than diamonds when she falls in love with a non-binary bluestocking. (978-1-63555-902-6)

Hot Days, Heated Nights by Renee Roman. When Cole and Lee meet, instant attraction quickly flares into uncontrollable passion, but their connection might be short lived as Lee's identity is tied to her life in the city. (978-1-63555-888-3)

Never Be the Same by MA Binfield. Casey meets Olivia and sparks fly in this opposites attract romance that proves love can be found in the unlikeliest places. (978-1-63555-938-5)

Quiet Village by Eden Darry. Something not quite human is stalking Collie and her niece, and she'll be forced to work with undercover reporter Emily Lassiter if they want to get out of Hyam alive. (978-1-63555-898-2)

Shaken or Stirred by Georgia Beers. Bar owner Julia Martini and home health aide Savannah McNally attempt to weather the storms brought on by a mysterious blogger trashing the bar, family feuds they knew nothing about, and way too much advice from way too many relatives. (978-1-63555-928-6)

The Fiend in the Fog by Jess Faraday. Can four people on different trajectories work together to save the vulnerable residents of East London from the terrifying fiend in the fog before it's too late? (978-1-63555-514-1)

The Marriage Masquerade by Toni Logan. A no strings attached marriage scheme to inherit a Maui B&B uncovers unexpected attractions and a dark family secret. (978-1-63555-914-9)

Flight SQA016 by Amanda Radley. Fastidious airline passenger Olivia Lewis is used to things being a certain way. When her routine is changed by a new, attractive member of the staff, sparks fly. (978-1-63679-045-9)

Home Is Where the Heart Is by Jenny Frame. Can Archie make the countryside her home and give Ash the fairytale romance she desires? Or will the countryside and small village life all be too much for her? (978-1-63555-922-4)

Moving Forward by PJ Trebelhorn. The last person Shelby Ryan expects to be attracted to is Iris Calhoun, the sister of the man who killed her wife four years and three thousand miles ago. (978-1-63555-953-8)

Poison Pen by Jean Copeland. Debut author Kendra Blake is finally living her best life until a nasty book review and exposed secrets threaten her promising new romance with aspiring journalist Alison Chatterley. (978-1-63555-849-4)

Seasons for Change by KC Richardson. Love, laughter, and trust develop for Shawn and Morgan throughout the changing seasons of Lake Tahoe. (978-1-63555-882-1)

Summer Lovin' by Julie Cannon. Three different women, three exotic locations, one unforgettable summer. What do you think will happen? (978-1-63555-920-0)

Unbridled by D. Jackson Leigh. A visit to a local stable turns into more than riding lessons between a novel writer and an equestrian with a taste for power play. (978-1-63555-847-0)

VIP by Jackie D. In a town where relationships are forged and shattered by perception, sometimes even love can't change who you really are. (978-1-63555-908-8)

Yearning by Gun Brooke. The sleepy town of Dennamore has an irresistible pull on those who've moved away. The mystery Darian Benson and Samantha Pike uncover will change them forever, but the love they find along the way just might be the key to saving themselves. (978-1-63555-757-2)

Bold Strokes Books
Quality and Diversity in LGBTQ Literature